3

THE GHOST-FEELER

-7.
8B

2

CU:

EDITH WHARTON

THE GHOST-FEELER

Stories of Terror and the Supernatural

Selected and Introduced by
Peter Haining

PETER OWEN
London and Chester Springs

PETER OWEN PUBLISHERS
73 Kenway Road, London SW5 0RE
Peter Owen books are distributed in the USA by
Dufour Editions Inc., Chester Springs PA 19425-0007

This collection first published 1996
This paperback edition published 2002
Selection and Introduction © Peter Haining 1996

A catalogue record for this book is available from
the British Library

ISBN 0 7206 1152 0

Printed and bound in Great Britain by
Bookmarque Ltd, Croydon, Surrey

Contents

What gives a ghost story its thrill? First I
think its *physical* sense and, secondly, a
moral twist.

Graham Greene
The Spectator, 1937

Introduction

It is a strange fact that for the first twenty-seven years of her life, a woman who is today regarded by several authorities on ghost fiction as one of the foremost writers of supernatural stories of her time, was quite unable to sleep in any room that contained so much as a single book of such tales. So unnerved was Edith Wharton by supernatural fiction that she later admitted to destroying any that she came across at home. But it was from her childhood traumas and anxieties that Wharton drew the inspiration for her stories of ghosts and terror to produce a steady flow of work that spanned her entire literary career and which today is worthy of the highest praise.

Born into a wealthy New York family in January 1862, this sensitive, responsive and obedient young lady led a cosseted and strictly disciplined life until a cathartic experience in the summer of 1870. On holiday in Europe in the Black Forest, Wharton suddenly collapsed and was diagnosed with typhoid fever. For several days she was close to death before finally rallying and beginning a long period of convalescence. To pass the time she asked for some books to read, and among those given to her was one from two friends which she could only later describe with a shudder as a 'robber story'. This book, with its tales of robbers and ghosts, deeply affected her 'intense Celtic sense of the supernatural' and not only caused a set-back in her recovery but opened up to her fevered imagination 'a world haunted by formless horrors'. For years thereafter, she said, a dark undefinable menace dogged her footsteps. 'I had been a naturally fearless child,' she explained, 'now I lived in a state of chronic fear. Fear of *what*?

I cannot say – and even at the time I was never able to formulate my terror.'

Wharton also had a fear of old houses. One of her aunts, a stern, humourless spinster lady who had also suffered a death-threatening illness as a child, lived in almost reclusive isolation in a twenty-four-roomed Gothic mansion at Rhinecliff, New York. The building was ugly, dark and uncomfortable and the little girl could never visit the place without having nightmares afterwards.

Both of these influences contributed to Wharton's overwhelming fear of ghost and horror stories, a fear that persisted through her childhood, into her teens, and even her early twenties. 'I could not sleep in a room with a book containing a ghost story,' she confessed later. 'I frequently had to burn books of this kind, because it frightened me to know that they were downstairs in the library!' When, however, the urge to write possessed the young woman, she determined to exorcize the ghosts and goblins that haunted her.

Later in her life when Wharton was firmly established as a famous novelist and double-winner of the Pulitzer Prize, she could write freely of the terrors that had so affected her imagination as well as her convictions about the supernatural world.

> The celebrated reply (I forget whose): 'No, I don't believe in ghosts, but I'm afraid of them,' is much more than the cheap paradox it seems to many. To 'believe', in that sense, is a conscious act of the intellect, and it is in the warm darkness of the pre-natal fluid far below our conscious reason that the faculty dwells with which we apprehend the ghosts we may not be endowed with the gift of seeing.

For this very reason, Edith Wharton considered herself not a 'ghost-seer' – to use the term so often applied to those people who claim to have witnessed a spirit – but rather a 'ghost-feeler', someone who *senses* what cannot be seen. It is this fact which determined my choice of a title for this collection.

Between youth and old age, Wharton had plucked up the courage to read the works by the great masters of the genre and listed among her favourites three British authors, Robert Louis Stevenson, Joseph Sheridan Le Fanu and Walter de la Mare, and two fellow Americans, Francis Marion Crawford and Fitz James O'Brien. At the very pinnacle, though, she placed Henry James and his novel, *The Turn of the Screw*; she considered no other writer had come near to equalling its imaginative handling of the supernatural. She might be considered biased, however, since James had, in fact, become her friend and the guiding light of her literary career.

Wharton has, in turn, earned her own coterie of admirers. The American critic George D. Meadows, for example, says that, 'Mrs. Wharton works with the sure touch of an Emily Brontë, although with more restraint'; while the English novelist Anita Brookner believes she had 'an abiding fascination for the comfortably established world of haunted houses and revenants, wives or husbands betrayed, or dead too soon'.

As I belong to this circle of admirers, assembling this collection has for me been a special pleasure. It has provided some surprises, too. For example, I spent one day wading through dusty copies of the early issues of *Harper's Monthly Magazine*, to which Wharton contributed a number of her short stories, in the hope that I might come across some undiscovered gems. And there, in the index to volume II (1851), I found an essay entitled 'The Ghost That Appeared to Mrs. Wharton'. Of course, it had been published ten years *before* Wharton was born, but in succeeding volumes I came across a number of other supernatural stories by anonymous writers. I could not help wondering whether this magazine, popular with her parents and always to be found in the family library, had been another – until now – unacknowledged source of her inspiration?

In the stories that follow, Edith Wharton demonstrates her feeling for the supernatural and her knowledge of terror, both garnered from personal experience.

* * *

'The Duchess at Prayer' is a story of terror and punishment that could just as easily have been written by Edgar Allan Poe, whose work clearly influenced Wharton. Both writers shared a love for the town of Newport, where both of them spent periods of their lives. It was here, during the summer of 1900, that 'The Duchess at Prayer' was written, and according to an anonymous reviewer in the American magazine, *Independent* (June 1901), the tale might have been based on an incident 'which Balzac once developed somewhat differently'. In the same year, *Harper's Monthly Magazine* called it a tale about 'the brute facts of sin' and added that 'it could only have been written by one who has truly known horror'. In her recent study, *Edith Wharton: An Extraordinary Life* (1994), Eleanor Dwight suggests that the story reflects a plight familiar to Wharton and many young wives of the period, that of 'The woman abandoned by her husband for long periods of time and then expected to be sexually available to him when he returns'.

There is little doubt that 'The Fullness of Life', published at the end of 1893, reflects the state of Wharton's own married life at the time. She had been wed in 1885 to Edward Wharton, a man thirteen years older than her, who had little feeling for literature and art, preferred the company of other male New York socialites, and quickly lost interest in the artistic and physical needs of his young bride. Soon, in fact, the unsatisfactory state of her marriage was to cause Edith to form several intense friendships, and in 1907 she had a deeply passionate affair with a New York journalist named Morton Fullerton which released her sensuality and also had a profound effect upon the tenor of her later writing.

Some years after its publication, Wharton described 'The Fullness of Life' to her editor at *Scribner's*, Edward Burlingame, as 'one long shriek – I may not write any better, but at least I hope that I write in a lower key'. And probably because of its intensely personal nature – not to mention the fact that it must have annoyed Teddy Wharton, who could hardly have failed to grasp its implict suggestion – Wharton suppressed the work from her subsequent collections of stories. I know of few other stories of the afterlife more absorbing than this one. Eleanor Dwight believes that the tale may also have been partly inspired by a supernatural experience the author had while visiting Florence. She marvelled at the architectural beauty of the Church of San Michele, 'when she experienced a wonderful vision and felt herself being "borne onwards along a mighty current"'.

Wharton returned to the subject of death in 'A Journey', published in June 1899. Here again, Wharton's sensitivity and the idea of death as a physical presence make the story memorable.

As in 'The Duchess at Prayer', there are elements of sexuality to be found in 'The Lady's Maid's Bell', written in 1904, and Wharton's first true ghost story. Readers on both sides of the Atlantic were deeply moved by this tale of adultery mingled with supernatural protection, with its superbly evoked atmosphere of dark and mysterious events occurring in an unstable household.

Just how successfully Wharton had confronted the demons of her childhood is evident in 'Afterwards', a tale written in 1910 and generally considered to be her most successful ghost story. Jack Sullivan, writing in *The Penguin Encyclopedia of Horror and the Supernatural* (1986), believes that Wharton 'converted the primal dread from her childhood into the haunted library scene', which is the setting for one of the pivotal moments in the story.

New England in the grip of a blizzard is the backdrop for 'The Triumph of Night', published in 1914, and featuring the innovation of a *doppelgänger*. The ugly, malevolent spirit is the double of a well-known financier who has virtually imprisoned a young man suffering from advanced tuberculosis, in the hope of benefiting from his death. When the snow drives another traveller into the company of this pair and the man sees the *doppelgänger* for himself, he is faced with a stark choice: to save the stricken boy or flee from the house.

Interestingly, this story had been written several years earlier while Wharton was far away from America, staying in Paris. The French capital was then almost flooded from torrential rain, and this may well have set the tone of a piece that features fiscal misdealings, mysterious death and bloodstained hands.

Wharton returned to the locale of New England for 'Bewitched', a tale of vampirism, then a subject virtually untouched by women writers. The importance of the story was spotted on publication by the *New York Times*'s critic who wrote on 2 May 1926: '"Bewitched" has much of the same tragic power which was the commanding feature of *Ethan Frome*.'

It is an atmospheric and disturbing tale about a distracted wife, Mrs Rutledge, who appeals to her local Deacon for help because her husband, Saul, is having an affair. But this is no ordinary affair: he is infatuated with a dead woman who is relentlessly draining away his vitality. Even in the superstitious backwoods of New England, the poor woman does not find it easy to come to terms with what is happening or to get others to take the necessary action to put a stop to the vampire's activities. The influence of this story can be seen in a number of subsequent tales of the undead written by women – not the least of them the sensual and exotic vampire novels of Anne Rice.

The deceptive title of 'A Bottle of Perrier', which Wharton wrote in 1930, lures the reader almost unsuspectingly into a tale of murder and suspense set in a new locality: the African desert. This story was greatly admired by the late doyen of mystery fiction, Ellery Queen, who republished it in his magazine in 1948 with the following illuminating preface:

It has been said of Edith Wharton's work that 'her characters are given sharp, clear, consistent shape'. You will find that true of 'A

Bottle of Perrier': young Medford, the velvet-foot Gosling, and especially the strange archaeologist, Henry Almodham, are sharp and clear and consistent against the shimmering background of the desert. It has also been said that Edith Wharton's style is a 'clear, luminous medium in which things are seen in precise and striking outline'. You will find that also true: the mystery and menace of the infinite sands, the enervating heat, the timelessness, the silence, the inaccessibility – all become luminous; but there is something else, something brooding and haunting, which becomes clear and finally emerges 'in precise and striking outline'. . . .

Small wonder that this story should have captivated many other literary figures including L. P. Hartley, who called it 'an ingenious exercise in sustained suspense' and Graham Greene, who referred to it as 'that superb horror story'.

Wharton's mentor, Henry James, was a particular admirer of the final story in this collection, 'The Looking-Glass', which he called a 'diabolical little cleverness'. The story was contributed to *The Century* in 1935 and, curiously, not included in the collections of Wharton's work published immediately prior to and just after her death. It also appeared under the title 'The Mirror', and its heroine, Moyra Attlee, recounts the strange and unexpected visions she witnesses in an old looking-glass.

Edith Wharton died on 11 August 1937 at her French home in St Brice-sous-Fôret, just north of Paris, and she was buried at Versailles. Three months later, in a tribute to her work in the supernatural genre, the English critic Desmond Shawe-Taylor neatly encapsulated the secret of why her stories of ghosts and terror deserved to be read then and still do today, over half a century later:

She is a story-teller whose speech is naturally quiet and unhurried. Her stories have a half-eerie, half-cosy charm of their own. You begin to feel the silence around your chair; she is a past mistress of that curious art which makes you put the book down for an instant, poke the fire, and settle back with the thought: 'Well, here I am, reading a ghost story – what could be more agreeable?'

There is nothing more for me to add beyond suggesting that the reader immediately take Mr Shawe-Taylor's advice.

PETER HAINING
Boxford, Suffolk

The Duchess at Prayer

I

Have you ever questioned the long shuttered front of an old Italian house, that motionless mask, smooth, mute, equivocal as the face of a priest behind which buzz the secrets of the confessional? Other houses declare the activities they shelter; they are the clear expressive cuticle of a life flowing close to the surface; but the old palace in its narrow street, the villa on its cypress-hooded hill, are as impenetrable as death. The tall windows are like blind eyes, the great door is a shut mouth. Inside there may be sunshine, the scent of myrtles, and a pulse of life through all the arteries of the huge frame; or a mortal solitude, where bats lodge in the disjointed stones and the keys rust in unused doors. . . .

II

From the loggia, with its vanishing frescoes, I looked down an avenue barred by a ladder of cypress shadows to the ducal escutcheon and mutilated vases of the gate. Flat noon lay on the gardens, on fountains, porticoes, and grottoes. Below the terrace, where a chrome-coloured lichen had sheeted the balustrade as with fine *laminæ* of gold, vineyards stooped to the rich valley clasped in hills. The lower slopes were strewn with white villages like stars spangling

13

a summer dusk; and beyond these, fold on fold of blue mountain, clear as gauze against the sky. The August air was lifeless, but it seemed light and vivifying after the atmosphere of the shrouded rooms through which I had been led. Their chill was on me and I hugged the sunshine.

'The Duchess's apartments are beyond,' said the old man.

He was the oldest man I had ever seen; so sucked back into the past that he seemed more like a memory than a living being. The one trait linking him with the actual was the fixity with which his small saurian eye held the pocket that, as I entered, had yielded a *lira* to the gatekeeper's child. He went on, without removing his eye:

'For two hundred years nothing has been changed in the apartments of the Duchess.'

'And no one lives her now?'

'No one, sir. The Duke goes to Como for the summer season.'

I had moved to the other end of the loggia. Below me, through hanging groves, white roofs and domes flashed like a smile.

'And that's Vicenza?'

'*Proprio!*' The old man extended fingers as lean as the hands fading from the walls behind us. 'You see the palace roof over there, just to the left of the Basilica? The one with the row of statues like birds taking flight? That's the Duke's town palace, built by Palladio.'

'And does the Duke come there?'

'Never. In winter he goes to Rome.'

'And the palace and the villa are always closed?'

'As you see – always.'

'How long has this been?'

'Since I can remember.'

I looked into his eyes; they were like tarnished metal mirrors reflecting nothing. 'That must be a long time,' I said involuntarily.

'A long time,' he assented.

I looked down on the gardens. An opulence of dahlias overran the box-borders, between cypresses that cut the sunshine like basalt shafts. Bees hung above the lavender; lizards sunned themselves on the benches and slipped through the cracks of the dry basins. Everywhere were vanishing traces of that fantastic horticulture of which our dull age has lost the art. Down the alleys maimed statues stretched their arms like rows of whining beggars; faun-eared terms grinned in the thickets, and above the laurustinus walls rose the mock ruin of a temple, falling into real ruin in the bright disintegrating air. The glare was blinding.

'Let us go in,' I said.

The old man pushed open a heavy door, behind which the cold lurked like a knife.

'The Duchess's apartments,' he said.

Overhead and around us the same evanescent frescoes, under foot the same scagliola volutes, unrolled themselves interminably. Ebony cabinets, with inlay of precious marbles in cunning perspective, alternated down the room with the tarnished efflorescence of gilt consoles supporting Chinese monsters; and from the chimney-panel a gentleman in the Spanish habit haughtily ignored us.

'Duke Ercole II,' the old man explained, 'by the Genoese Priest.'

It was a narrow-browed face, sallow as a wax effigy, high-nosed and cautious-lidded, as though modelled by priestly hands; the lips weak and vain rather than cruel; a quibbling mouth that would have snapped at verbal errors like a lizard catching flies, but had never learned the shape of a round yes or no. One of the Duke's hands rested on the head of a dwarf, a simian creature with pearl ear-rings and fantastic dress; the other turned the pages of a folio propped on a skull.

'Beyond is the Duchess's bedroom,' the old man reminded me.

Here the shutters admitted but two narrow shafts of light, gold bars deepening the subaqueous gloom. On a daïs the bedstead, grim, nuptial, official, lifted its baldachin; a yellow Christ agonized between the curtains, and across the room a lady smiled at us from the chimney-breast.

The old man unbarred a shutter and the light touched her face. Such a face it was, with a flicker of laughter over it like the wind on a June meadow, and a singular tender pliancy of mien, as though one of Tiepolo's lenient goddesses had been busked into the stiff sheath of a seventeenth-century dress!

'No one has slept here', said the old man, 'since the Duchess Violante.'

'And she was —?'

'The lady there – first Duchess of Duke Ercole II.'

He drew a key from his pocket and unlocked a door at the farther end of the room. 'The chapel,' he said. 'This is the Duchess's balcony.' As I turned to follow him the Duchess tossed me a sidelong smile.

I stepped into a grated tribune above a chapel festooned with stucco. Pictures of bituminous saints mouldered between the pilasters; the artificial roses in the altar vases were grey with dust and age, and under the cobwebby rosettes of the vaulting a bird's nest clung. Before the altar stood a row of tattered armchairs and I drew back at sight of a figure kneeling near them.

'The Duchess,' the old man whispered. 'By the Cavaliere Bernini.'

It was the image of a woman in furred robes and spreading *fraise*, her hand lifted, her face addressed to the tabernacle. There was a strangeness in the sight of that immovable presence locked in prayer before an abandoned shrine. Her face was hidden, and I wondered whether it were grief or gratitude that raised her hands and drew her eyes to the altar, where no living prayer joined her marble invocation. I followed my guide down the tribune steps, impatient to see what mystic version of such terrestrial graces the ingenious artist had found – the Cavaliere was master of such arts. The Duchess's attitude was one of transport, as though heavenly airs fluttered her laces and the love-locks escaping from her coif. I saw how admirably the sculptor had caught the pose of her head, the tender slope of the shoulder; then I crossed over and looked into her face – it was a frozen horror. Never have hate, revolt, and agony so possessed a human countenance. . . .

The old man crossed himself and shuffled his feet on the marble.

'The Duchess Violante,' he repeated.

'The same as in the picture?'

'Eh – the same.'

'But the face – what does it mean?'

He shrugged his shoulders and turned deaf eyes on me. Then he shot a glance round the sepulchral place, clutched my sleeve and said, close to my ear: 'It was not always so.'

'What was not?'

'The face – so terrible.'

'The Duchess's face?'

'The statue's. It changed after —"

'After?'

'It was put here.'

'The statue's face *changed* —?'

He mistook my bewilderment for incredulity, and his confidential finger dropped from my sleeve. 'Eh, that's the story. I tell what I've heard. What do I know?' He resumed his senile shuffle across the marble. 'This is a bad place to stay in – no one comes here. It's too cold. But the gentleman said, *I must see everything?*'

I let the *lire* sound. 'So I must – and hear everything. This story, now – from whom did you have it?'

His hand stole back. 'One that saw it, by God!'

'That saw it?'

'My grandmother, then. I'm a very old man.'

'You grandmother? Your grandmother was —?'

'The Duchess's serving girl, with respect to you.'

'Your grandmother? Two hundred years ago?'

'Is it too long ago? That's as God pleases. I am a very old man, and she was a very old woman when I was born. When she died she was as black as a miraculous virgin, and her breath whistled like the wind in a keyhole. She told me the story when I was a little boy. She told it to me out there in the garden, on a bench by the fish pond, one summer night of the year she died. It must be true, for I can show you the very bench we sat on. . . .'

III

Noon lay heavier on the gardens; not our live humming warmth but the stale exhalation of dead summers. The very statues seemed to drowse like watches by a deadbed. Lizards shot out of the cracked soil like flames, and the bench in the laurustinus niche was strewn with the blue varnished bodies of dead flies. Before us lay the fish pond, a yellow marble slab above rotting secrets. The villa looked across it, composed as a dead face, with the cypresses flanking it for candles. . . .

IV

'Impossible, you say, that my mother's mother should have been the Duchess's maid? What do I know? It is so long since anything has happened here that the old things seem nearer, perhaps, than to those who live in cities. . . . But how else did she know about the statue then? Answer me that, sir! That she saw with her eyes, I can swear to, and never smiled again, so she told me, till they put her first child in her arms; . . . for she was taken to wife by the steward's son, Antonio, the same who had carried the letters. . . . But where am I? Ah, well . . . she was a mere slip, you understand, my grandmother, when the Duchess died, a niece of the upper maid, Nencia, and suffered about the Duchess because of her pranks and the funny songs she knew. It's possible, you think, she may have heard from others what she afterward fancied she had seen herself? How that is, it's not for an unlettered man to say; though indeed I myself seem to have seen many of the things she told me. This is a strange place. No one comes here, nothing changes, and the old memories stand up as distinct as the statues in the garden. . . .

'It began the summer after they came back from the Brenta. Duke Ercole had married the lady from Venice, you must know; it was a gay city, then, I'm told, with laughter and music on the water, and the days slipped by like boats running with the tide. Well, to humour her, he took her back the first autumn to the Brenta. Her father, it appears, had a grand palace there, with such gardens, bowling-alleys, grottoes, and casinos as never were; gondolas bobbing at the water-gates, a stable full of gilt coaches, a theater full of players, and kitchens and offices full of cooks and lackeys to serve up chocolate all day long to the fine ladies in masks and furbelows, with their pet dogs and their blackamoors and their *abates*. Eh! I know it all as if I'd been there; for Nencia, you see, my grandmother's aunt, travelled with the Duchess, and came back with her eyes round as platters, and not a word to say for the rest of the year to any of the lads who'd courted her here in Vicenza.

'What happened there I don't know – my grandmother could never get at the rights of it, for Nencia was mute as a fish where her lady was concerned – but when they came back to Vicenza the Duke ordered the villa set in order; and in the spring he brought the Duchess here and left her. She looked happy enough, my grandmother said, and seemed no object for pity. Perhaps, after all, it was better than being shut up in Vicenza, in the tall painted rooms where priests came and went as softly as cats prowling for birds, and the Duke was for ever closeted in his library, talking with learned men. The Duke was a scholar; you noticed he was painted with a book? Well, those that can read 'em make out that they're full of wonderful things; as a man that's been to a fair across the mountains will always tell his people at home it was beyond anything *they'll* ever see. As for the Duchess, she was all for music, play-acting, and young company. The Duke was a silent man, stepping quietly, with his eyes down, as though he'd just come from confession; when the Duchess's lap-dog yapped at his heels he danced like a man in a swarm of hornets; when the Duchess laughed he winced as if you'd drawn a diamond across a window-pane. And the Duchess was always laughing.

'When she first came to the villa she was very busy laying out the gardens, designing grottoes, planting groves and planning all manner of agreeable surprises in the way of water-jets that drenched you unexpectedly, and hermits in caves, and wild men that jumped at you out of thickets. She had a very pretty taste in such matters, but after a while she tired of it, and there being no one for her to talk to but her maids and the chaplain – a clumsy man deep in his books – why, she would have strolling players out from Vicenza, mountebanks and fortune-tellers from the market-place, travelling doctors and astrologers, and all manner of trained animals. Still it could be seen that the poor lady pined for company, and her waiting women, who loved her, were glad when the Cavaliere Ascanio, the Duke's cousin, came to live at the vineyard across the valley – you see the pinkish house over there in the mulberries, with a red roof and a pigeon-cote?

'The Cavaliere Ascanio was a cadet of one of the great Venetian houses, *pezzi grossi* of the Golden Book. He had been meant for the Church, I believe, but what! he set fighting above praying, and cast in his lot with the captain of the Duke of Mantua's *bravi*, himself a Venetian of good standing, but a little at odds with the law. Well, the next I know, the Cavaliere was in Venice again, perhaps not in good odour on account of his connection with the gentleman I speak of. Some say he tried to carry off a nun from the convent of Santa Croce; how that may be I can't say; but my grandmother declared he had enemies there, and the end of it was that on some pretext or other the Ten banished him to Vicenza. There, of course, the Duke, being his kinsman, had to show him a civil face; and that was how he first came to the villa.

'He was a fine young man, beautiful as a Saint Sebastian, a rare musician, who sang his own songs to the lute in a way that used to make my grandmother's heart melt and run through her body like mulled wine. He had a good word for everybody, too, and was always dressed in the French fashion, and smelt as sweet as a bean-field, and every soul about the place welcomed the sight of him.

'Well, the Duchess, it seemed, welcomed it too; youth will have youth, and laughter turns to laughter; and the two matched each other like the candlesticks on an altar. The Duchess – you've seen her portrait – but to hear my grandmother, sir, it no more approached her than a weed comes up to a rose. The Cavaliere, indeed, as became a poet, paragoned her in his song to all the pagan goddesses of antiquity; and doubtless these were finer to look at than mere women; but so, it seemed, was she; for, to believe my grandmother, she made other women look no more than the big French fashion-doll that used to be shown on Ascension days in the Piazza. She was one, at any rate, that needed no outlandish finery to beautify her; whatever dress she wore became her as feathers fit the bird; and her hair didn't get its colour by bleaching on the housetop. It glittered of itself like the threads in an Easter chasuble, and her skin was whiter than fine wheaten bread and her mouth as sweet as a ripe fig. . . .

'Well, sir, you could no more keep them apart than the bees and the lavender. They were always together, singing, bowling, playing cup and ball, walking in the gardens, visiting the aviaries, and petting her Grace's trick-dogs and monkeys. The Duchess was as gay as a foal, always playing pranks and laughing, tricking out her animals like comedians, disguising herself as a peasant or a nun (you should have seen her one day pass herself off to the chaplain as a mendicant sister), or teaching the lads and girls of the vineyards to dance and sing madrigals together. The Cavaliere had a singular ingenuity in planning such entertainments, and the days were hardly long enough for their diversions. But towards the end of the summer the Duchess fell quiet and would hear only sad music, and the two sat together much in the gazebo at the end of the garden. It was there the Duke found them one day when he drove out from Vicenza in his gilt coach. He came but once or twice a year to the villa, and it was, as my grandmother said, just a part of her poor lady's ill-luck to be wearing that day the Venetian habit, which uncovered the shoulders in a way the Duke always scowled at, and her curls loose and powdered with gold. Well, the three drank chocolate in the gazebo, and what happened no one knew, except that the Duke, on taking leave, gave his cousin a seat in his carriage; but the Cavaliere never returned.

'Winter approaching, and the poor lady thus finding herself

once more alone, it was surmised among her women that she must fall into a deeper depression of spirits. But far from this being the case, she displayed such cheerfulness and equanimity of humour that my grandmother, for one, was half-vexed with her for giving no more thought to the poor young man who, all this time, was eating his heart out in the house across the valley. It is true she quitted her gold-laced gowns and wore a veil over her head; but Nencia would have it she looked the lovelier for the change, and so gave the Duke greater displeasure. Certain it is that the Duke drove out oftener to the villa, and though he found his lady always engaged in some innocent pursuit, such as embroidery or music, or playing games with her young women, yet he always went away with a sour look and a whispered word to the chaplain. Now as to the chaplain, my grandmother owned there had been a time when her Grace had not handled him over-wisely. For, according to Nencia, it seems that his reverence, who seldom approached the Duchess, being buried in his library like a mouse in a cheese – well, one day he made bold to appeal to her for a sum of money, a large sum, Nencia said, to buy certain tall books, a chest full of them, that a foreign pedlar had brought him; whereupon the Duchess, who could never abide a book, breaks out at him with a laugh and a flash of her old spirit – "Holy Mother of God, must I have more books about me? I was nearly smothered with them in the first year of my marriage"; and the chaplain turning red at the affront, she added: "You may buy them and welcome, my good chaplain, if you can find the money; but as for me, I am yet seeking a way to pay for my turquoise necklace, and the statue of Daphne at the end of the bowling-green, and the Indian parrot that my black boy brought me last Michaelmas from the Bohemians – so you see I've no money to waste on trifles"; and as he backs out awkwardly she tosses at him over her shoulder: "You should pray to Saint Blandina to open the Duke's pocket!" to which he returned very quietly; "Your Excellency's suggestion is an admirable one, and I have already entreated that blessed martyr to open the Duke's understanding."

'Thereat, Nencia said (who was standing by), the Duchess flushed wonderfully red and waved him out of the room; and then "Quick!" she cried to my grandmother (who was too glad to run on such errands). "Call me Antonio, the gardener's boy, to the box-garden; I've a word to say to him about the new clove-carnations. . . ."

'Now I may not have told you, sir, that in the crypt under the chapel there has stood, for more generations than a man can count, a stone coffin containing a thigh-bone of the blessed Saint Blandina of Lyons, a relic offered, I've been told, by some great Duke of France to one of our own dukes when they fought the Turk together; and the object, ever since, of particular veneration in this illustrious family. Now, since the Duchess had been left to herself, it was observed she affected a fervent devotion to this relic, praying often in the chapel and even causing the stone slab that covered the entrance to the crypt to be replaced by a wooden one, that she might at will descend and kneel by the coffin. This was matter of edification to all the household, and should have been peculiarly pleasing to the chaplain; but, with respect to you, he was the kind of man who brings a sour mouth to the eating of the sweetest apple.

'However that may be, the Duchess, when she dismissed him, was seen running to the garden, where she talked earnestly with the boy Antonio about the new clove-carnations, and the rest of the day she sat indoors and played sweetly on the virginal. Now Nencia always had it in mind that her Grace had made a mistake in refusing that request of the chaplain's; but she said nothing, for to talk reason to the Duchess was of no more use than praying for rain in a drought.

'Winter came early that year, there was snow on the hills by All Souls, the wind stripped the gardens, and the lemon-trees were nipped in the lemon-house. The Duchess kept her room in this black season, sitting over the fire, embroidering, reading books of devotion (which was a thing she had never done), and praying frequently in the chapel. As for the chaplain, it was a place he never set foot in but to say mass in the morning, with the Duchess overhead in the tribune, and the servants aching with rheumatism on the marble floor. The chaplain himself hated the cold, and galloped through the mass like a man with witches after him. The rest of the day he spent in his library, over a brazier, with his eternal books. . . .

'You'll wonder, sir, if I'm ever to get to the gist of the story; and I've gone slowly, I own, for fear of what's coming. Well, the winter was long and hard. When it fell cold the Duke ceased to come out from Vicenza, and not a soul had the Duchess to speak to but her maid-servants and the gardeners about the place. Yet it was wonderful, my grandmother said, how she kept her brave colours and her spirits; only it was remarked that she prayed longer in the chapel, where a brazier was kept burning for her all day. When the young are denied their natural pleasures they turn often enough to religion; and it was a mercy, as my grandmother said, that she, who had scarce a live sinner to speak to, should take such comfort in a dead saint.

'My grandmother seldom saw her that winter, for though she showed a brave front to all, she kept more and more to herself, choosing to have only Nencia about her, and dismissing even her when she went to pray. For her devotion has that mark of true piety, that she wished it not to be observed; so that Nencia had strict orders, on the chaplain's approach, to warn her mistress if she happened to be in prayer.

'Well, the winter passed, and spring was well forward, when my grandmother one evening had a bad fright. That it was her own fault I won't deny, for she'd been down the lime-walk with Antonio when her aunt fancied her to be stitching in her chamber; and seeing a sudden light in Nencia's window, she took fright lest her disobedience be found out, and ran up quickly through the laurel-grove to the house. Her way lay by the chapel, and as she crept past it, meaning to slip in through the scullery, and groping her way, for the dark had fallen and the moon was scarce up, she heard a crash close behind her, as though some one had dropped from a window of the chapel. The young fool's heart turned over, but she looked round as she ran, and there, sure enough, was a man scuttling across the terrace; and as he doubled the corner of the house my grandmother swore she caught the whisk of the chaplain's skirts. Now that was a strange thing, certainly; for why should the chaplain be getting out of the chapel window when he might have passed through the door? For you may have noticed, sir, there's a door leads from the chapel into the saloon on the ground floor; the only other way out being through the Duchess's tribune.

'Well, my grandmother turned the matter over, and next time she met Antonio in the lime-walk (which, by reason of her fright, was not for some days) she laid before him what had happened; but to her surprise he only laughed and said: "You little simpleton, he wasn't getting out of the window, he was trying to look in"; and not another word could she get from him.

'So the reason moved on to Easter, and news came the Duke had gone to Rome for that holy festivity. His comings and goings made no change at the villa, and yet there was no one there but felt easier to think his yellow face was on the far side of the Apennines, unless perhaps it was the chaplain.

'Well, it was one day in May that the Duchess, who had walked long with Nencia on the terrace, rejoicing at the sweetness of the prospect and the pleasant scent of the gillyflowers in the stone vases, the Duchess towards mid-day withdrew to her rooms, giving orders that her dinner should be served in her bedchamber. My grandmother helped to carry in the dishes, and observed, she said, the singular beauty of the Duchess, who in honour of the fine weather had put on a gown of shot-silver and hung her bare shoulders with pearls, so that she looked fit to dance at court with an emperor. She had ordered, too, a rare repast for a lady that heeded so little what she ate – jellies, game-pasties, fruits in syrup, spiced cakes and a flagon of Greek wine; and she nodded and clapped her hands as the women set it before her, saying again and again, "I shall eat well today."

'But presently another mood seized her, she turned from the table, called for her rosary, and said to Nencia: "The fine weather has made me neglect my devotions. I must say a litany before I dine."

'She ordered the women out and barred the door, as her custom was; and Nencia and my grandmother went downstairs to work in the linen-room.

'Now the linen-room gives on the courtyard, and suddenly my grandmother saw a strange sight approaching. First up the avenue came the Duke's carriage (whom all thought to be in Rome), and after it, drawn by a long string of mules and oxen, a cart carrying what looked like a kneeling figure wrapped in death-clothes. The strangeness of it struck the girl dumb, and the Duke's coach was at the door before she had the wit to cry out that it was coming. Nencia, when she saw it, went white and ran out of the room. My grandmother followed, scared by her face, and the two fled along the corridor to the chapel. On the way they met the chaplain, deep in a book, who asked in surprise where they were running, and when they said to announce the Duke's arrival, he fell into such astonishment, and asked them so many questions, and uttered such Ohs and Ahs, that by the time he let them by the Duke was at their heels. Nencia reached the chapel-door first, and cried out that the Duke was coming; and before she had a reply he was at her side, with the chaplain following.

'A moment later the door opened and there stood the Duchess. She held her rosary in one hand and had drawn a scarf over her shoulders; but they shone through it like the moon in a mist, and her countenance sparkled with beauty.

'The Duke took her hand with a bow. "Madam," he said, "I could have had no greater happiness than thus to surprise you at your devotions."

'"My own happiness", she replied, "would have been greater had your Excellency prolonged it by giving me notice of your arrival."

'"Had you expected me, Madam," said he, "your appearance could scarcely have been more fitted to the occasion. Few ladies of your youth and beauty array themselves to venerate a saint as they would to welcome a lover."

'"Sir," she answered, "having never enjoyed the latter opportunity, I am constrained to make the most of the former. — What's that?" she cried, falling back, and the rosary dropped from her hand.

'There was a loud noise at the other end of the saloon, as of a heavy object being dragged down the passage; and presently a dozen men were seen hauling across the threshold the shrouded thing from the ox-cart. The Duke waved his hand toward it. "That," said he, "Madam, is a tribute to your extraordinary piety. I have heard, with peculiar satisfaction of your devotion to the blessed relics in this chapel, and to commemorate a zeal which neither the rigours of winter nor the sultriness of summer could abate, I have ordered a sculptured image of you, marvellously executed by the Cavaliere Bernini, to be placed before the altar over the entrance to the crypt."

'The Duchess, who had grown pale, nevertheless smiled playfully at this. "As to commemorating my piety," she said, "I recognize there one of your Excellency's pleasantries—"

'"A pleasantry?" the Duke interrupted; and he made a sign to the men, who had now reached the threshold of the chapel. In an instant the wrappings fell from the figure, and there knelt the Duchess to the life. A cry of wonder rose from all, but the Duchess herself stood whiter than the marble.

'"You will see," says the Duke, "this is no pleasantry, but a triumph of the incomparable Bernini's chisel. The likeness was done from your miniature portrait by the divine Elisabetta Sirani, which I sent to the master some six months ago, with what results all must admire."

'"Six months!" cried the Duchess, and seemed about to fall; but his Excellency caught her by the hand.

'"Nothing," he said, "could better please me than the excessive emotion you display, for true piety is ever modest, and your thanks could not take a form that better became you. And now," says he to the men, "let the image be put in place."

'By this time, life seemed to have returned to the Duchess, and she answered him with a deep reverence. "That I should be overcome by so unexpected a grace, your Excellency admits to be natural; but what honours you accord it is my privilege to accept, and I entreat only that in mercy to my modesty the image be placed in the remotest part of the chapel."

'At that the Duke darkened. "What! You would have this masterpiece of a renowned chisel, which, I disguise not, cost me the price of a good vineyard in gold pieces, you would have it thrust out of sight like the work of a village stonecutter?"

'"It is my semblance, not the sculptor's work, I desire to conceal."

'"If you are fit for my house, Madam, you are fit for God's, and entitled to the place of honour in both. Bring the statue forward, you dawdlers!" he called out to the men.

'The Duchess fell back submissively. "You are right, sir, as always; but I would at least have the image stand on the left of the altar, that, looking up, it may behold your Excellency's seat in the tribune."

'"A pretty thought, Madam, for which I thank you; but I design before long to put my companion image on the other side of the altar; and the wife's place, as you know, is at her husband's right hand."

'"True, my Lord – but, again, if my poor presentment is to have the unmerited honour of kneeling beside yours, why not place both before the altar, where it is our habit to pray in life?"

'"And where, Madam, should we kneel if they took our places? Besides," says the Duke, still speaking very blandly, "I have a more particular purpose in placing your image over the entrance to the crypt; for not only would I thereby mark your special devotion to the blessed saint who rests there, but, by sealing up the opening in the pavement, would assure the perpetual preservation of that holy martyr's bones, which hitherto have been too thoughtlessly exposed to sacrilegious attempts."

'"What attempts, my Lord?" cries the Duchess. "No one enters this chapel without my leave."

'"So I have understood, and can well believe from what I have learned of your piety; yet at night a malefactor might break in through a window, Madam, and your Excellency not know it."

'"I'm a light sleeper," said the Duchess.

'The Duke looked at her gravely. "Indeed?" said he. "A bad sign at your age. I must see that you are provided with a sleeping-draught."

'The Duchess's eyes filled. "You would deprive me, then, of the consolation of visiting those venerable relics?"

'"I would have you keep eternal guard over them, knowing no one to whose care they may more fittingly be entrusted."

'At this the image was brought close to the wooden slab that covered the entrance to the crypt, when the Duchess, springing forward, placed herself in the way.

'"Sir, let the statue be put in place tomorrow, and suffer me, tonight, to say a last prayer beside those holy bones."

'The Duke stepped instantly to her side. "Well thought, Madam; I will go down with you now, and we will pray together."

'"Sir, your long absences have, alas! given me the habit of solitary devotion, and I confess that any presence is distracting."

'"Madam, I accept your rebuke. Hitherto, it is true, the duties of my station have constrained me to long absences; but henceforward I remain with you while you live. Shall we go down into the crypt together?"

'"No; for I fear for your Excellency's ague. The air there is excessively damp."

'"The more reason you should no longer be exposed to it; and to prevent the intemperance of your zeal I will at once make the place inaccessible."

'The Duchess at this fell on her knees on the slab, weeping excessively and lifting her hands to Heaven.

'"Oh" she cried, "you are cruel, sir, to deprive me of access to the sacred relics that have enabled me to support with resignation the solitude to which your Excellency's duties have condemned me; and if prayer and meditation give me any authority to pronounce on such matters, suffer me to warn you, sir, that I fear the blessed Saint Blandina will punish us for thus abandoning her venerable remains!"

'The Duke at this seemed to pause, for he was a pious man, and my grandmother thought she saw him exchange a glance with the chaplain; who, stepping timidly forward, with his eyes on the ground, said; "There is indeed much wisdom in her Excellency's words, but I would suggest, sir, that her pious wish might be met, and the saint more conspicuously honoured, by transferring the relics from the crypt to a place beneath the altar."

'"True!" cried the Duke, "and it shall be done at once."

'But thereat the Duchess rose to her feet with a terrible look.

'"No," she cried, "by the body of God! For it shall not be said that, after your Excellency has chosen to deny every request I addressed to him, I owe his consent to the solicitation of another!"

'The chaplain turned red and the Duke yellow, and for a moment neither spoke.

'Then the Duke said, "Here are words enough, Madam. Do you wish the relics brought up from the crypt?"

'"I wish nothing that I owe to another's intervention!"

'"Put the image in place then," says the Duke furiously; and handed her Grace to a chair.

'She sat there, my grandmother said, straight as an arrow, her hands locked, her head high, her eyes on the Duke, while the statue was dragged to its place; then she stood up and turned away. As she passed by Nencia, "Call me Antonio," she whispered; but before the words were out of her mouth the Duke stepped between them.

'"Madam," says he, all smiles now, " I have travelled straight from Rome to bring you the sooner this proof of my esteem. I lay last night at Monselice, and have been on the road since daybreak. Will you not invite me to supper?"

'"Surely, my Lord," said the Duchess. "It shall be laid in the dining-parlour within the hour."

'"Why not in your chamber and at once, Madam? Since I believe it is your custom to sup there."

'"In my chamber?" says the Duchess, in disorder.

'"Have you anything against it?" he asked.

'"Assuredly not, sir, if you will give me time to prepare myself."

'"I will wait in your cabinet," said the Duke.

'At that, said my grandmother, the Duchess gave one look, as the souls in hell may have looked when the gates closed on our Lord; then she called Nencia and passed to her chamber.

'What happened there my grandmother could never learn, but that the Duchess, in great haste, dressed herself with extraordinary splendour, powdering her hair with gold, painting her face and bosom, and covering herself with jewels till she shone like our Lady of Loretto; and hardly were these preparations complete when the Duke entered from the cabinet, followed by the servants carrying supper. Thereupon the Duchess dismissed Nencia, and what follows my grandmother learned from a pantry-lad who brought up the dishes and waited in the cabinet; for only the Duke's body-servant entered the bedchamber.

'Well, according to this boy, sir, who was looking and listening with his whole body, as it were, because he had never before been suffered so near the Duchess, it appears that the noble couple sat down in great good humour, the Duchess playfully reproving her husband for his long absence, while the Duke swore that to look so beautiful was the best way of punishing him. In this tone the talk continued, with such gay sallies on the part of the Duchess, such tender advances on the Duke's, that the lad declared they were for all the world like a pair of lovers courting on a summer's night in the vineyard; and so it went till the servant brought in the mulled wine.

'"Ah," the Duke was saying at that moment, "this agreeable evening repays me for the many dull ones I have spent away from you; nor do I remember to have enjoyed such laughter since the afternoon last year when we drank chocolate in the gazebo with my cousin Ascanio. And that reminds me," he said, "is my cousin in good health?"

'"I have no reports of it," says the Duchess. "But your Excellency should taste these figs stewed in malmsey — "

'"I am in the mood to taste whatever you offer," said he; and as she helped him to the figs, he added, "if my enjoyment were not complete as it is, I could almost wish my cousin Ascanio were with us. The fellow is rare good company at supper. What do you say, Madam? I hear he's still in the country; shall we send for him to join us?"

'"Ah," said the Duchess, with a sigh and a languishing look, "I see your Excellency wearies of me already."

'"I, Madam? Ascanio is a capital good fellow, but to my mind his chief merit at this moment is his absence. It inclines me so tenderly to him that, by God, I could empty a glass to his good health."

'With that the Duke caught up his goblet and signed to the servant to fill the Duchess's.

'"Here's to the cousin," he cried, standing, "who has the good taste to stay away when he's not wanted. I drink to his very long life — and you, Madam?"

'At this the Duchess, who had sat staring at him with a changed face, rose also and lifted her glass to her lips.

'"And I to his happy death," says she in a wild voice; and as she spoke the empty goblet dropped from her hand and she fell down on the floor.

'The Duke shouted to her women that she had swooned, and they came and lifted her to the bed. . . . She suffered horribly all night, Nencia said, twisting herself like a heretic at the stake, but without a word escaping her. The Duke watched by her, and toward daylight sent for the chaplain; but by then she was unconscious, and, her teeth being locked, our Lord's body could not be passed through them.

'The Duke announced to his relations that his lady had died after partaking too freely of spiced wine and an omelette of carp's roe, at a supper she had prepared in honour of his return; and the next year he brought home a new Duchess, who gave him a son and five daughters. . . .'

V

The sky had turned to a steel grey, against which the villa stood out sallow and inscrutable. A wind strayed through the gardens, loosening here and there a yellow leaf from the sycamores; and the hills across the valley were purple as thunder clouds.

* * *

'And the statue —?' I asked.

'Ah, the statue. Well, sir, this is what my grandmother told me, here on this very bench where we're sitting. The poor child, who worshipped the Duchess as a girl of her years will worship a beautiful kind mistress, spent a night of horror, you may fancy, shut out from her lady's room, hearing the cries that came from it, and seeing, as she crouched in her corner, the women rush to and fro with wild looks, the Duke's lean face in the door, and the chaplain skulking in the antechamber with his eyes on his breviary. No one minded her that night or the next morning; and towards dusk, when it became known the Duchess was no more, the poor girl felt the pious wish to say a prayer for her dead mistress. She crept to the chapel and stole in unobserved. The place was empty and dim, but as she advanced she heard a low moaning, and coming in front of the statue she saw that its face, the day before so sweet and smiling, had the look on it that you know – and the moaning seemed to come from its lips. My grandmother turned cold, but something she said afterward, kept her from calling or shrieking out, and she turned and ran from the place. In the passage she fell in a swoon; and when she came to her senses, in her own chamber, she heard that the Duke had locked the chapel door and forbidden any to set foot there. . . . The place was never opened again till the Duke died, some ten years later; and then it was that the other servants, going in with the new heir, saw for the first time the horror that my grand-mother had kept in her bosom. . . .'

'And the crypt?' I asked. 'Has it never been opened?'

'Heaven forbid, sir!' cried the old man, crossing himself. 'Was it not the Duchess's express wish that the relics should not be disturbed?'

The Fullness of Life

I

For hours she had lain in a kind of gentle torpor, not unlike that sweet lassitude which masters one in the hush of a midsummer noon, when the heat seems to have silenced the very birds and insects, and, lying sunk in the tasselled meadowgrasses, one looks up through a level roofing of maple-leaves at the vast, shadowless, and unsuggestive blue. Now and then, at ever-lengthening intervals, a flash of pain darted through her, like the ripple of sheet-lightning across such a midsummer sky; but it was too transitory to shake her stupor, that calm, delicious, bottomless stupor into which she felt herself sinking more and more deeply, without a disturbing impulse of resistance, an effort of reattachment to the vanishing edges of consciousness.

The resistance, the effort, had known their hour of violence; but now they were at an end. Through her mind, long harried by grotesque visions, fragmentary images of the life that she was leaving, tormenting lines of verse, obstinate presentiments of pictures once beheld, indistinct impressions of rivers, towers, and cupolas, gathered in the length of journeys half forgotten – through her mind there now only moved a few primal sensations of colourless well-being; a vague satisfaction in the thought that she had swallowed her noxious last draught of medicine . . . and that she should never again hear the creaking of her husband's boots – those horrible boots – and that no one would come to bother her about the

32

next day's dinner . . . or the butcher's book. . . .

At last even these dim sensations spent themselves in the thickening obscurity which enveloped her; a dusk now filled with pale geometric roses, circling softly, interminably before her, now darkened to a uniform blue-blackness, the hue of a summer night without stars. And into this darkness she felt herself sinking, sinking, with the gentle sense of security of one upheld from beneath. Like a tepid tide it rose around her, gliding ever higher and higher, folding in its velvety embrace her relaxed and tired body, now submerging her breast and shoulders, now creeping gradually, with soft inexorableness, over her throat to her chin, to her ears, to her mouth. . . . Ah, now it was rising too high; the impulse to struggle was renewed; . . . her mouth was full; . . . she was choking. . . . Help!

'It is all over,' said the nurse, drawing down the eyelids with official composure.

The clock struck three. They remembered it afterwards. Someone opened the window and let in a blast of that strange, neutral air which walks the earth between darkness and dawn; someone else led the husband into another room. He walked vaguely, like a blind man, on his creaking boots.

II

She stood, as it seemed, on a threshold, yet no tangible gateway was in front of her. Only a wide vista of light, mild yet penetrating as the gathered glimmer of innumerable stars, expanded gradually before her eyes, in blissful contrast to the cavernous darkness from which she had of late emerged.

She stepped forward, not frightened, but hesitating, and as her eyes began to grow more familiar with the melting depths of light about her, she distinguished the outlines of landscape, at first swimming in the opaline uncertainty of Shelley's vaporous creations, then gradually resolved into distincter shape – the vast unrolling of a sunlit plain, aërial forms of mountains, and presently the silver crescent of a river in the valley, and a blue stencilling of trees along its curve – something suggestive in its ineffable hue of an azure background of Leonardo's, strange, enchanting, mysterious, leading on the eye and the imagination into regions of fabulous delight. As she gazed, her heart beat with a soft and rapturous surprise; so exquisite a promise she read in the summons of that hyaline distance.

'And so death is not the end after all,' in sheer gladness she heard herself exclaiming aloud. 'I always knew that it couldn't be. I believed in Darwin, of course. I do still; but then Darwin himself said that he wasn't sure about the soul – at least, I think he did – and Wallace was a spiritualist; and then there was St George Mivart —'

Her gaze lost itself in the ethereal remoteness of the mountains.

'How beautiful! How satisfying!' she murmured. 'Perhaps now I shall really know what it is to live.'

As she spoke she felt a sudden thickening of her heartbeats, and looking up she was aware that before her stood the Spirit of Life.

'Have you never really known what it is to live?' the Spirit of Life asked her.

'I have never known', she replied, 'that fullness of life which we all feel ourselves capable of knowing; though my life has not been without scattered hints of it, like the scent of earth which comes to one sometimes far out at sea.'

'And what do you call the fullness of life?' the Spirit asked again.

'Oh, I can't tell you, if you don't know,' she said, almost reproachfully. 'Many words are supposed to define it – love and sympathy are those in commonest use, but I am not even sure that they are the right ones, and so few people really know what they mean.'

'You were married,' said the Spirit, 'yet you did not find the fullness of life in your marriage?'

'Oh, dear, no,' she replied, with an indulgent scorn, 'my marriage was a very incomplete affair.'

'And yet you were fond of your husband?'

'You have hit upon the exact word; I was fond of him, yes, just as I was fond of my grandmother, and the house that I was born in, and my old nurse. Oh, I was fond of him, and we were counted a very happy couple. But I have sometimes thought that a woman's nature is like a great house full of rooms: there is the hall, through which everyone passes in going in and out; the drawing-room, where one receives formal visits; the sitting-room, where the members of the family come and go as they list; but beyond that, far beyond, are other rooms, the handles of whose doors perhaps are never turned; no one knows the way to them, no one knows whither they lead; and in the innermost room, the holy of holies, the soul sits alone and waits for a footstep that never comes.'

'And your husband', asked the Spirit, after a pause, 'never got beyond the family sitting-room?'

'Never,' she returned, impatiently; 'and the worst of it was that he was quite content to remain there. He thought it perfectly beautiful, and sometimes, when he was admiring its commonplace furniture, insignificant as the chairs and tables of a hotel parlour, I felt like crying out to him: "Fool, will you never guess that close at hand are rooms full of treasures and wonders, such as the eye of man hath not seen, rooms that no step has crossed, but that might be yours to live in, could you but find the handle of the door?"'

'Then,' the Spirit continued, 'those moments of which you lately spoke, which seemed to come to you like scattered hints of the fullness of life, were not shared with your husband?'

'Oh, no – never. He was different. His boots creaked, and he always slammed the door when he went out, and he never read anything but railway novels and the sporting advertisements in the papers – and – and, in short, we never understood each other in the least.'

'To what influence, then, did you owe those exquisite sensations?'

'I can hardly tell. Sometimes to the perfume of a flower; sometimes to a verse of Dante or of Shakespeare; sometimes to a picture or a sunset, or to one of those calm days at sea, when one seems to be lying in the hollow of a blue pearl; sometimes, but rarely, to a word spoken by someone who chanced to give utterance, at the right moment, to what I felt but could not express.'

'Someone whom you loved?' asked the Spirit.

'I never loved anyone, in that way,' she said, rather sadly, 'nor was I thinking of any one person when I spoke, but of two or three who, by touching for an instant upon a certain chord of my being, had called forth a single note of that strange melody which seemed sleeping in my soul. It has seldom happened, however, that I have owed such feelings to people; and no one ever gave me a moment of such happiness as it was my lot to feel one evening in the Church of Or San Michele, in Florence.'

'Tell me about it,' said the Spirit.

'It was near sunset on a rainy spring afternoon in Easter week. The clouds had vanished, dispersed by a sudden wind, and as we entered the church the fiery panes of the high windows shone out like lamps through the dusk. A priest was at the high altar, his white cope a livid spot in the incense-laden obscurity, the light of the candles flickering up and down like fireflies about his head; a few people knelt near by. We stole behind them and sat down on a bench close to the tabernacle of Orcagna.

'Strange to say, though Florence was not new to me, I had never been in the church before; and in that magical light I saw for the first time the inlaid steps, the fluted columns, the sculptured bas-reliefs and canopy of the marvellous shrine. The marble, worn and mellowed by the subtle hand of time, took on an unspeakable rosy hue, suggestive in some remote way of the honey-coloured columns of the Parthenon, but more mystic, more complex, a colour not born of the sun's inveterate kiss, but made up of cryptal twilight, and the flame of candles upon martyrs' tombs, and gleams of sunset through symbolic panes of chrysoprase and ruby; such a light as illumines the missals in the library of Siena, or burns like a hidden fire through the Madonna of Gian Bellini in the Church of the Redeemer, at Venice; the light of the Middle Ages, richer, more solemn, more significant than the limpid sunshine of Greece.

'The church was silent, but for the wail of the priest and the occasional scraping of a chair against the floor, and as I sat there, bathed in that light, absorbed in rapt contemplation of the marble miracle which rose before me, cunningly wrought as a casket of ivory and enriched with jewel-like incrustations and tarnished gleams of gold, I felt myself borne onward along a mighty current, whose source seemed to be in the very beginning of things, and whose tremendous waters gathered as they went all the mingled streams of human passion and endeavor. Life in all its varied manifestations of beauty and strangeness seemed weaving a rhythmical dance around me as I moved, and wherever the spirit of man had passed I knew that my foot had once been familiar.

'As I gazed, the mediæval bosses of the tabernacle of Orcagna seemed to melt and flow into their primal forms, so that the folded lotus of the Nile and the Greek acanthus were braided with the runic knots and fish-tailed monsters of the North, and all the plastic terror and beauty born of man's hand from the Ganges to the Baltic quivered and mingled in Orcagna's apotheosis of Mary. And so the river bore me on, past the alien face of antique civilizations and the familiar wonders of Greece, till I swam upon the fiercely rushing tide of the Middle Ages, with its swirling eddies of passion, its heaven-reflecting pools of poetry and art; I heard the rhythmic blow of the craftsmen's hammers in the goldsmiths' workshops and on the walls of churches, the party-cries of armed factions in the narrow streets, the organ-roll of Dante's verse, the crackle of the faggots around Arnold of Brescia, the twitter of the swallows to which St Francis preached, the laughter of the ladies listening on the hillside to the quips of the Decameron, while plague-struck Florence howled beneath them – all this and much more I heard, joined in strange unison with voices earlier and more remote, fierce, passionate, or tender, yet subdued to such awful harmony that I thought of the song that the morning stars sang together and felt as though it were sounding in my ears. My heart beat to suffocation, the tears burned my lids, the joy, the mystery of it seemed too intolerable to be borne. I could not understand even then the words of the song; but I knew that if there had been someone at my side who could have heard it with me, we might have found the key to it together.

'I turned to my husband, who was sitting beside me in an attitude of patient dejection, gazing into the bottom of his hat; but at that moment he rose, and stretching his stiffened legs, said, mildly: "Hadn't we better be going? There doesn't seem to be much to see here, and you know the table d'hôte dinner is at half-past six o'clock."'

Her recital ended, there was an interval of silence; then the Spirit of Life said: 'There is a compensation in store for such needs as you have expressed.'

'Oh, then you *do* understand?' she exclaimed. 'Tell me what compensation, I entreat you!'

'It is ordained', the Spirit answered, 'that every soul which seeks in vain on earth for a kindred soul to whom it can lay bare its inmost being shall find that soul here and be united to it for eternity.'

A glad cry broke from her lips.

'Ah, shall I find him at last?' she cried, exultant.

'He is here,' said the Spirit of Life.

She looked up and saw that a man stood near whose soul (for in that unwonted light she seemed to see his soul more clearly than his face) drew her towards him with an invincible force.

'Are you really he?' she murmured.

'I am he,' he answered.

She laid her hand in his and drew him towards the parapet which overhung the valley.

'Shall we go down together,' she asked him, 'into that marvellous country; shall we see it together, as if with the selfsame eyes, and tell each other in the same words all that we think and feel?'

'So', he replied, 'have I hoped and dreamed.'

'What?' she asked, with rising joy. 'Then you, too, have looked for me?'

'All my life.'

'How wonderful! And did you never, never find anyone in the other world who understood you?'

'Not wholly – not as you and I understand each other.'

'Then you feel it, too? Oh, I am happy,' she sighed.

They stood, hand in hand, looking down over the parapet upon the shimmering landscape which stretched forth beneath them into sapphirine space, and the Spirit of Life, who kept watch near the threshold, heard now and then a floating fragment of their talk blown backwards like the stray swallows which the wind sometimes separates from their migratory tribe.

'Did you never feel at sunset —'

'Ah, yes; but I never heard anyone else say so. Did you?'

'Do you remember that line in the third canto of the "Inferno"?'

'Ah, that line – my favourite always. Is it possible —'

'You know the stooping Victory in the frieze of the Nike Apteros?'

'You mean the one who is tying her sandal? Then you have noticed, too, that all Botticelli and Mantegna are dormant in those flying folds of her drapery?'

'After a storm in autumn have you never seen —'

'Yes, it is curious how certain flowers suggest certain painters – the perfume of the carnation, Leonardo; that of the rose, Titian; the tuberose, Crivelli —'

'I never supposed that anyone else had noticed it.'

'Have you never thought —'

'Oh, yes, often and often; but I never dreamed that anyone else had.'

'But surely you must have felt —'

'Oh, yes, yes; and you, too —'

'How beautiful! How strange —'

Their voices rose and fell, like the murmur of two fountains answering each other across a garden full of flowers. At length, with a certain tender impatience, he turned to her and said: 'Love, why should we linger here? All eternity lies before us. Let us go down into that beautiful country together and make a home for ourselves on some blue hill above the shining river.'

As he spoke, the hand she had forgotten in his was suddenly withdrawn, and he felt that a cloud was passing over the radiance of her soul.

'A home,' she repeated, slowly, 'a home for you and me to live in for all eternity?'

'Why not, love? Am I not the soul that yours has sought?'

'Y-yes – yes, I know – but, don't you see, home would not be like home to me, unless —'

'Unless?' he wonderingly repeated.

She did not answer, but she thought to herself, with an impulse of whimsical inconsistency, 'Unless you slammed the door and wore creaking boots.'

But he had recovered his hold upon her hand, and by imperceptible degrees was leading her towards the shining steps which descended to the valley.

'Come, O my soul's soul,' he passionately implored; 'why delay a moment? Surely you feel, as I do, that eternity itself is too short to hold such bliss as ours. It seems to me that I can see our home already. Have I not always seen it in my dreams? It is white, love, is it not, with polished columns, and a sculptured cornice against the blue? Groves of laurel and oleander and thickets of roses surround it; but from the terrace where we walk at sunset, the eye looks out over woodlands and cool meadows where, deep-bowered under ancient boughs, a stream goes delicately towards the river. Indoors our favourite pictures hang upon the walls and the rooms are lined with books. Think, dear, at last we shall have time to read them all. With which shall we begin? Come, help me to choose. Shall it be "Faust" or the *Vita Nuova*, the "Tempest" or "Les Caprices de Marianne," or the thirty-first canto of the *Paradise*, or "Epipsychidion" or "Lycidas"? Tell me, dear, which one?'

As he spoke he saw the answer trembling joyously upon her lips; but it died in the ensuing silence, and she stood motionless, resisting the persuasion of his hand.

'What is it?' he entreated.

'Wait a moment,' she said, with a strange hesitation in her voice. 'Tell me first, are you quite sure of yourself? Is there no one on earth whom you sometimes remember?'

'Not since I have seen you,' he replied; for, being a man, he had indeed forgotten.

Still she stood motionless, and he saw that the shadow deepened on her soul.

'Surely, love,' he rebuked her, 'it was not that which troubled you? For my part I have walked through Lethe. The past has melted like a cloud before the moon. I never lived until I saw you.'

She made no answer to his pleadings, but at length, rousing herself with a visible effort, she turned away from him and moved towards the Spirit of Life, who still stood near the threshold.

'I want to ask you a question,' she said, in a troubled voice.

'Ask,' said the Spirit.

'A little while ago,' she began, slowly, 'you told me that every soul which has not found a kindred soul on earth is destined to find one here.'

'And have you not found one?' asked the Spirit.

'Yes; but will it be so with my husband's soul also?'

'No,' answered the Spirit of Life, 'for your husband imagined that he had found his soul's mate on earth in you; and for such delusions eternity itself contains no cure.'

She gave a little cry. Was it of disappointment or triumph?

'Then – then what will happen to him when he comes here?'

'That I cannot tell you. Some field of activity and happiness he will doubtless find, in due measure to his capacity for being active and happy.'

She interrupted, almost angrily: 'He will never be happy without me.'

'Do not be too sure of that,' said the Spirit.

She took no notice of this, and the Spirit continued: 'He will not understand you here any better than he did on earth.'

'No matter,' she said; 'I shall be the only sufferer, for he always thought that he understood me.'

'His boots will creak just as much as ever —'

'No matter.'

'And he will slam the door —'

'Very likely.'

'And continue to read railway novels —'

She interposed, impatiently: 'Many men do worse than that.'

'But you said just now', said the Spirit, 'that you did not love him.'

'True,' she answered, simply; 'but don't you understand that I shouldn't feel at home without him? It is all very well for a week or two – but for eternity! After all, I never minded the creaking of his boots, except when my head ached, and I don't suppose it will ache *here*; and he was always so sorry when he had slammed the door, only he never *could* remember not to. Besides, no one else would know how to look after him, he is so helpless. His inkstand would never be filled, and he would always be out of stamps and visiting-cards. He would never remember to have his umbrella recovered, or to ask the price of anything before he bought it. Why, he wouldn't even know what novels to read. I always had to choose the kind he liked, with a murder or a forgery and a successful detective.'

She turned abruptly to her kindred soul, who stood listening with a mien of wonder and dismay.

'Don't you see', she said, 'that I can't possibly go with you?'

'But what do you intend to do?' asked the Spirit of Life.

'What do I intend to do?' she returned, indignantly. 'Why, I mean to wait for my husband, of course. If he had come here first *he* would have waited for me for years and years; and it would break his heart not to find me here when he comes.' She pointed with a contemptuous gesture to the magic vision of hill and vale sloping away to the translucent mountains. 'He wouldn't give a fig for all that,' she said, 'if he didn't find me here.'

'But consider,' warned the Spirit, 'that you are now choosing for eternity. It is a solemn moment.'

'Choosing!' she said, with a half-sad smile. 'Do you still keep up here that old fiction about choosing? I should have thought that *you* knew better than that. How can I help myself? He will expect to find me here when he comes, and he would never believe you if you told him that I had gone away with someone else – never, never.'

'So be it,' said the Spirit. 'Here, as on earth, each one must decide for himself.'

She turned to her kindred soul and looked at him gently, almost wistfully. 'I am sorry,' she said. 'I should have liked to talk with you again; but you will understand, I know, and I dare say you will find someone else a great deal cleverer —'

And without pausing to hear his answer she waved him a swift farewell and turned back towards the threshold.

'Will my husband come soon?' she asked the Spirit of Life.

'That you are not destined to know,' the Spirit replied.

'No matter,' she said, cheerfully; 'I have all eternity to wait in.'

And still seated alone on the threshold, she listens for the creaking of his boots.

A Journey

❦

As she lay in her berth, staring at the shadows overhead, the rush of the wheels was in her brain, driving her deeper and deeper into circles of wakeful lucidity. The sleeping-car had sunk into its night-silence. Through the wet window-pane she watched the sudden lights, the long stretches of hurrying blackness. Now and then she turned her head and looked through the opening in the hangings at her husband's curtains across the aisle. . . .

She wondered restlessly if he wanted anything and if she could hear him if he called. His voice had grown very weak within the last months and it irritated him when she did not hear. This irritability, this increasing childish petulance seemed to give expression to their imperceptible estrangement. Like two faces looking at one another through a sheet of glass they were close together, almost touching, but they could not hear or feel each other: the conductivity between them was broken. She, at least, had this sense of separation, and she fancied sometimes that she saw it reflected in the look with which he supplemented his failing words. Doubtless the fault was hers. She was too impenetrably healthy to be touched by the irrelevancies of disease. Her self-reproachful tenderness was tinged with the sense of his irrationality: she had a vague feeling that there was a purpose in his helpless tyrannies. The suddenness of the change had found her so unprepared. A year ago their pulses had beat to one robust measure; both had the same prodigal confidence in an exhaustless future. Now their energies no longer kept step: hers still bounded ahead of life, pre-empting unclaimed regions of hope and activity, while his lagged behind, vainly struggling to overtake her.

When they married, she had such arrears of living to make up: her days had been as bare as the whitewashed schoolroom where she forced innutritious facts upon reluctant children. His coming had broken in on the slumber of circumstance, widening the present till it became the encloser of remotest chances. But imperceptibly the horizon narrowed. Life had a grudge against her: she was never to be allowed to spread her wings.

At first the doctors had said that six weeks of mild air would set him right; but when he came back this assurance was explained as having of course included a winter in a dry climate. They gave up their pretty house, storing the wedding presents and new fur-niture, and went to Colorado. She had hated it there from the first. Nobody knew her or cared about her; there was no one to wonder at the good match she had made, or to envy her the new dresses and the visiting-cards which were still a surprise to her. And he kept growing worse. She felt herself beset with difficulties too evasive to be fought by so direct a temperament. She still loved him, of course; but he was gradually, undefinably ceasing to be himself. The man she had married had been strong, active, gently masterful: the male whose pleasure it is to clear a way through the material obstructions of life; but now it was she who was the protector, he who must be shielded from importunities and given his drops or his beef-juice though the skies were falling. The routine of the sick-room bewildered her; this punctual ad-ministering of medicine seemed as idle as some uncomprehended religious mummery.

There were moments, indeed, when warm gushes of pity swept away her instinctive resentment of his condition, when she still found his old self in his eyes as they groped for each other through the dense medium of his weakness. But these moments had grown rare. Sometimes he frightened her: his sunken expressionless face seemed that of a stranger; his voice was weak and hoarse; his thin-lipped smile a mere muscular contraction. Her hand avoided his damp soft skin, which had lost the familiar roughness of health: she caught herself furtively watching him as she might have watched a strange animal. It frightened her to feel that this was the man she loved; there were hours when to tell him what she suffered seemed the one escape from her fears. But in general she judged herself more leniently, reflecting that she had perhaps been too long alone with him, and that she would feel differently when they were at home again, surrounded by her robust and buoyant family. How she had rejoiced when the doctors at last gave their consent to his going home! She knew, of course, what the decision meant; they both knew. It meant that he was to die; but they dressed the truth in hopeful euphuisms, and at times, in the joy of preparation, she really forgot the purpose of their journey, and slipped into an eager allusion to next year's plans.

At last the day of leaving came. She had a dreadful fear that they would never get away; that somehow at the last moment he would fail her; that the doctors held one of their accustomed treacheries in reserve; but nothing happened. They drove to the station, he was installed in a seat with a rug over his knees and a cushion at his back, and she hung out of the window waving unregretful farewells to the acquaintances she had really never liked till then.

The first twenty-four hours had passed off well. He revived a little and it amused him to look out of the window and to observe the humours of the car. The second day he began to grow weary and to chafe under the dispassionate stare of the freckled child with the lump of chewing-gum. She had to explain to the child's mother that her husband was too ill to be disturbed: a statement received by that lady with a resentment visibly supported by the maternal sentiment of the whole car. . . .

That night he slept badly and the next morning his temperature frightened her: she was sure he was growing worse. The day passed slowly, punctuated by the small irritations of travel. Watching his tired face, she traced in its contractions every rattle and jolt of the train, till her own body vibrated with sympathetic fatigue. She felt the others observing him too, and hovered restlessly between him and the line of interrogative eyes. The freckled child hung about him like a fly; offers of candy and picture-books failed to dislodge her: she twisted one leg around the other and watched him imperturbably. The porter, as he passed, lingered with vague proffers of help, probably inspired by philanthropic passengers swelling with the sense that 'something ought to be done'; and one nervous man in a skull-cap was audibly concerned as to the possible effect on his wife's health.

The hours dragged on in a dreary inoccupation. Towards dusk she sat down beside him and he laid his hand on hers. The touch startled her. He seemed to be calling her from far off. She looked at him helplessly and his smile went through her like a physical pang.

'Are you very tired?' she asked.

'No, not very.'

'We'll be there soon now.'

'Yes, very soon.'

'This time tomorrow –'

He nodded and they sat silent. When she had put him to bed and crawled into her own berth she tried to cheer herself with the thought that in less than twenty-four hours they would be in New York. Her people would all be at the station to meet her – she pictured their round unanxious faces pressing through the crowd. She only hoped they would not tell him too loudly that he was looking splendidly and would be all right in no time: the subtler sympathies developed by long contact with suffering were making her aware of a certain coarseness of texture in the family sensibilities.

Suddenly she thought she heard him call. She parted the curtains and listened. No, it was only a man snoring at the other end of the car. His snores had a greasy sound, as though they passed through tallow. She lay down and tried to sleep. . . . Had she not heard him move? She started up trembling. . . . The silence frightened her more than any sound. He might not be able to make her hear – he might be calling her now. . . . What made her think of such things? It was merely the familiar tendency of an overtired mind to fasten itself on the most intolerable chance within the range of its forebodings. . . . Putting her head out, she listened; but she could not distinguish his breathing from that of the other pairs of lungs about her. She longed to get up and look at him, but she knew the impulse was a mere vent for her restlessness, and the fear of disturbing him restrained her. . . . The regular movement of his curtain reassured her, she knew not why; she remembered that he had wished her a cheerful good-night; and the sheer inability to endure her fears a moment longer made her put them from her with an effort of her whole sound tired body. She turned on her side and slept.

She sat up stiffly, staring out at the dawn. The train was rushing through a region of bare hillocks huddled against a lifeless sky. It looked like the first day of creation. The air of the car was close, and she pushed up her window to let in the keen wind. Then she looked at her watch: it was seven o'clock, and soon the people about her would be stirring. She slipped into her clothes, smoothed her dishevelled hair and crept to the dressing-room. When she had washed her face and adjusted her dress she felt more hopeful. It was always a struggle for her not to be cheerful in the morning. Her cheeks burned deliciously under the coarse towel and the wet hair about her temples broke into strong upward tendrils. Every inch of her was full of life and elasticity. And in ten hours they would be at home!

She stepped to her husband's berth: it was time for him to take his early glass of milk. The window-shade was down, and in the dusk of the curtained enclosure she could just see that he lay sideways, with his face away from her. She leaned over him and drew up the shade. As she did so she touched one of his hands. It felt cold. . . .

She bent closer, laying her hand on his harm and calling him by name. He did not move. She spoke again more loudly; she grasped his shoulder and gently shook it. He lay motionless. She caught hold of his hand again: it slipped from her limply, like a dead thing. A dead thing?. . . Her breath caught. She must see his face. She leaned forward, and hurriedly, shrinkingly, with a sickening reluctance of the flesh, laid her hands on his shoulders and turned him over. His head fell back; his face looked small and smooth; he gazed at her with steady eyes.

She remained motionless for a long time, holding him thus; and they looked at each other. Suddenly she shrank back: the longing to scream, to call out, to fly from him, had almost overpowered her. But a strong hand arrested her. Good God! If it were known that he was dead they would be put off the train at the next station–

In a terrifying flash of remembrance there arose before her a scene she had once witnessed in travelling, when a husband and wife, whose child had died in the train, had been thrust out at some chance station. She saw them standing on the platform with the child's body between them; she had never forgotten the dazed look with which they followed the receding train. And this was what would happen to her. Within the next hour she might find herself on the platform of some strange station, alone with her husband's body.... Anything but that! It was too horrible– She quivered like a creature at bay.

As she cowered there, she felt the train moving more slowly. It was coming then – they were approaching a station! She saw again the husband and wife standing on the lonely platform; and with a violent gesture she drew down the shade to hide her husband's face.

Feeling dizzy, she sank down on the edge of the berth, keeping away from his outstretched body, and pulling the curtains close, so that he and she were shut into a kind of sepulchral twilight. She tried to think. At all costs she must conceal the fact that he was dead. But how? Her mind refused to act: she could not plan, combine. She could think of no way but to sit there, clutching the curtains, all day long....

She heard the porter making up her bed; people were beginning to move about the car; the dressing-room door was being opened and shut. She tried to rouse herself. At length with a supreme effort she rose to her feet, stepping into the aisle of the car and drawing the curtains tight behind her. She noticed that they still parted slightly with the motion of the car, and finding a pin in her dress she fastened them together. Now she was safe. She looked round and saw the porter. She fancied he was watching her.

'Ain't he awake yet?' he enquired.

'No,' she faltered.

'I got his milk all ready when he wants it. You know you told me to have it for him by seven.'

She nodded silently and crept into her seat.

At half-past eight the train reached Buffalo. By this time the other passengers were dressed and the berths had been folded back for the day. The porter, moving to and fro under his burden of sheets and pillows, glanced at her as he passed. At length he said: 'Ain't he going to get up? You know we're ordered to make up the berths as early as we can.'

She turned cold with fear. They were just entering the station.

'Oh, not yet,' she stammered. 'Not till he's had his milk. Won't you get it, please?'

'All right. Soon as we start again.'

When the train moved on he reappeared with the milk. She took it from him and sat vaguely looking at it: her brain moved slowly from one idea to another, as though there were stepping-stones set far apart across a whirling flood. At length she became aware that the porter still hovered expectantly.

'Will I give it to him?' he suggested.

'Oh, no,' she cried, rising. 'He – he's asleep yet, I think–'

She waited till the porter had passed on; then she unpinned the curtains and slipped behind them. In the semi-obscurity her husband's face stared up at her like a marble mask with agate eyes. The eyes were dreadful. She put out her hand and drew down the lids. Then she remembered the glass of milk in her other hand: what was she to do with it? She thought of raising the window and throwing it out; but to do so she would have to lean across his body and bring her face close to his. She decided to drink the milk.

She returned to her seat with the empty glass and after a while the porter came back to get it.

'When'll I fold up his bed? he asked.

'Oh, not now – not yet; he's ill – he's very ill. Can't you let him stay as he is? The doctor wants him to lie down as much as possible.'

He scratched his head. 'Well, if he's *really* sick–'

He took the empty glass and walked away, explaining to the passengers that the party behind the curtains was too sick to get up just yet.

She found herself the centre of sympathetic eyes. A motherly woman with an intimate smile sat down beside her.

'I'm real sorry to hear your husband's sick. I've had a remarkable amount of sickness in my family and maybe I could assist you. Can I take a look at him?'

'Oh, no – no, please! He mustn't be disturbed.'

The lady accepted the rebuff indulgently.

'Well, it's just as you say, of course, but you don't look to me as if you'd had much experience in sickness and I'd have been glad to assist you. What do you generally do when you husband's taken this way?'

'I – I let him sleep.'

'Too much sleep ain't any too healthful either. Don't you give him any medicine?'

'Ye – yes.'

'Don't you wake him to take it?'

'Yes.'

'When does he take the next dose?'

'Not for – two hours–'

The lady looked disappointed. 'Well, if I was you I'd try giving it oftener. That's what I do with my folks.'

After that many faces seemed to press upon her. The passengers were on their way to the dining-car, and she was conscious that as they passed down the aisle they glanced curiously at the closed curtains. One lantern-jawed man with prominent eyes stood still and tried to shoot his projecting glance through the division between the folds. The freckled child, returning from breakfast, waylaid the passers with a buttery clutch, saying in a loud whisper, 'He's sick'; and once the conductor came by, asking for tickets. She shrank into her corner and looked out of the window at the flying trees and houses, meaningless hieroglyphs of an endlessly unrolled papyrus.

Now and then the train stopped, and the newcomers on entering the car stared in turn at the closed curtains. More and more people seemed to pass – their faces began to blend fantastically with the images surging in her brain. . . .

Later in the day a fat man detached himself from the mist of faces. He had a creased stomach and soft pale lips. As he pressed himself into the seat facing her she noticed that he was dressed in black broadcloth, with a soiled white tie.

'Husband's pretty bad this morning, is he?'

'Yes.'

'Dear, dear! Now that's terribly distressing, ain't it?' an apostolic smile revealed his gold-filled teeth.

'Of course you know there's no such thing as sickness. Ain't that a lovely thought? Death itself is but a delusion of our grosser senses. On'y lay yourself open to the influx of the sperrit, submit yourself passively to the action of the divine force, and disease and dissolution will cease to exist for you. If you could indooce your husband to read this little pamphlet–'

The faces about her again grew indistinct. She had a vague recollection of hearing the motherly lady and the parent of the freckled child ardently disputing the relative advantages of trying several medicines at once, or of taking each in turn; the motherly lady maintaining that the competitive system saved time; the other objecting that you couldn't tell which remedy had effected the cure; their voices went on and on, like bell-buoys droning through a fog. . . . The porter came up now and then with questions that she did not understand, but that somehow she must have answered since he went away again without repeating them; every two hours the motherly lady reminded her that her husband ought to have his drops; people left the car and others replaced them. . . .

Her head was spinning and she tried to steady herself by clutching at her thoughts as they swept by, but they slipped away from her like bushes on the side of a sheer precipice down which she seemed to be falling. Suddenly her mind grew clear again and she found herself vividly picturing what would happen when the train reached New York. She shuddered as it occurred to her that he would be quite cold and that some one might perceive he had been dead since morning.

She thought hurriedly: – 'If they see I am not surprised they will suspect something. They will ask questions, and if I tell them the truth they won't believe me – no one would believe me! It will be terrible' – and she kept repeating to herself: –'I must pretend I don't know. I must pretend I don't know. When they open the curtains I must go up to him quite naturally – and then I must scream.' . . . She had an idea that the scream would be very hard to do.

Gradually new thoughts crowded upon her, vivid and urgent; she tried to separate and retrain them, but they beset her clamorously, like her schoolchildren at the end of a hot day, when she was too tired to silence them. Her head grew confused, and she felt a sick fear of forgetting her part, of betraying herself by some unguarded word or look.

'I must pretend I don't know,' she went on murmuring. The words had lost their significance, but she repeated them mechanically, as though they had been a magic formula, until suddenly she heard herself saying: 'I can't remember, I can't remember!'

Her voice sounded very loud, and she looked about her in terror; but no one seemed to notice that she had spoken.

As she glanced down the car her eye caught the curtains of her husband's berth, and she began to examine the monotonous arabesques woven through their heavy folds. The pattern was intricate and difficult to trace; she gazed fixedly at the curtains and as she did so the thick stuff grew transparent and through it she saw her husband's face – his dead face. She struggled to avert

her look, but her eyes refused to move and her head seemed to
be held in a vice. At last, with an effort that left her weak and
shaking, she turned away; but it was of no use; close in front of
her, small and smooth, was her husband's face. It seemed to be
suspended in the air between her and the false braids of the woman
who sat in front of her. With an uncontrollable gesture she stretched
out her hand to push the face away, and suddenly she felt the
touch of his smooth skin. She repressed a cry and half started
from her seat. The woman with the false braids looked around,
and feeling that she must justify her movement in some way she
rose and lifted her travelling-bag from the opposite seat. She unlocked
the bag and looked into it; but the first object her hand met was
a small flask of her husband's, thrust there at the last moment, in
the haste of departure. She locked the bag and closed her eyes . . .
his face was there again, hanging between her eyeballs and lids
like a waxen mask against a red curtain. . . .

She roused herself with a shiver. Had she fainted or slept? Hours
seemed to have elapsed; but it was still broad day, and the people
about her were sitting in the attitudes as before.

A sudden sense of hunger made her aware that she had eaten
nothing since morning. The thought of food filled her with disgust,
but she dreaded a return of faintness, and remembering that she
has some biscuits in her bag she took one out and ate it. The dry
crumbs choked her, and she hastily swallowed a little brandy from
her husband's flask. The burning sensation in her throat acted as
a counter-irritant, momentarily relieving the dull ache of her nerves.
Then she felt a gently stealing warmth, as though a soft air fanned
her, and the swarming fears relaxed their clutch, receding through
the stillness that enclosed her, a stillness soothing as the spacious
quietude of a summer day. She slept.

Through her sleep she felt the impetuous rush of the train. It
seemed to be life itself that was sweeping her on with headlong
inexorable force – sweeping her into darkness and terror, and the
awe of unknown days.– Now all at once everything was still –
not a sound, not a pulsation. . . . She was dead in her turn, and
lay beside him with smooth upstaring face. How quiet it was! –
and yet she heard feet coming, the feet of the men who were to
carry them away. . . . She could feel too – she felt a sudden prolonged
vibration, a series of hard rocks, and then another plunge into
darkness: the darkness of death this time – a black whirlwind on

which they were both spinning like leaves, in wild uncoiling spirals, with millions and millions of the dead. . . .

She sprang up in terror. Her sleep must have lasted a long time, for the winter day had paled and the lights had been lit. The car was in confusion, and as she regained her self-possession she saw that the passengers were gathering up their wraps and bags. The woman with the false braids had brought from the dressing-room a sickly ivy-plant in a bottle, and the Christian Scientist was reversing his cuffs. The porter passed down the aisle with his impartial brush. An impersonal figure with a gold-banded cap asked for her husband's ticket. A voice shouted 'Baig-gage *ex*press!' and she heard the clicking of metal as the passengers handed over their checks.

Presently her window was blocked by an expanse of sooty wall, and the train passed into the Harlem tunnel. The journey was over; in a few minutes she would see her family pushing their joyous way through the throng at the station. Her heart dilated. The worst terror was past. . . .

'We'd better get him up now, hadn't we?' asked the porter, touching her arm.

He had her husband's hat in his hand and was meditatively revolving it under his brush.

She looked at the hat and tried to speak; but suddenly the car grew dark. She flung up her arms, struggling to catch at something, and fell face downward, striking her head against the dead man's berth.

The Lady's Maid's Bell

It was the autumn after I had the typhoid. I'd been three months in hospital, and when I came out I looked so weak and tottery that the two or three ladies I applied to were afraid to engage me. Most of my money was gone, and after I'd boarded for two months, hanging about the employment-agencies, and answering any advertisement that looked any way respectable, I pretty nearly lost heart, for fretting hadn't made me fatter, and I didn't see why my luck should ever turn. It did though – or I thought so at the time. A Mrs Railton, a friend of the lady that first brought me out to the States, met me one day and stopped to speak to me: she was one that had always a friendly way with her. She asked me what ailed me to look so white, and when I told her, 'Why, Hartley,' says she, 'I believe I've got the very place for you. Come in tomorrow and we'll talk about it.'

The next day, when I called, she told me the lady she'd in mind was a niece of hers, a Mrs Brympton, a youngish lady, but something of an invalid, who lived all the year round at her country-place on the Hudson, owing to not being able to stand the fatigue of town life.

'Now, Hartley,' Mrs Railton said, in that cheery way that always made me feel things must be going to take a turn for the better – 'now understand me; it's not a cheerful place I'm sending you to. The house is big and gloomy; my niece is nervous, vapourish; her husband – well, he's generally away; and the two children are dead. A year ago I would as soon have thought of shutting a rosy active girl like you into a vault; but you're not particularly brisk yourself just now, are you? and a quiet place, with country air and wholesome food and early hours, ought to be the very thing for you. Don't mistake me,' she added, for I suppose I looked a trifle downcast; 'you may find it dull, but you won't be unhappy. My niece is an angel. Her former maid, who died last spring, had been with her twenty years and worshipped the ground she walked on. She's a kind mistress to all, and where the mistress is kind, as you know, the servants are generally good-humoured, so you'll probably get on well enough with the rest of the household. And you're the very woman I want for my niece: quiet, well-mannered, and educated above your station. You read aloud well, I think? That's a good thing; my niece likes to be read to. She wants a maid that can be something of a companion: her last was, and I can't say how she misses her. It's a lonely life. . . . Well, have you decided?'

'Why, ma'am,' I said, 'I'm not afraid of solitude.'

'Well, then, go; my niece will take you on my recommendation. I'll telegraph her at once and you can take the afternoon train. She has no one to wait on her at present, and I don't want you to lose any time.'

I was ready enough to start, yet something in me hung back; and to gain time I asked, 'And the gentleman, ma'am?'

'The gentleman's almost always away, I tell you,' said Mrs Railton, quick-like – 'and when he's there,' says she suddenly, 'you've only to keep out of his way.'

I took the afternoon train and got out at D— station at about four o'clock. A groom in a dog-cart was waiting, and we drove off at a smart pace. It was a dull October day, with rain hanging close overhead, and by the time we turned into Brympton Place woods the daylight was almost gone. The drive wound through the woods for a mile or two, and came out on a gravel court shut in with thickets of tall black-looking shrubs. There were no lights in the windows and the house *did* look a bit gloomy.

I had asked no questions of the groom, for I never was one to get my notion of new masters from their other servants: I prefer to wait and see for myself. But I could tell by the look of everything that I had got into the right kind of house, and that things were

done handsomely. A pleasant-faced cook met me at the back door
and called the housemaid to show me up to my room. 'You'll see
madam later,' she said. 'Mrs Brympton has a visitor.'

I hadn't fancied Mrs Brympton was a lady to have many visitors,
and somehow the words cheered me. I followed the housemaid
upstairs, and saw, through a door on the upper landing, that the
main part of the house seemed well furnished, with dark panel-
ling and a number of old portraits. Another flight of stairs led us
up to the servants' wing. It was almost dark now, and the housemaid excused herself for not having brought a light. 'But there's
matches in your room,' she said, 'and if you go careful you'll be
all right. Mind the step at the end of the passage. Your room is
just beyond.'

I looked ahead as she spoke, and half-way down the passage I
saw a woman standing. She drew back into a doorway as we
passed and the housemaid didn't appear to notice her. She was a
thin woman with a white face, and a darkish stuff gown and
apron. I took her for the housekeeper and thought it odd that she
didn't speak, but just gave me a long look as she went by. My
room opened into a square hall at the end of the passage. Facing
my door was another which stood open; the housemaid exclaimed
when she saw it:

'There – Mrs Blinder's left that door open again!' said she,
closing it.

'Is Mrs Blinder the housekeeper?'

'There's no housekeeper: Mrs Blinder's the cook.'

'And is that her room?'

'Laws, no,' said the housemaid, cross-like. 'That's nobody's room.
It's empty, I mean, and the door hadn't ought to be open. Mrs
Brympton wants it kept locked.'

She opened my door and led me into a neat room, nicely furnished,
with a picture or two on the walls; and having lit a candle she
took leave, telling me that the servants'-hall tea was at six, and
that Mrs Brympton would see me afterwards.

I found them a pleasant-spoken set in the servants' hall, and by
what they let fall I gathered that, as Mrs Railton had said, Mrs
Brympton was the kindest of ladies; but I didn't take much notice
of their talk, for I was watching to see the pale woman in the
dark gown come in. She didn't show herself, however, and I wondered if she ate apart; but if she wasn't the housekeeper, why

should she? Suddenly it struck me that she might be a trained nurse, and in that case her meals would of course be served in her room. If Mrs Brympton was an invalid it was likely enough she had a nurse. The idea annoyed me, I own, for they're not always the easiest to get on with, and if I'd known I shouldn't have taken the place. But there I was and there was no use pulling a long face over it; and not being one to ask questions I waited to see what would turn up.

When tea was over the housemaid said to the footman: 'Has Mr Ranford gone?' and when he said yes, she told me to come up with her to Mrs Brympton.

Mrs Brympton was lying down in her bedroom. Her lounge stood near the fire and beside it was a shaded lamp. She was a delicate-looking lady, but when she smiled I felt there was nothing I wouldn't do for her. She spoke very pleasantly, in a low voice, asking me my name and age and so on, and if I had everything I wanted, and if I wasn't afraid of feeling lonely in the country.

'Not with you I wouldn't be, madam,' I said, and the words surprised me when I'd spoken them, for I'm not an impulsive person; but it was just as if I'd thought aloud.

She seemed pleased at that, and said she hoped I'd continue in the same mind; then she gave me a few directions about her toilet, and said Agnes the housemaid would show me next morning where things were kept.

'I am tired tonight, and shall dine upstairs,' she said. 'Agnes will bring me my tray, that you may have time to unpack and settle yourself; and later you may come and undress me.'

'Very well, ma'am,' I said. 'You'll ring, I suppose?'

I thought she looked odd.

'No – Agnes will fetch you,' says she quickly, and took up her book again.

Well – that was certainly strange: a lady's maid having to be fetched by the housemaid whenever her lady wanted her! I wondered if there were no bells in the house; but the next day I satisfied myself that there was one in every room, and a special one ringing from my mistress's room to mine; and after that it did strike me as queer that, whenever Mrs Brympton wanted anything, she rang for Agnes, who had to walk the whole length of the servants' wing to call me.

But that wasn't the only queer thing in the house. The very

next day I found out that Mrs Brympton had no nurse; and then I asked Agnes about the woman I had seen in the passage the afternoon before. Agnes said she had seen no one, and I saw that she thought I was dreaming. To be sure, it was dusk when we went down the passage, and she had excused herself for not bringing a light; but I had seen the woman plain enough to know her again if we should meet. I decided that she must have been a friend of the cook's, or of one of the other women servants; perhaps she had come down from town for a night's visit, and the servants wanted it kept secret. Some ladies are very stiff about having their servants' friends in the house overnight. At any rate, I made up my mind to ask no more questions.

In a day or two another odd thing happened. I was chatting one afternoon with Mrs Blinder, who was a friendly-disposed woman, and had been longer in the house than the other servants, and she asked me if I was quite comfortable and had everything I needed. I said I had no fault to find with my place or with my mistress, but I thought it odd that in so large a house there was no sewing-room for the lady's maid.

'Why,' says she, 'there *is* one: the room you're in is the old sewing-room.'

'Oh,' said I; 'and where did the other lady's maid sleep?'

At that she grew confused, and said hurriedly that the servants' rooms had all been changed last year, and she didn't rightly remember.

That struck me as peculiar, but I went on as if I hadn't noticed: 'Well, there's a vacant room opposite mine, and I mean to ask Mrs Brympton if I mayn't use that as a sewing-room.'

To my astonishment, Mrs Blinder went white and gave my hand a kind of squeeze. 'Don't do that, my dear,' said she, trembling-like. 'To tell you the truth, that was Emma Saxon's room, and my mistress has kept it closed ever since her death.'

'And who was Emma Saxon?'

'Mrs Brympton's former maid.'

'The one that was with her so many years?' said I, remembering what Mrs Railton had told me.

Mrs Blinder nodded.

'What sort of woman was she?'

'No better walked the earth,' said Mrs Blinder. 'My mistress loved her like a sister.'

'But I mean – what did she look like?'

Mrs Blinder got up and gave me a kind of angry stare. 'I'm no great hand at describing,' she said; 'and I believe my pastry's rising.' And she walked off into the kitchen and shut the door after her.

II

I had been near a week at Brympton before I saw my master. Word came that he was arriving one afternoon, and a change passed over the whole household. It was plain that nobody loved him below stairs. Mrs Blinder took uncommon care with the dinner that night, but she snapped at the kitchen-maid in a way quite unusual with her; and Mr Wace, the butler, a serious low-spoken man, went about his duties as if he'd been getting ready for a funeral. He was a great Bible-reader, Mr Wace was, and had a beautiful assortment of texts at his command; but that day he used such dreadful language that I was about to leave the table, when he assured me it was all out of Isaiah; and I noticed that whenever the master came Mr Wace took to the prophets.

About seven, Agnes called me to my mistress's room; and there I found Mr Brympton. He was standing on the hearth; a big, fair, bull-necked man, with a red face and little bad-tempered blue eyes: the kind of man a young simpleton might have thought handsome, and would have been like to pay dear for thinking it.

He swung about when I came in, and looked me over in a trice. I knew what the look meant, from having experienced it once or twice in my former places. Then he turned his back on me, and went on talking to his wife; and I knew what *that* meant, too. I was not the kind of morsel he was after. The typhoid had served me well enough in one way: it kept that kind of gentleman at arm's-length.

'This is my new maid, Hartley,' says Mrs Brympton in her kind voice; and he nodded and went on with what he was saying.

In a minute or two he went off, and left my mistress to dress for dinner, and I noticed as I waited on her that she was white, and chill to the touch.

Mr Brympton took himself off the next morning, and the whole house drew a long breath when he drove away. As for my mistress, she put on her hat and furs (for it was a fine winter morning) and went out for a walk in the gardens, coming back quite fresh and rosy, so that for a minute, before her colour faded, I could guess what a pretty young lady she must have been, and not so long ago, either.

She had met Mr Ranford in the grounds, and the two came back together, I remember, smiling and talking as they walked along the terrace under my window. That was the first time I saw Mr Ranford, though I had often heard his name mentioned in the hall. He was a neighbour, it appeared, living a mile or two beyond Brympton, at the end of the village; and as he was in the habit of spending his winters in the country he was almost the only company my mistress had at that season. He was a slight tall gentleman of about thirty, and I thought him rather melancholy-looking till I saw his smile, which had a kind of surprise in it, like the first warm day in spring. He was a great reader, I heard, like my mistress, and the two were for ever borrowing books of one another, and sometimes (Mr Wace told me) he would read aloud to Mrs Brympton by the hour, in the big dark library where she sat in the winter afternoons. The servants all liked him, and perhaps that's more of a compliment than the masters suspect. He had a friendly word for every one of us, and we were all glad to think that Mrs Brympton had a pleasant companionable gentleman like that to keep her company when the master was away. Mr Ranford seemed on excellent terms with Mr Brympton too; though I couldn't but wonder that two gentlemen so unlike each other should be so friendly. But then I knew how the real quality can keep their feelings to themselves.

As for Mr Brympton, he came and went, never staying more than a day or two, cursing the dullness and the solitude, grumbling at everything, and (as I soon found out) drinking a deal more than was good for him. After Mrs Brympton left the table he would sit half the night over the old Brympton port and madeira, and once, as I was leaving my mistress's room rather later than usual, I met him coming up the stairs in such a state that I turned sick to think of what some ladies have to endure and hold their tongues about.

The servants said very little about their master; but from what they let drop I could see it had been an unhappy match from the beginning. Mr Brympton was coarse, loud, and pleasure-loving; my mistress quiet, retiring, and perhaps a trifle cold. Not that she was not always pleasant-spoken to him: I thought her wonderfully forbearing; but to a gentleman as free as Mr Brympton I dare say she seemed a little offish.

Well, things went on quietly for several weeks. My mistress was kind, my duties were light, and I got on well with the other servants. In short, I had nothing to complain of; yet there was always a weight on me. I can't say why it was so, but I know it was not the loneliness that I felt. I soon got used to that; and being still languid from the fever I was thankful for the quiet and the good country air. Nevertheless, I was never quite easy in my mind. My mistress, knowing I had been ill, insisted that I should take my walk regular, and often invented errands for me – a yard of ribbon to be fetched from the village, a letter posted, or a book returned to Mr Ranford. As soon as I was out of doors my spirits rose, and I looked forward to my walks through the bare moist-smelling woods; but the moment I caught sight of the house again my heart dropped down like a stone in a well. It was not a gloomy house exactly, yet I never entered it but a feeling of gloom came over me.

Mrs Brympton seldom went out in winter; only on the finest days did she walk an hour at noon on the south terrace. Excepting Mr Ranford, we had no visitors but the doctor, who drove over from D— about once a week. He sent for me once or twice to give me some trifling direction about my mistress, and though he never told me what her illness was, I thought, from a waxy look she had now and then of a morning, that it might be the heart that ailed her. The season was soft and unwholesome, and in January we had a long spell of rain. That was a sore trial to me, I own, for I couldn't go out, and sitting over my sewing all day, listening to the drip, drip of the eaves, I grew so nervous that the least sound made me jump. Somehow, the thought of that locked room across the passage began to weigh on me. Once or twice, in the long rainy nights, I fancied I heard noises there; but that was nonsense, of course, and the daylight drove such notions out of my head. Well, one morning Mrs Brympton gave me quite a start of pleasure by telling me she wished me to go to town for some shopping. I hadn't known till then how low my spirits had fallen. I set off in high glee, and my first sight of the crowded streets and the cheerful-looking shops quite took me out of myself. Towards afternoon, however, the noise and confusion began to tire me, and I was actually looking forward to the quiet of Brympton, and thinking how I should enjoy the drive home through the dark woods, when I ran across an old acquaintance, a maid I had once been in service with. We had lost sight of each other for a number of years, and I had to stop and tell her what had happened to me in the interval. When I mentioned where I was living she rolled up her eyes and pulled a long face.

'What! The Mrs Brympton that lives all the year at her place on the Hudson? My dear, you won't stay there three months.'

'Oh, but I don't mind the country,' says I, offended somehow at her tone. 'Since the fever I'm glad to be quiet.'

She shook her head. 'It's not the country I'm thinking of. All I know is she's had four maids in the last six months, and the last one, who was a friend of mine, told me nobody could stay in the house.'

'Did she say why?' I asked.

'No – she wouldn't give me her reason. But she says to me, *Mrs Ansey*, she says, *if ever a young woman as you know of thinks of going there, you tell her it's not worth while to unpack her boxes.*'

'Is she young and handsome?' said I, thinking of Mr Brympton.

'Not her! She's the kind that mothers engage when they've gay young gentlemen at college.'

Well, though I knew the woman was an idle gossip, the words stuck in my head, and my heart sank lower than ever as I drove up to Brympton in the dusk. There *was* something about the house – I was sure of it now. . . .

When I went in to tea I heard that Mr Brympton had arrived, and I saw at a glance that there had been a disturbance of some kind. Mrs Blinder's hand shook so that she could hardly pour the tea, and Mr Wace quoted the most dreadful texts full of brimstone. Nobody said a word to me then, but when I went up to my room, Mrs Blinder followed me.

'Oh, my dear,' says she, taking my hand, 'I'm so glad and thankful you've come back to us!'

That struck me, as you may imagine. 'Why,' said I, 'did you think I was leaving for good?'

'No, no, to be sure,' said she, a little confused, 'but I can't a-bear to have madam left alone for a day even.' She pressed my hand hard, and, 'Oh, Miss Hartley,' says she, 'be good to your mistress, as you're a Christian woman.' And with that she hurried away, and left me staring.

A moment later Agnes called me to Mrs Brympton. Hearing Mr Brympton's voice in her room, I went round by the dressing-room, thinking I would lay out her dinner-gown before going in. The dressing-room is a large room with a window over the portico that looks toward the gardens. Mr Brympton's apartments are beyond. When I went in, the door into the bedroom was ajar, and I heard Mr Brympton saying angrily: 'One would suppose he was the only person fit for you to talk to.'

'I don't have many visitors in winter,' Mrs Brympton answered quietly.

'You have *me*!' he flung at her, sneeringly.

'You are here so seldom,' said she.

'Well – whose fault is that? You make the place about as lively as the family vault—'

With that I rattled the toilet-things, to give my mistress warning, and she rose and called me in.

The two dined alone, as usual, and I knew by Mr Wace's manner at supper that things must be going badly. He quoted the prophets something terrible, and worked on the kitchen-maid so that she declared she wouldn't go down alone to put the cold meat in the ice-box. I felt nervous myself, and after I had put my mistress to bed I was half-tempted to go down again and persuade Mrs Blinder to sit up a while over a game of cards. But I heard her door closing for the night and so I went on to my own room. The rain had begun again, and the drip, drip, drip seemed to be dropping into my brain. I lay awake listening to it, and turning over what my friend in town had said. What puzzled me was that it was always the maids who left. . . .

After a while I slept; but suddenly a loud noise wakened me. My bell had rung. I sat up, terrified by the unusual sound, which seemed to go on jangling through the darkness. My hands shook so that I couldn't find the matches. At length I struck a light and jumped out of bed. I began to think I must have been dreaming; but I looked at the bell against the wall, and there was the little hammer still quivering.

I was just beginning to huddle on my clothes when I heard another sound. This time it was the door of the locked room opposite mine softly opening and closing. I heard the sound distinctly, and it frightened me so that I stood stock-still. Then I heard a footstep hurrying down the passage toward the main house. The floor being carpeted, the sound was very faint, but I was quite sure it was a woman's step. I turned cold with the thought of it, and for a minute or two I dursn't breathe or move. Then I came to my senses.

'Alice Hartley,' says I to myself, 'someone left that room just now and ran down the passage ahead of you. The idea isn't pleasant, but you may as well face it. Your mistress has rung for you, and to answer her bell you've got to go the way that other woman has gone.'

Well – I did it. I never walked faster in my life, yet I thought I should never get to the end of the passage or reach Mrs Brympton's room. On the way I heard nothing and saw nothing: all was dark and quiet as the grave. When I reached my mistress's door the silence was so deep that I began to think I must be dreaming, and was half-minded to turn back. Then a panic seized me, and I knocked.

There was no answer, and I knocked again, loudly. To my astonishment the door was opened by Mr Brympton. He started back when he saw me, and in the light of my candle his face looked red and savage.

'*You?*' he said, in a queer voice. '*How many of you are there, in God's name?*'

At that I felt the ground give under me; but I said to myself that he had been drinking, and answered as steadily as I could: 'May I go in, sir? Mrs Brympton has rung for me.'

'You may all go in, for what I care,' says he, and, pushing by me, walked down the hall to his own bedroom. I looked after him as he went, and to my surprise I saw that he walked as straight as a sober man.

I found my mistress lying very weak and still but she forced a smile when she saw me, and signed to me to pour out some drops for her. After that she lay without speaking, her breath coming quick, and her eyes closed. Suddenly she groped out with her hand, and '*Emma,*' says she, faintly.

'It's Hartley, madam,' I said. 'Do you want anything?'

She opened her eyes wide and gave me a startled look.

'I was dreaming,' she said. 'You may go now, Hartley, and thank you kindly. I'm quite well again, you see.' And she turned her face away from me.

III

There was no more sleep for me that night, and I was thankful when daylight came.

Soon afterwards, Agnes called me to Mrs Brympton. I was afraid she was ill again, for she seldom sent for me before nine, but I found her sitting up in bed, pale and drawn-looking, but quite herself.

'Hartley,' says she quickly, 'will you put on your things at once and go down to the village for me? I want this prescription made up' – here she hesitated a minute and blushed – 'and I should like you to be back again before Mr Brympton is up.'

'Certainly, madam,' I said.

'And – stay a moment' – she called me back as if an idea had just struck her – 'while you're waiting for the mixture, you'll have time to go on to Mr Ranford's with this note.'

It was a two-mile walk to the village, and on my way I had time to turn things over in my mind. It struck me as peculiar that my mistress should wish that prescription made up without Mr Brympton's knowledge; and, putting this together with the scene of the night before, and with much else that I had noticed and suspected, I began to wonder if the poor lady was weary of her life, and had come to the mad resolve of ending it. The idea took such hold on me that I reached the village on a run, and dropped breathless into a chair before the chemist's counter. The good man, who was just taking down his shutters, stared at me so hard that it brought me to myself.

'Mr Limmel,' I says, trying to speak indifferent, 'will you run your eye over this, and tell me if it's quite right?'

He put on his spectacles and studied the prescription.

'Why, it's one of Dr Walton's,' says he. 'What should be wrong with it?'

'Well – is it dangerous to take?'

'Dangerous – how do you mean?'

I could have shaken the man for his stupidity.

'I mean – if a person was to take too much of it – by mistake of course—' says I, my heart in my throat.

'Lord bless you, no. It's only lime-water. You might feed it to a baby by the bottleful.'

I gave a great sigh of relief and hurried on to Mr Ranford's.

But on the way another thought struck me. If there was nothing to conceal about my visit to the chemist's, was it my other errand that Mrs Brympton wished me to keep private? Somehow, that thought frightened me worse than the other. Yet the two gentlemen seemed fast friends, and I would have staked my head on my mistress's goodness. I felt ashamed of my suspicions, and concluded that I was still disturbed by the strange events of the night. I left the note at Mr Ranford's, and hurrying back to Brympton, slipped in by a side door without being seen, as I thought.

An hour later, however, as I was carrying in my mistress's breakfast, I was stopped in the hall by Mr Brympton.

'What were you doing out so early?' he says, looking hard at me.

'Early – me, sir?' I said, in a tremble.

'Come, come,' he says, an angry red spot coming out on his forehead, 'didn't I see you scuttling home through the shrubbery an hour or more ago?'

I'm a truthful woman by nature, but at that a lie popped out ready-made. 'No, sir, you didn't,' said I, and looked straight back at him.

He shrugged his shoulders and gave a sullen laugh. 'I suppose you think I was drunk last night?' he asked suddenly.

'No, sir, I don't,' I answered, this time truthfully enough.

He turned away with another shrug. 'A pretty notion my servants have of me!' I heard him mutter as he walked off.

Not till I had settled down to my afternoon's sewing did I realize how the events of the night had shaken me. I couldn't pass that locked door without a shiver. I knew I had heard someone come out of it, and walk down the passage ahead of me. I thought of speaking to Mrs Blinder or to Mr Wace, the only two in the house who appeared to have an inkling of what was going on, but I had a feeling that if I questioned them they would deny everything, and that I might learn more by holding my tongue and keeping my eyes open. The idea of spending another night opposite the locked room sickened me, and once I was seized with the notion of packing my trunk and taking the first train to town; but it wasn't in me to throw over a kind mistress in that manner, and I tried to go on with my sewing as if nothing had happened. I hadn't worked ten minutes before the sewing machine broke down. It was one I had found in the house, a good machine but a trifle out of order; Mrs Blinder said it had never been used since Emma Saxon's death. I stopped to see what was wrong, and as I was working at the machine a drawer which I had never been able to open slid forward, and a photograph fell out. I picked it up and sat looking at it in a maze. It was a woman's likeness, and I knew I had seen the face somewhere – the eyes had an asking look that I had felt on me before. And suddenly I remembered the pale woman in the passage.

I stood up, cold all over, and ran out of the room. My heart seemed to be thumping in the top of my head, and I felt as if I should never get away from the look in those eyes. I went straight to Mrs Blinder. She was taking her afternoon nap, and sat up with a jump when I came in.

'Mrs Blinder,' said I, 'who is that?' And I held out the photograph. She rubbed her eyes and stared.

'Why, Emma Saxon,' says she. 'Where did you find it?'

I looked hard at her for a minute. 'Mrs Blinder,' I said, 'I've seen that face before.'

Mrs Blinder got up and walked over to the looking-glass. 'Dear me! I must have been asleep,' she says. 'My front is all over one ear. And now do run along, Miss Hartley, dear, for I hear the clock striking four, and I must go down this very minute and put on the Virginia ham for Mr Brympton's dinner.'

IV

To all appearances, things went on as usual for a week or two. The only difference was that Mr Brympton stayed on, instead of going off as he usually did, and that Mr Ranford never showed himself. I heard Mr Brympton remark on this one afternoon when he was sitting in my mistress's room before dinner.

'Where's Ranford?' says he. 'He hasn't been near the house for a week. Does he keep away because I'm here?'

Mrs Brympton spoke so low that I couldn't catch her answer.

'Well,' he went on, 'two's company and three's trumpery; I'm sorry to be in Ranford's way, and I suppose I shall have to take myself off again in a day or two and give him a show.' And he laughed at his own joke.

The very next day, as it happened, Mr Ranford called. The footman said the three were very merry over their tea in the library,

and Mr Brympton strolled down to the gate with Mr Ranford
when he left.

I have said that things went on as usual; and so they did with
the rest of the household; but as for myself, I had never been the
same since the night my bell had rung. Night after night I used to
lie awake, listening for it to ring again, and for the door of the
locked room to open stealthily. But the bell never rang, and I
heard no sound across the passage. At last the silence began to be
more dreadful to me than the most mysterious sounds. I felt that
someone was cowering there, behind the locked door, watching
and listening as I watched and listened, and I could almost have
cried out, 'Whoever you are, come out and let me see you face to
face, but don't lurk there and spy on me in the darkness!'

Feeling as I did, you may wonder I didn't give warning. Once
I very nearly did so; but at the last moment something held me
back. Whether it was compassion for my mistress, who had grown
more and more dependent on me, or unwillingness to try a new
place, or some other feeling that I couldn't put a name to, I lingered
on as if spellbound, though every night was dreadful to me, and
the days but little better.

For one thing, I didn't like Mrs Brympton's looks. She had
never been the same since that night, no more than I had. I thought
she would brighten up after Mr Brympton left, but though she
seemed easier in her mind, her spirits didn't revive, nor her strength
either. She had grown attached to me and seemed to like to have
me about; and Agnes told me one day that, since Emma Saxon's
death, I was the only maid her mistress had taken to. This gave
me a warm feeling for the poor lady, though after all there was
little I could do to help her.

After Mr Brympton's departure Mr Ranford took to coming
again, though less often than formerly. I met him once or twice in
the grounds, or in the village, and I couldn't but think there was
a change in him too; but I set it down to my disordered fancy.

The weeks passed, and Mr Brympton had now been a month
absent. We heard he was cruising with a friend in the West Indies,
and Mr Wace said that was a long way off, but though you had
the wings of a dove and went to the uttermost parts of the earth,
you couldn't get away from the Almighty. Agnes said that as
long as he stayed away from Brympton the Almighty might have
him and welcome; and this raised a laugh, though Mrs Blinder

tried to look shocked, and Mr Wace said the bears would eat us.

We were all glad to hear that the West Indies were a long way off, and I remember that, in spite of Mr Wace's solemn looks, we had a very merry dinner that day in the hall. I don't know if it was because of my being in better spirits, but I fancied Mrs Brympton looked better too, and seemed more cheerful in her manner. She had been for a walk in the morning, and after luncheon she lay down in her room, and I read aloud to her. When she dismissed me I went to my own room feeling quite bright and happy, and for the first time in weeks walked past the locked door without thinking of it. As I sat down to my work I looked out and saw a few snowflakes falling. The sight was pleasanter than the eternal rain, and I pictured to myself how pretty the bare gardens would look in their white mantle. It seemed to me as if the snow would cover up all the dreariness, indoors as well as out.

The fancy had hardly crossed my mind when I heard a step at my side. I looked up, thinking it was Agnes.

'Well, Agnes—' said I, and the words froze on my tongue; for there, in the door, stood Emma Saxon.

I don't know how long she stood there. I only know I couldn't stir or take my eyes from her. Afterwards I was terribly frightened, but at the time it wasn't fear I felt, but something deeper and quieter. She looked at me long and long, and her face was just one dumb prayer to me – but how in the world was I to help her? Suddenly she turned, and I heard her walk down the passage. This time I wasn't afraid to follow – I felt that I must know what she wanted. I sprang up and ran out. She was at the other end of the passage, and I expected her to take the turn towards my mistress's room; but instead of that she pushed open the door that led to the back stairs. I followed her down the stairs, and across the passageway to the back door. The kitchen and hall were empty at that hour, the servants being off duty, except for the footman, who was in the pantry. At the door she stood still a moment, with another look at me; then she turned the handle, and stepped out. For a minute I hesitated. Where was she leading me to? The door had closed softly after her, and I opened it and looked out, half-expecting to find that she had disappeared. But I saw her a few yards off hurrying across the courtyard to the path through the woods. Her figure looked black and lonely in the snow, and for a second my heart failed me and I thought of turning back.

But all the while she was drawing me after her; and catching up an old shawl of Mrs Blinder's I ran out into the open.

Emma Saxon was in the wood-path now. She walked on steadily, and I followed at the same pace till we passed out of the gates and reached the highroad. Then she struck across the open fields to the village. By this time the ground was white, and as she climbed the slope of a bare hill ahead of me I noticed that she left no footprints behind her. At sight of that my heart shrivelled up within me and my knees were water. Somehow it was worse here than indoors. She made the whole countryside seem lonely as the grave, with none but us two in it, and no help in the wide world.

Once I tried to go back; but she turned and looked at me, and it was as if she had dragged me with ropes. After that I followed her like a dog. We came to the village and she led me through it, past the church and the blacksmith's shop, and down the lane to Mr Ranford's. Mr Ranford's house stands close to the road: a plain old-fashioned building, with a flagged path leading to the door between box-borders. The lane was deserted, and as I turned into it I saw Emma Saxon pause under the old elm by the gate. And now another fear came over me. I saw that we had reached the end of our journey, and that it was my turn to act. All the way from Brympton I had been asking myself what she wanted of me, but I had followed in a trance, as it were, and not till I saw her stop at Mr Ranford's gate did my brain begin to clear itself. I stood a little way off in the snow, my heart beating fit to strangle me, and my feet frozen to the ground; and she stood under the elm and watched me.

I knew well enough that she hadn't led me there for nothing. I felt there was something I ought to say or do – but how was I to guess what it was? I had never thought harm of my mistress and Mr Ranford, but I was sure now that, from one cause or another, some dreadful thing hung over them. *She* knew what it was; she would tell me if she could; perhaps she would answer if I questioned her.

It turned me faint to think of speaking to her; but I plucked up heart and dragged myself across the few yards between us. As I did so, I heard the house door open and saw Mr Ranford approaching. He looked handsome and cheerful, as my mistress had looked that morning, and at sight of him the blood began to flow again in my veins.

'Why, Hartley,' said he, 'what's the matter? I saw you coming down the lane just now, and came out to see if you had taken root in the snow.' He stopped and stared at me. 'What are you looking at?' he says.

I turned towards the elm as he spoke, and his eyes followed me; but there was no one there. The lane was empty as far as the eye could reach.

A sense of helplessness came over me. She was gone, and I had not been able to guess what she wanted. Her last look had pierced me to the marrow; and yet it had not told me! All at once, I felt more desolate than when she had stood there watching me. It seemed as if she had left me all alone to carry the weight of the secret I couldn't guess. The snow went round me in great circles, and the ground fell away from me. . . .

A drop of brandy and the warmth of Mr Ranford's fire soon brought me to, and I insisted on being driven back at once to Brympton. It was nearly dark, and I was afraid my mistress might be wanting me. I explained to Mr Ranford that I had been out for a walk and had been taken with a fit of giddiness as I passed his gate. This was true enough; yet I never felt more like a liar than when I said it.

When I dressed Mrs Brympton for dinner she remarked on my pale looks and asked what ailed me. I told her I had a headache, and she said she would not require me again that evening, and advised me to go to bed.

It was a fact that I could scarcely keep on my feet; yet I had no fancy to spend a solitary evening in my room. I sat downstairs in the hall as long as I could hold my head up; but by nine I crept upstairs, too weary to care what happened if I could but get my head on a pillow. The rest of the household went to bed soon afterwards; they kept early hours when the master was away, and before ten I heard Mrs Blinder's door close, and Mr Wace's soon after.

It was a very still night, earth and air all muffled in snow. Once in bed I felt easier, and lay quiet, listening to the strange noises that come out in a house after dark. Once I thought I heard a door open and close again below: it might have been the glass door that led to the gardens. I got up and peered out of the window; but it was in the dark of the moon, and nothing visible outside but the streaking of snow against the panes.

I went back to bed and must have dozed, for I jumped awake

to the furious ringing of my bell. Before my head was clear I had
sprung out of bed and was dragging on my clothes. *It is going to
happen now*, I heard myself saying; but what I meant I had no
notion. My hands seemed to be covered with glue – I thought I
should never get into my clothes. At last I opened my door and
peered down the passage. As far as my candle-flame carried, I
could see nothing unusual ahead of me. I hurried on, breathless;
but as I pushed open the baize door leading to the main hall my
heart stood still, for there at the head of the stairs was Emma
Saxon, peering dreadfully down into the darkness.

For a second I couldn't stir; but my hand slipped from the
door, and as it swung shut the figure vanished. At the same instant
there came another sound from below stairs – a stealthy mysterious
sound, as of a latch-key turning in the house door. I ran to Mrs
Brympton's room and knocked.

There was no answer, and I knocked again. This time I heard
someone moving in the room; the bolt slipped back and my mistress
stood before me. To my surprise, I saw that she had not undressed
for the night. She gave me a startled look.

'What is this, Hartley?' she says in a whisper. 'Are you ill?
What are you doing here at this hour?'

'I am not ill, madam; but my bell rang.'

At that she turned pale, and seemed about to fall.

'You are mistaken,' she said harshly; 'I didn't ring. You must
have been dreaming.' I had never heard her speak in such a tone.
'Go back to bed,' she said, closing the door on me.

But as she spoke I heard sounds again in the hall below; a
man's step this time; and the truth leaped out on me.

'Madam,' I said, pushing past her, 'there is someone in the
house—'

'Someone—?'

'Mr Brympton, I think – I hear his step below—'

A dreadful look came over her, and without a word, she dropped
flat at my feet. I fell on my knees and tried to lift her: by the way
she breathed I saw it was no common faint. But as I raised her
head there came quick steps on the stairs and across the hall: the
door was flung open, and there stood Mr Brympton, in his travelling-
clothes, the snow dripping from him. He drew back with a start
as he saw me kneeling by my mistress.

'What the devil is this?' he shouted. He was less high-coloured than usual, and the red spot came out on his forehead.

'Mrs Brympton has fainted, sir,' said I.

He laughed unsteadily and pushed by me. 'It's a pity she didn't choose a more convenient moment. I'm sorry to disturb her, but—'

I raised myself up, aghast at the man's action.

'Sir,' said I, 'are you mad? What are you doing?'

'Going to meet a friend,' said he, and seemed to make for the dressing-room.

At that my heart turned over. I don't know what I thought or feared; but I sprang up and caught him by the sleeve.

'Sir, sir,' said I, 'for pity's sake look to your wife!'

He shook me off furiously.

'It seems that's done for me,' says he, and caught hold of the dressing-room door.

At that moment I heard a slight noise inside. Slight as it was, he heard it too, and tore the door open; but as he did so he dropped back. On the threshold stood Emma Saxon. All was dark behind her, but I saw her plainly, and so did he. He threw up his hands as if to hide his face from her; and when I looked again she was gone.

He stood motionless, as if the strength had run out of him; and in the stillness my mistress suddenly raised herself, and opening her eyes fixed a look on him. Then she fell back, and I saw the death-flutter pass over her. . . .

We buried her on the third day, in a driving snowstorm. There were few people in the church, for it was bad weather to come from town, and I've a notion my mistress was one that hadn't many near friends. Mr Ranford was among the last to come, just before they carried her up the aisle. He was in black, of course, being such a friend of the family, and I never saw a gentleman so pale. As he passed me I noticed that he leaned a trifle on a stick he carried; and I fancy Mr Brympton noticed it too, for the red spot came out sharp on his forehead, and all through the service he kept staring across the church at Mr Ranford, instead of following the prayers as a mourner should.

When it was over and we went out to the graveyard, Mr Ranford had disappeared, and as soon as my poor mistress's body was underground, Mr Brympton jumped into the carriage nearest the gate and drove off without a word to any of us. I heard him call out, 'To the station,' and we servants went back alone to the house.

Afterwards

❦

'Oh, there *is* one, of course, but you'll never know it.' The assertion, laughingly flung out six months earlier in a bright June garden, came back to Mary Boyne with a new perception of its significance as she stood, in the December dusk, waiting for the lamps to be brought into the library.

The words had been spoken by their friend Alida Stair, as they sat at tea on her lawn at Pangbourne, in reference to the very house of which the library in question was the central, the pivotal, 'feature'. Mary Boyne and her husband, in quest of a country place in one of the southern or south-western counties, had, on their arrival in England, carried their problem straight to Alida Stair, who had successfully solved it in her own case; but it was not until they had rejected, almost capriciously, several practical and judicious suggestions, that she threw out: 'Well, there's Lyng, in Dorsetshire. It belongs to Hugo's cousins, and you can get it for a song.'

The reason she gave for its being obtainable on these terms – its remoteness from a station, its lack of electric light, hot-water pipes, and other vulgar necessities – were exactly those pleasing in its favour with two romantic Americans perversely in search of the economic drawbacks which were associated, in their tradition, with unusual architectural felicities.

'I should never believe I was living in an old house unless I was

thoroughly uncomfortable,' Ned Boyne, the more extravagant of
the two, had jocosely insisted; 'the least hint of "convenience"
would make me think it had been bought out of an exhibition,
with the pieces numbered, and set up again.' And they had proceeded
to enumerate, with humorous precision, their various doubts and
demands, refusing to believe that the house their cousin recommended
was *really* Tudor till they learned it had no heating system, or
that the village church was literally in the grounds, and till she
assured them of the deplorable uncertainty of the water-supply.

'It's too uncomfortable to be true!' Edward Boyne had continued to exult as the avowel of each disadvantage was successively
wrung from her; but he had cut short his rhapsody to ask, with
a relapse to distrust: 'And the ghost? You've been concealing from
us the fact that there is no ghost!'

Mary, at the moment, had laughed with him, yet almost with
her laugh, being possessed of several sets of independent perceptions,
had been struck by a note of flatness in Alida's answering hilarity.

'Oh, Dorsetshire's full of ghosts, you know.'

'Yes, yes; but that won't do. I don't want to have to drive ten
miles to see somebody else's ghost. I want one of my own on the
premises. *Is* there a ghost at Lyng?'

His rejoinder had made Alida laugh again, and it was then that
she had flung back tantalizing: 'Oh, there *is* one, of course, but
you'll never know it.'

'Never know it?' Boyne pulled her up. 'But what in the world
constitutes a ghost except the fact of its being known for one?'

'I can't say. But that's the story.'

'That there's a ghost, but that nobody know it's a ghost?'

'Well – not till afterwards, at any rate.'

'Till afterwards?'

'Not till long, long afterwards.'

'But if it's once been identified as an unearthly visitant, why
hasn't its *signalement* been handed down in the family? How has
it managed to preserve its incognito?'

Alida could only shake her head. 'Don't ask me. But it has.'

'And then suddenly' – Mary spoke up as if from cavernous
depths of divination – 'suddenly, long afterwards, one says to
oneself, *That was it!*'

She was startled at the sepulchral sound with which her question
fell on the banter of the other two, and she saw the shadow of

the same surprise flit across Alida's pupils. 'I suppose so. One just has to wait.'

'Oh, hang waiting!' Ned broke in. 'Life's too short for a ghost who can only be enjoyed in retrospect. Can't we do better than that, Mary?'

But it turned out that in the event they were not destined to, for within three months of their conversation with Mrs Stair they were settled at Lyng, and the life they had yearned for, to the point of planning it in advance in all its daily details, had actually begun for them.

It was to sit, in the thick December dusk, by just such a wide-hooded fireplace, under just such black oak rafters, with the sense that beyond the mullioned panes the downs were darkened to a deeper solitude: it was for the ultimate indulgence of such sensations that Mary Boyne, abruptly exiled from New York by her husband's business, had endured for nearly fourteen years the soul-deadening ugliness of a Middle Western town, and that Boyne had ground on doggedly at his engineering till, with a suddenness that still made her blink, the prodigious windfall of the Blue Star Mine had put them at a stroke in possession of life and the leisure to taste it. They had never for a moment meant their new state to be one of idleness; but they meant to give themselves only to harmonious activities. She had her vision of painting and gardening (against a background of grey walls), he dreamed of the production of his long-planned book on the *Economic Basis of Culture*, and with such absorbing work ahead no existence could be too sequestered: they could not get far enough from the world, or plunge deep enough into the past.

Dorsetshire had attracted them from the first by an air of remoteness out of all proportion to its geographical position. But to the Boynes it was one of the ever-recurring wonders of the whole incredibly compressed island – a nest of counties, as they put it – that for the production of its effects so little of a given quality went so far: that so few miles made a distance, and so short a distance a difference.

'It's that,' Ned had once enthusiastically explained, 'that gives such depth to their efforts, such relief to their contrasts. They've been able to lay the butter so thick on every delicious mouthful.'

The butter had certainly been laid on thick at Lyng: the old house hidden under a shoulder of the downs had almost all the

finer marks of commerce with a protracted past. The mere fact
that it was neither large nor exceptional made it, to the Boynes,
abound the more completely in its special charm – the charm of
having been for centuries a deep, dim reservoir of life. The life
had probably not been of the most vivid order: for long periods,
no doubt, it had fallen as noiselessly into the past as the quiet
drizzle of autumn fell, hour after hour, into the fish-pond between
the yews; but these backwaters of existence sometimes breed, in
their sluggish depths, strange acuities of emotion, and Mary Boyne
had felt from the first the mysterious stir of intenser memories.

The feeling had never been stronger than on this particular
afternoon when, waiting in the library for the lamps to come, she
rose from her seat and stood among the shadows of the hearth.
Her husband had gone off, after luncheon, for one of his long
tramps on the downs. She had noticed of late that he preferred to
go alone; and, in the tried security of their personal relations, had
been driven to conclude that his book was bothering him, and
that he needed the afternoons to turn over in solitude the problems
left from the morning's work. Certainly the book was not going
as smoothly as she had thought it would, and there were lines of
perplexity between his eyes such as had never been there in his
engineering days. He had often, then, looked fagged to the verge
of illness, but the native demon of 'worry' had never branded his
brow. Yet the few pages he had so far read to her – the introduction,
and a summary of the opening chapter – showed a firm hold on
his subject, and an increasing confidence in his powers.

The fact threw her into deeper perplexity, since, now that he
had done with 'business' and its disturbing contingencies, the one
other possible source of anxiety was eliminated. Unless it were
his health, then? But physically he had gained since they had come
to Dorsetshire, grown robuster, ruddier and fresher-eyed. It was
only within the last week that she had felt in him the undefinable
change which made her restless in his absence, and as tongue-tied
in his presence as though it were *she* who had a secret to keep
from him!

The thought that there *was* a secret somewhere between them
struck her with a sudden rap of wonder, and she looked about
her down the long room.

'Can it be the house?' she mused.

The room itself might have been full of secrets. They seemed to be piling themselves up, as evening fell, like the layers and layers of velvet shadow dropping from the low ceiling, the row of books, the smoke-blurred sculpture of the hearth.

'Why, of course – the house is haunted!' she reflected.

The ghost – Alida's imperceptible ghost – after figuring largely in the banter of their first month or two at Lyng, had been gradually left aside as too ineffectual for imaginative use. Mary had, indeed, as became the tenant of a haunted house, made the customary inquiries among her rural neighbours, but, beyond a vague 'They dü say so, ma'am,' the villagers had nothing to impart. The elusive spectre had apparently never had sufficient identity for a legend to crystallize about it, and after a time the Boynes had set the matter down to their profit-and-loss account, agreeing that Lyng was one of the few houses good enough in itself to dispense with supernatural enhancements.

'And I suppose, poor ineffectual demon, that's why it beats its beautiful wings in vain in the void,' Mary had laughingly concluded.

'Or, rather,' Ned answered in the same strain, 'why, amid so much that's ghostly, it can never affirm its separate existence as *the* ghost.' And thereupon their visible housemate had finally dropped out of their references, which were numerous enough to make them soon unaware of the loss.

Now, as she stood on the hearth, the subject of their earlier curiosity revived in her with a new sense of its meaning – a sense gradually acquired through daily contact with the scene of the lurking mystery. It was the house itself, of course, that possessed the ghost-seeing faculty, that communed visually but secretly with its own past; if one could only get into close enough communion with the house one might surprise its secret, and acquire the ghost-sight on one's own account. Perhaps, in his long hours in this very room, where she never trespassed till the afternoon, her husband *had* acquired it already, and was silently carrying about the weight of whatever it had revealed to him. Mary was too well versed in the code of the spectral world not to know that one could not talk about the ghosts one saw: to do so was almost as great a breach of taste as to name a lady in a club. But this explanation did not really satisfy her. 'What, after all, except for the fun of the shudder', she reflected, 'would he really care for any of their old ghosts?' And thence she was thrown back once more on the fundamental dilemma: the fact that one's greater or less susceptibility to spectral influences had no particular bearing on the case, since, when one *did* see a ghost at Lyng, one did not know it.

'Not till long afterwards,' Alida Stair had said. Well, supposing Ned *had* seen one when they first came, and had known only within the last week what had happened to him? More and more under the spell of the hour, she threw back her thoughts to the early days of their tenancy, but at first only to recall a lively confusion of unpacking, settling, arranging of books, and calling to each other from remote corners of the house as, treasure after treasure, it revealed itself to them. It was in this particular connection that she presently recalled a certain soft afternoon of the previous October, when, passing from the first rapturous flurry of exploration to a detailed inspection of the old house, she had pressed (like a novel heroine) a panel that opened on a flight of corkscrew stairs leading to a flat ledge of the roof – the roof which, from below, seemed to slope away on all sides too abruptly for any but practised feet to scale.

The view from this hidden coign was enchanting, and she had flown down to snatch Ned from his papers and give him the freedom of her discovery. She remembered still how, standing at her side, he had passed his arm about her while their gaze flew to the long tossed horizon-line of the downs, and then dropped contentedly back to trace the arabesque of yew hedges about the fish-pond, and the shadow of the cedar on the lawn.

'And now the other way,' he had said, turning her about within his arm; and closely pressed to him, she had absorbed, like some long satisfying draught, the picture of the grey-walled court, the squat lions on the gates, and the lime-avenue reaching up to the high-road under the downs.

It was just then, while they gazed and held each other, that she had felt his arms relax, and heard a sharp 'Hullo!' that made her turn to glance at him.

Distinctly, yes, she now recalled that she had seen, as she glanced, a shadow of anxiety, of perplexity, rather, fall across his face; and, following his eyes, had beheld the figure of a man – a man in loose greyish clothes, as it appeared to her – who was sauntering down the lime-avenue to the court with the doubtful gait of a stranger who seeks his way. Her short-sighted eyes had given her but a blurred impression of slightness and greyishness, with something foreign, or at least unlocal, in the cut of the figure or its dress; but her husband had apparently seen more – seen enough to make him push past her with a hasty 'Wait!' and dash down the stairs without pausing to give her a hand.

A slight tendency to dizziness obliged her, after a provisional clutch at the chimney against which they had been leaning, to follow him first more cautiously; and when she had reached the landing she paused again, for a less definite reason, leaning over the banister to strain her eyes through the silence of the brown sun-flecked depths. She lingered there until, somewhere in those depths she heard the closing of a door; then, mechanically impelled, she went down the shallow flight of steps till she reached the lower hall.

The front door stood open on the sunlight of the court, and hall and court were empty. The library door was open, too, and after listening in vain for any sound of voices within, she crossed the threshold and found her husband alone, vaguely fingering the papers on his desk.

He looked up, as if surprised at her entrance, but the shadow of anxiety had passed from his face, leaving it even, as she fancied, a little brighter and clearer than usual.

'What was it? Who was it?' she asked.

'Who?' he repeated, with the surprise still all on his side.

'The man we saw coming towards the house.'

He seemed to reflect. 'The man? Why, I thought I saw Peters; I dashed after him to say a word about the stable drains, but he had disappeared before I could get down.'

'Disappeared? But he seemed to be walking so slowly when we saw him.'

Boyne shrugged his shoulders. 'So I thought; but he must have got up steam in the interval. What do you say to our trying a scramble up Meldon Steep before sunset?'

That was all. At the time the occurrence had been less than nothing, had, indeed, been immediately obliterated by the magic of their first vision from Meldon Steep, a height which they had dreamed of climbing ever since they had first seen its bare spine rising above the roof of the Lyng. Doubtless it was the mere fact of the other incident's having occurred on the very day of their ascent to Meldon that had kept it stored away in the fold of memory from which it now emerged; for in itself it had no mark of the portentous. At the moment there could have been nothing more natural than that Ned should dash down from the roof in pursuit of dilatory tradesmen. It was the period when they were always on the watch for one or the other of the specialists employed about the place; always lying in wait for them, and rushing out at them with questions, reproaches, or reminders. And certainly in the distance the grey figure had looked like Peters.

Yet now, as she reviewed the scene, she felt her husband's explanation of it to have been invalidated by the look of anxiety on his face. Why had the familiar appearance of Peters made him anxious? Why, above all, if it was of such prime necessity to confer with him on the subject of the stable drains, had the failure to find him produced such a look of relief? Mary could not say that any one of these questions had occurred to her at the time, yet, from the promptness with which they now marshalled themselves at her summons, she had a sense that they must all along have been there, waiting their hour.

II

Weary with her thoughts, she moved to the window. The library was now quite dark, and she was surprised to see how much faint light the outer world still held.

As she peered out into it across the court, a figure shaped itself far down the perspective of bare limes: it looked a mere blot of deeper grey in the greyness, and for an instant, as it moved towards her, her heart thumped to the thought, 'It's the ghost!'

She had time, in that long instant, to feel suddenly that the man of whom, two months earlier, she had had a distant vision from the roof, was now, at his predestined hour, about to reveal himself as *not* having been Peters; and her spirit sank under the impending fear of the disclosure. But almost with the next tick of the clock the figure, gaining substance and character, showed itself even to her weak sight as her husband's; and she turned to meet him, as he entered, with the confession of her folly.

'It's really too absurd,' she laughed out, 'but I never *can* remember!'

'Remember what?' Boyne questioned as they drew together.

'That when one sees the Lyng ghost one never knows it.'

Her hand was on his sleeve, and he kept it there, but with no response in his gesture or in the lines of his preoccupied face.

'Did you think you'd seen it?' he asked, after an appreciable interval.

'Why, I actually took *you* for it, my dear, in my mad determination to spot it!'

'Me – just now?' His arm dropped away, and he turned from her with a faint echo of her laugh. 'Really, dearest, you'd better give it up, if that's the best you can do.'

'Oh yes, I give it up. Have *you*?' she asked, turning round on him abruptly.

The parlour-maid had entered with letters and a lamp, and the light struck up into Boyne's face as he bent above the tray she presented.

'Have *you*?' Mary perversely insisted, when the servant had disappeared on her errand of illumination.

'Have I what?' he rejoined absently, the light bringing out the sharp stamp of worry between his brows as he turned over the letters.

'Given up trying to see the ghost.' Her heart beat a little at the experiment she was making.

Her husband, laying his letters aside, moved away into the shadow of the hearth.

'I never tried,' he said, tearing open the wrapper of a newspaper.

'Well, of course,' Mary persisted, 'the exasperating thing is that there's no use trying, since one can't be sure until so long afterwards.'

He was unfolding the paper as if he had hardly heard her; but after a pause, during which the sheets rustled spasmodically between his hands, he looked up to ask, 'Have you any idea *how long*?'

Mary had sunk into a low chair beside the fireplace. From her seat she glanced over, startled, at her husand's profile, which was projected against the circle of lamplight.

'No; none. Have *you*?' she retorted, repeating her former phrase with an added stress of intention.

Boyne crumpled the paper into a bunch, and then, inconsequently, turned back with it towards the lamp.

'Lord, no! I only meant,' he explained, with a faint tinge of impatience, 'is there any legend, any tradition as to that?'

'Not that I know of,' she answered; but the impulse to add, 'What makes you ask?' was checked by the reappearance of the parlour-maid, with tea and a second lamp.

With the dispersal of shadows, and the repetition of the daily domestic office, Mary Boyne felt herself less oppressed by that sense of something mutely imminent which had darkened her afternoon. For a few moments she gave herself to the details of her task, and when she looked up from it she was struck to the point of bewilderment by the change in her husband's face. He had seated himself near the farther lamp, and was absorbed in the perusal of his letters; but was it something he had found in them, or merely the shifting of her own point of view, that had restored his features to their normal aspect? The longer she looked the more definitely the change affirmed itself. The lines of tension had vanished, and such traces of fatigue as lingered were of the kind easily attributable to steady mental effort. He glanced up, as if drawn by her gaze, and met her eyes with a smile.

'I'm dying for my tea, you know; and here's a letter for you,' he said.

She took the letter he held out in exchange for the cup she proffered him, and, returning to her seat, broke the seal with the languid gesture of the reader whose interests are all enclosed in the circle of one cherished presence.

Her next conscious motion was that of starting to her feet, the letter falling to them as she rose, while she held out to her husband a newspaper clipping.

'Ned! What's this? What does this mean?'

He had risen at the same instant, almost as if hearing her cry before she uttered it; and for a perceptible space of time he and she studied each other, like adversaries watching for an advantage, across the space between her chair and his desk.

'What's what? You fairly made me jump!' Boyne said at length, moving towards her with a sudden half-exasperated laugh. The shadow of apprehension was on his face again, not now a look of fixed foreboding, but a shifting vigilance of lips and eyes that gave her the sense of feeling himself invisibly surrounded.

Her hand shook so that she could hardly give him the clipping.

'This article – from the *Waukesha Sentinel* – that a man named Elwell has brought suit against you – that there was something wrong about the Blue Star Mine. I can't understand more than half.'

They continued to face each other as she spoke, and to her astonishment she saw that her words had the almost immediate effect of dissipating the strained watchfulness of his look.

'Oh, *that*!' he glanced down the printed slip, and then folded it with the gesture of one who handles something harmless and familiar. 'What's the matter with you this afternoon, Mary? I thought you'd got bad news.'

She stood before him with her undefinable terror subsiding slowly under the reassurance of his tone.

'You knew about this, then – it's all right?'

'Certainly I knew about it; and it's all right.'

'But what *is* it? I don't understand. What does this man accuse you of?'

'Pretty nearly every crime in the calendar.' Boyne had tossed the clipping down and thrown himself into an armchair near the fire. 'Do you want to hear the story? It's not particularly interesting – just a squabble over interests in the Blue Star.'

'But who is this Elwell? I don't know the name.'

'Oh, he's a fellow I put into it – gave him a hand up. I told you about him at the time.'

'I dare say, I must have forgotten.' Vainly she strained back among her memories. 'But if you helped him, why does he make this return?'

'Probably some shyster lawyer got hold of him and talked him over. It's all rather technical and complicated. I thought that kind of thing bored you.'

His wife felt a sting of compunction. Theoretically, she deprecated the American wife's detachment from her husband's professional interests, but in practice she had always found it difficult to fix her attention on Boyne's report of the transactions in which his varied interests involved him. Besides, she had felt during their years of exile, that, in a community where the amenities of living could be obtained only at the cost of efforts as arduous as her husband's professional labours, such brief leisure as he and she could command should be used as an escape from immediate preoccupations, a flight to the life they always dreamed of living. Once or twice, now that this new life had actually drawn its magic circle about them, she had asked herself if she had done right; but hitherto such conjectures had been no more than the retrospective excursions of an active fancy. Now, for the first time, it startled her a little to find how little she knew of the material foundation on which her happiness was built.

She glanced at her husband, and was again reassured by the

composure of his face; yet she felt the need of more definite grounds for her reassurance.

'But doesn't this suit worry you? Why have you never spoken to me about it?'

He answered both questions at once. 'I didn't speak of it at first because it *did* worry me – annoyed me, rather. But it's all ancient history now. Your correspondent must have got hold of a back number of the *Sentinel.*'

She felt a quick thrill of relief. 'You mean it's over? He's lost his case?'

There was a just perceptible delay in Boyne's reply. 'The suit's been withdrawn – that's all.'

But she persisted, as if to exonerate herself from the inward charge of being too easily put off. 'Withdrawn it because he saw he had no chance?'

'Oh, he had no chance,' Boyne answered.

She was still struggling with a dimly felt perplexity at the back of her thoughts.

'How long ago was it withdrawn?'

He paused, as if with a slight return of his former uncertainty. 'I've just had the news now; but I've been expecting it.'

'Just now – in one of your letters?'

'Yes; in one of my letters.'

She made no answer and was aware only, after a short interval of waiting, that he had risen and, strolling across the room, had placed himself on the sofa at her side. She felt him, as he did so, pass an arm about her, she felt his hand seek hers and clasp it, and turning slowly, drawn by the warmth of his cheek, she met his smiling eyes.

'It's all right – it's all right?' she questioned, through the flood of her dissolving doubts; and, 'I give you my word it was never righter!' he laughed back at her, holding her close.

III

One of the strangest things she was afterward to recall out of all the next day's strangeness was the sudden and complete recovery of her sense of security.

It was in the air when she awoke in her low-ceiled, dusky room; it went with her downstairs to the breakfast-table, flashed out at her from the fire, and reduplicated itself from the flanks of the urn and the sturdy flutings of the Georgian tea-pot. It was as if, in some roundabout way, all her diffused fears of the previous day, with their moment of sharp concentration about the newspaper article – as if this dim questioning of the future, and startled return upon the past, had between them liquidated the arrears of some haunting moral obligation. If she had indeed been careless of her husband's affairs, it was, her new state seemed to prove, because her faith in him instinctively justified such carelessness; and his right to her faith had now affirmed itself in the very face of menace and suspicion. She had never seen him more untroubled, more naturally and unconsciously himself, than after the cross-examination to which she had subjected him: it was almost as if he had been aware of her doubts, and had wanted the air cleared as much as she did.

It was as clear, thank heaven, as the bright outer light that surprised her almost with a touch of summer when she issued from the house for her daily round of the gardens. She had left Boyne at his desk, indulging herself, as she passed the library door, by a last peep at his quiet face, where he bent, pipe in mouth, above his papers; and now she had her own morning's task to perform. The task involved, on such charmed winter days, almost as much happy loitering about the different quarters of her demesne as if spring were already at work there. There were such endless possibilities still before her, such opportunities to bring out the latent graces of the old place, without a single irreverent touch of alteration, that the winter was all too short to plan what spring and autumn executed. And her recovered sense of safety gave, on this particular morning, a peculiar zest to her progress through the sweet, still place. She went first to the kitchen garden, where the espaliered pear trees drew complicated patterns on the walls, and pigeons were fluttering and preening about the silvery-slated roof of their cote.

There was something wrong about the piping of the hot house and she was expecting an authority from Dorchester, who was to drive out between trains and make a diagnosis of the boiler. But when she dipped into the damp heat of the greenhouses, among the spiced scents and waxy pinks and reds of old-fashioned exotics – even the flora of Lyng was in the note! – she learned that the great man had not arrived, and, the day being too rare to waste in an artificial atmosphere, she came out again and paced along the springy turf of the bowling-green to the gardens behind the house. At their farther end rose a grass terrace, looking across the fish-pond and yew hedges to the long house-front with its twisted chimney-stacks and blue roof angles all drenched in the pale-gold moisture of the air.

Seen thus, across the level tracery of the gardens, it sent her, from open windows and hospitably smoking chimneys, the look of some warm human presence, of a mind slowly ripened on a sunny wall of experience. She had never before had such a sense of her intimacy with it, such a conviction that its secrets were all beneficent, kept, as they said to children, 'for one's own good', such a trust in its power to gather up her life and Ned's into the harmonious pattern of the long, long story it sat there weaving in the sun.

She heard steps behind her, and turned, expecting to see the gardener accompanied by the engineer from Dorchester. But only one figure was in sight, that of a youngish, slightly built man, who, for reasons she could not on the spot have given, did not remotely resemble her notion of an authority on hothouse boilers. The newcomer, on seeing her, lifted his hat, and paused with the air of a gentleman – perhaps a traveller – who wishes to make it known that his intrusion is involuntary. Lyng occasionally attracted the more cultivated traveller, and Mary half expected to see the stranger dissemble a camera, or justify his presence by producing it. But he made no gesture of any sort, and after a moment she asked, in a tone responding to the courteous hesitation of his attitude: 'Is there anyone you wish to see?'

'I came to see Mr Boyne,' he answered. His intonation, rather than his accent, was faintly American, and Mary, at the note, looked at him more closely. The brim of his soft felt hat cast a shade on his face, which, thus obscured, wore, to her short-sighted gaze, a look of seriousness, as of a person arriving 'on business', and civilly but firmly aware of his rights.

Past experience had made her equally sensible to such claims; but she was jealous of her husband's morning hours, and doubtful of his having given anyone the right to intrude on them.

'Have you an appointment with my husband?' she asked.

The visitor hesitated, as if unprepared for the question.

'I think he expects me,' he replied.

It was Mary's turn to hesitate. 'You see, this is his time for work: he never sees anyone in the morning.'

He looked at her a moment without answering; then, as if accepting her decision, he began to move away. As he turned, Mary saw him pause and glance up at the peaceful house-front. Something in his air suggested weariness and disappointment, the dejection of the traveller who has come from far off and whose hours are limited by the timetable. It occurred to her that if this were the case her refusal might have made his errand vain, and a sense of compunction caused her to hasten after him.

'May I ask if you have come a long way?'

He gave her the same grave look. 'Yes – I have come a long way.'

'Then, if you'll go to the house, no doubt my husband will see you now. You'll find him in the library.'

She did not know why she had added the last phrase, except from a vague impulse to atone for her previous inhospitality. The visitor seemed about to express his thanks, but her attention was distracted by the approach of the gardener with a companion who bore all the marks of being the expert from Dorchester.

'This way,' she said, waving the stranger to the house; and an instant later she had forgotten him in the absorption of her meeting with the boiler-maker.

The encounter led to such far-reaching results that the engineer ended by finding it expedient to ignore his train, and Mary was beguiled into spending the remainder of the morning in absorbed confabulation among the flower-pots. When the colloquy ended, she was surprised to find that it was nearly luncheon-time, and she half expected, as she hurried back to the house, to see her husband coming out to meet her. But she found no one in the court but an under-gardener raking the gravel, and the hall, when she entered it, was so silent that she guessed Boyne to be still at work.

Not wishing to disturb him, she turned into the drawing-room, and there, at her writing-table, lost herself in renewed calculations of the outlay to which the morning's conference had pledged her. The fact that she could permit herself such follies had not yet lost its novelty; and somehow, in contrast to the vague fears of the previous days, it now seemed an element of her recovered security, of the sense that, as Ned had said, things in general had never been 'righter'.

She was still luxuriating in a lavish play of figures when the parlour-maid, from the threshold, roused her with an inquiry as to the expediency of serving luncheon. It was one of their jokes that Trimmle announced luncheon as if she were divulging a State secret, and Mary, intent upon her papers, merely murmured an absent-minded assent.

She felt Trimmle wavering doubtfully on the threshold, as if in rebuke of such unconsidered assent; then her retreating steps sounded down the passage, and Mary, pushing away her papers, crossed the hall and went to the library door. It was still closed, and she wavered in her turn, disliking to disturb her husband, yet anxious that he should not exceed his usual measure of work. As she stood there, balancing her impulses, Trimmle returned with the announcement of luncheon, and Mary, thus impelled, opened the library door.

Boyne was not at his desk, and she peered about her, expecting to discover him before the bookshelves, somewhere down the length of the room; but her call brought no response, and gradually it became clear to her that he was not there.

She turned back to the parlour-maid.

'Mr Boyne must be upstairs. Please tell him that luncheon is ready.'

Trimmle appeared to hesitate between the obvious duty of obedience and an equally obvious conviction of the foolishness of the injunction laid on her. The struggle resulted in her saying: 'If you please, madam, Mr Boyne's not upstairs.'

'Not in his room? Are you sure?'

'I'm sure, madam.'

Mary consulted the clock. 'Where is he, then?'

'He's gone out,' Trimmle announced, with the superior air of one who has respectfully waited for the question that a well-ordered mind would have put first.

Mary's conjecture had been right, then; Boyne must have gone to the gardens to meet her, and since she had missed him, it was clear that he had taken the shorter way by the south door, instead of going round to the court. She crossed the hall to the french window opening directly on the yew garden, but the parlour-maid, after another moment of inner conflict, decided to bring out: 'Please, madam, Mr Boyne didn't go that way.'

Mary turned back. 'Where *did* he go? And when?'

'He went out of the front door, up the drive, madam.' It was a matter of principle with Trimmle never to answer more than one question at a time.

'Up the drive? At this hour?' Mary went to the door herself and glanced across the court through the tunnel of bare limes. But its perspective was as empty as when she had scanned it on entering.

'Did Mr Boyne leave no message?'

Trimmle seemed to surrender herself to a last struggle with the forces of chaos.

'No, madam. He just went out with the gentleman.'

'The gentleman? What gentleman?' Mary wheeled about, as if to front this new factor.

'The gentleman who called, madam,' said Trimmle resignedly.

'When did a gentleman call? Do explain yourself, Trimmle!'

Only the fact that Mary was very hungry, and that she wanted to consult her husband about the greenhouses, would have caused her to lay so unusual an injunction on her attendant; and even now she was detached enough to note in Trimmle's eye the dawning defiance of the respectful subordinate who has been pressed too hard.

'I couldn't exactly say the hour, madam, because I didn't let the gentleman in,' she replied, with an air of discreetly ignoring the irregularity of her mistress's course.

'You didn't let him in?'

'No, madam. When the bell rang I was dressing, and Agnes —'

'Go and ask Agnes, then,' said Mary.

Trimmle still wore her look of patient magnanimity. 'Agnes would not know, madam, for she had unfortunately burnt her hand in trimming the wick of the new lamp from town' – Trimmle, as Mary was aware, had always been opposed to the new lamp – 'and so Mrs Dockett sent the kitchen-maid instead.'

Mary looked again at the clock. 'It's after two. Go and ask the kitchen-maid if Mr Boyne left any word.'

She went into luncheon without waiting, and Trimmle presently brought to her there the kitchen-maid's statement that the gentleman had called about eleven o'clock, and that Mr Boyne had gone out with him without leaving any message. The kitchen-maid did not even know the caller's name, for he had written it on a slip of paper, which he had folded and handed to her with the injunction to deliver it at once to Mr Boyne.

Mary finished her luncheon, still wondering, and when it was over and Trimmle had brought the coffee to the drawing-room, her wonder had deepened to a first faint tinge of disquietude. It was unlike Boyne to absent himself without explanation at so unwonted an hour, and the difficulty of identifying the visitor whose summons he had apparently obeyed made his disappearance the more unaccountable. Mary Boyne's experience as the wife of a busy engineer, subject to sudden calls and compelled to keep irregular hours, had trained her to the philosophic acceptance of surprises; but since Boyne's withdrawal from business he had adopted a Benedictine regularity of life. As if to make up for the dispersed and agitated years, with their 'stand-up' lunches and dinners rattled down to the joltings of the dining-cars, he cultivated the last refinements of punctuality and monotony, discounting his wife's fancy for the unexpected, and declaring that to a delicate taste there were infinite gradations of pleasure in the recurrences of habit.

Still, since no life can completely defend itself from the unforeseen, it was evident that all Boyne's precautions would sooner or later prove unavailable, and Mary concluded that he had cut short a tiresome visit by walking with his caller to the station, or at least accompanying him for part of the way.

This conclusion relieved her from farther preoccupation, and she went out herself to take up her conference with the gardener. Thence she walked to the village post office, a mile or so away; and when she turned towards home the early twilight was setting in.

She had taken a footpath across the downs, and as Boyne, meanwhile, had probably returned from the station by the highroad, there was little likelihood of their meeting. She felt sure, however, of his having reached the house before her; so sure that, when she entered it herself, without even pausing to inquire of Trimmle, she made directly for the library. But the library was still empty, and with an unwonted exactness of visual memory she observed that the papers on her husband's desk lay precisely as they had lain when she had gone in to call him to luncheon.

Then of a sudden she was seized by a vague dread of the unknown. She had closed the door behind her on entering, and as she stood alone in the long, silent room, her dread seemed to take shape and sound, to be there breathing and lurking among the shadows. Her short-sighted eyes strained through them, half discerning an actual presence, something aloof, that watched and knew; and in the recoil from that intangible presence she threw herself on the bell-rope and gave it a sharp pull.

The sharp summons brought Trimmle in precipitately with a lamp, and Mary breathed again at this sobering reappearance of the usual.

'You may bring tea if Mr Boyne is in,' she said, to justify her ring.

'Very well, madam. But Mr Boyne is not in,' said Trimmle, putting down the lamp.

'Not in? You mean he's come back and gone out again?'

'No, madam. He's never been back.'

The dread stirred again, and Mary knew that now it had her fast.

'Not since he went out with – the gentleman?'

'Not since he went out with the gentleman.'

'But who *was* the gentleman?' Mary insisted, with the shrill note of someone trying to be heard through a confusion of noises.

'That I couldn't say, madam.' Trimmle, standing there by the lamp, seemed suddenly to grow less round and rosy, as though eclipsed by the same creeping shade of apprehension.

'But the kitchen-maid knows – wasn't it the kitchen-maid who let him in?'

'She doesn't know either, madam, for he wrote his name on a folded paper.'

Mary, through her agitation, was aware that they were both designating the unknown visitor by a vague pronoun, instead of the conventional formula which, till then, had kept their allusions within the bounds of conformity. And at the same moment her mind caught at the suggestion of the folded paper.

'But he must have a name! Where's the paper?'

She moved to the desk and began to turn over the documents that littered it. The first that caught her eye was an unfinished letter in her husband's hand, with his pen lying across it, as though dropped there at a sudden summons.

My dear Parvis – who was Parvis? – *I have just received your letter announcing Elwell's death, and while I suppose there is now no further risk of trouble, it might be safer —*

She tossed the sheet aside, and continued her search; but no folded paper was discoverable among the letters and pages of manuscript which had been swept together in a heap, as if by a hurried or a startled gesture.

'But the kitchen-maid *saw* him. Send her here,' she commanded, wondering at her dullness in not thinking sooner of so simple a solution.

Trimmle vanished in a flash, as if thankful to be out of the room, and when she reappeared, conducting the agitated underling, Mary had regained her self-possession and had her questions ready.

The gentleman was a stranger, yes – that she understood. But what had he said? And, above all, what had he looked like? The first question was easily enough answered, for the disconcerting reason that he had said so little – had merely asked for Mr Boyne, and, scribbling something on a bit of paper, had requested that it should at once be carried in to him.

'Then you don't know what he wrote? You're not sure it *was* his name?'

The kitchen-maid was not sure, but supposed it was, since he had written it in answer to her inquiry as to whom she should announce.

'And when you carried the paper in to Mr Boyne, what did he say?'

The kitchen-maid did not think that Mr Boyne had said anything, but she could not be sure, for just as she had handed him the paper and he was opening it, she had become aware that the visitor had followed her into the library, and she had slipped out, leaving the two gentlemen together.

'But, then, if you left them in the library, how do you know that they went out of the house?'

This question plunged the witness into a momentary inarticulateness, from which she was rescued by Trimmle, who, by means of ingenious circumlocutions, elicited the statement that before she could cross the hall to the back passage she had heard the two gentlemen behind her, and had seen them go out to the front door together.

'Then, if you saw the strange gentleman twice, you must be able to tell me what he looked like.'

But with this final challenge to her powers of expression it became clear that the limit of the kitchen-maid's endurance had been reached. The obligation of going to the front door to 'show

in' a visitor was in itself so subversive of the fundamental order
of things that it had thrown her faculties into hopeless disarray,
and she could only stammer out, after various panting efforts:
'His hat, mum, was different-like, as you might say —'

'Different? How different?' Mary flashed out, her own mind, in
the same instant, leaping back to an image left on it that morning,
and then lost under layers of subsequent impressions.

'His hat had a wide brim, you mean, and his face was pale – a
youngish face?' Mary pressed her, with a white-lipped intensity
of interrogation. But if the kitchen-maid found any adequate answer
to this challenge, it was swept away for her listener down the
rushing current of her own convictions. The stranger – the stranger
in the garden! Why had not Mary thought of him before? She
needed no one now to tell her that it was he who had called for
her husband and gone away with him. But who was he, and why
had Boyne obeyed him?

IV

It leaped out at her suddenly, like a grin out of the dark, that
they had often called England so little – 'such a confoundedly
hard place to get lost in'.

A confoundedly hard place to get lost in! That had been her
husband's phrase. And now, with the whole machinery of official
investigation sweeping its flashlights from shore to shore, and across
the dividing straits; now, with Boyne's name blazing from the
walls of every town and village, his portrait (how that wrung
her!) hawked up and down the country like the image of a hunted
criminal; now the little, compact, populous island, so policed,
surveyed and administered, revealed itself as a Sphinx-like guardian
of abysmal mysteries, staring back into his wife's anguished eyes
as if with the wicked joy of knowing something they would never
know!

In the fortnight since Boyne's disappearance there had been no
word of him, no trace of his movements. Even the usual mislead-
ing reports that raise expectancy in tortured bosoms had been
few and fleeting. No one but the kitchen-maid had seen Boyne
leave the house, and no one else had seen the 'gentleman' who
accompanied him. All inquiries in the neighbourhood failed to
elicit the memory of a stranger's presence that day in the

neighbourhood of Lyng. And no one had met Edward Boyne, either alone or in company, in any of the neighbouring villages, or on the road across the downs, or at either of the local railway stations. The sunny English noon had swallowed him as completely as if he had gone out into Cimmerian night.

Mary, while every official means of investigation was working at its highest pressure, had ransacked her husband's papers for any trace of antecedent complications, of entanglements or obligations unknown to her, that might throw a ray into the darkness. But if any such had existed in the background of Boyne's life, they had vanished like the slip of paper on which the visitor had written his name. There remained no possible thread of guidance except – if it were indeed an exception – the letter which Boyne had apparently been in the act of writing when he received his mysterious summons. That letter, read and re-read by his wife, and submitted by her to the police, yielded little enough to feed conjecture.

'I have just heard of Elwell's death, and while I suppose there is now no further risk of trouble, it might be safer' — That was all. The 'risk of trouble' was easily explained by the newspaper clipping which had apprised Mary of the suit brought against her husband by one of his associates in the Blue Star enterprise. The only new information conveyed by the letter was the fact of its showing Boyne, when he wrote it, to be still apprehensive of the results of the suit, though he had told his wife that it had been withdrawn, and though the letter itself proved that the plaintiff was dead. It took several days of cabling to fix the identity of the 'Parvis' to whom the fragment was addressed, but even after these inquiries had shown him to be a Waukesha lawyer, no new facts concerning the Elwell suit were elicited. He appeared to have had no direct concern in it, but to have been conversant with the facts merely as an acquaintance, and possible intermediary; and he declared himself unable to guess with what object Boyne intended to seek his assistance.

This negative information, sole fruit of the first fortnight's search, was not increased by a jot during the slow weeks that followed. Mary knew that the investigations were still being carried on, but she had a vague sense of their gradually slackening, as the actual march of time seemed to slacken. It was as though the days, flying horror-struck from the shrouded image of the one inscrutable day, gained assurance as the distance lengthened, till as last they fell back into their normal gait. And so with the human imaginations at work on the dark event. No doubt it occupied them still, but week by week and hour by hour it grew less absorbing, took up less space, was slowly but inevitably crowded out of the foreground of consciousness by the new problems perpetually bubbling up from the cloudy cauldron of human experience.

Even Mary Boyne's consciousness gradually felt the same lowering of velocity. It still swayed with the incessant oscillations of conjecture; but they were slower, more rhythmical in their beat. There were even moments of weariness when, like the victim of some poison which leaves the brain clear, but holds the body motionless, she saw herself domesticated with the Horror, accepting its perpetual presence as one of the fixed conditions of life.

These moments lengthened into hours and days, till she passed into a phase of stolid acquiescence. She watched the routine of daily life with the incurious eye of a savage on whom the meaningless processes of civilization make but the faintest impression. She had come to regard herself as part of the routine, a spoke of the wheel, revolving with its motion; she felt almost like the furniture of the room in which she sat, an insensate object to be dusted and pushed about with the chairs and tables. And this deepening apathy held her fast at Lyng, in spite of the entreaties of friends and the usual medical recommendation of 'change'. Her friends supposed that her refusal to move was inspired by the belief that her husband would one day return to the spot from which he had vanished, and a beautiful legend grew up about this imaginary state of waiting. But in reality she had no such belief: the depths of anguish enclosing her were no longer lighted by flashes of hope. She was sure that Boyne would never come back, that he had gone out of her sight as completely as if death itself had waited that day on the threshold. She had even renounced, one by one, the various theories as to his disappearance which had been advances by the Press, the police, and her own agonized imagination. In sheer lassitude her mind turned from these alternatives of horror, and sank back into the blank fact that he was gone.

No, she would never know what had become of him – no one would ever know. But the house *knew*; the library in which she spent her long, lonely evenings knew. For it was here that the last scene had been enacted, here that the stranger had come and spoken the word which had caused Boyne to rise and follow him.

The floor she trod had felt his tread; the books on the shelves had seen his face; and there were moments when the intense consciousness of the old dusky walls seemed about to break out into some audible revelation of their secret. But the revelation never came, and she knew it would never come. Lyng was not one of the garrulous old houses that betray the secrets entrusted to them. Its very legend proved that it had always been the mute accomplice, the incorruptible custodian, of the mysteries it had surprised. And Mary Boyne, sitting face to face with its silence, felt the futility of seeking to break it by any human means.

V

'I don't say it *wasn't* straight, and yet I don't say it *was* straight. It was business.'

Mary, at the words, lifted her head with a start and looked intently at the speaker.

When, half an hour before, a card with 'Mr Parvis' on it had been brought up to her, she had been immediately aware that the name had been a part of her consciousness ever since she had read it at the head of Boyne's unfinished letter. In the library she had found awaiting her a small, sallow man with a bald head and gold eyeglasses, and it sent a tremor through her to know that this was the person to whom her husband's last known thought had been directed.

Parvis, civilly, but without vain preamble – in the manner of a man who has his watch in his hand – had set forth the object of his visit. He had 'run over' to England on business, and finding himself in the neighbourhood of Dorchester, had not wished to leave without paying his respects to Mrs Boyne; and without asking her, if the occasion offered, what she meant to do about Bob Elwell's family.

The words touched the spring of some obscure dread in Mary's bosom. Did her visitor, after all, know what Boyne had meant by his unfinished phrase? She asked for an elucidation of his question, and noticed at once that he seemed surprised at her continued ignorance of the subject. Was it possible that she really knew as little as she said?

'I know nothing – you just tell me,' she faltered out; and her visitor thereupon proceeded to unfold his story. It threw, even to

her confused perceptions and imperfectly initiated vision, a lurid
glare on the whole hazy episode of the Blue Star Mine. Her husband
had made his money in that brilliant speculation at the cost of
'getting ahead' of someone less alert to seize the chance; and the
victim of his ingenuity was young Robert Elwell, who had 'put
him on' to the Blue Star scheme.

Parvis, at Mary's first cry, had thrown her a sobering glance
through his impartial glasses.

'Bob Elwell wasn't smart enough, that's all; if he had been, he
might have turned round and served Boyne the same way. It's the
kind of thing that happens every day in business. I guess it's what
the scientists call the survival of the fittest – see?' said Mr Parvis,
evidently pleased with the aptness of his analogy.

Mary felt a physical shrinking from the next question she tried
to frame: it was as though the words on her lips had a taste that
nauseated her.

'But then – you accuse my husband of doing something dis-
honourable?'

Mr Parvis surveyed the question dispassionately. 'Oh no, I don't.
I don't even say it wasn't straight.' He glanced up and down the
long lines of books, as if one of them might have supplied him
with the definition he sought. 'I don't say it *wasn't* straight, and
yet I don't say it *was* straight. It was business.' After all, no definition
in his category could be more comprehensive than that.

Mary sat staring at him with a look of terror. He seemed to
her like the indifferent emissary of some evil power.

'But Mr Elwell's lawyers apparently did not take your view,
since I suppose the suit was withdrawn by their advice.'

'Oh yes; they knew he hadn't a leg to stand on, technically. It
was when they advised him to withdraw the suit that he got
desperate. You see, he'd borrowed most of the money he lost in
the Blue Star, and he was up a tree. That's why he shot himself
when they told him he had no show.'

The horror was sweeping over Mary in great deafening waves.

'He shot himself? He killed himself because of *that*?'

'Well, he didn't kill himself, exactly. He dragged on two months
before he died.' Parvis emitted the statement as unemotionally as
a gramophone grinding out its 'record'.

'You mean that he tried to kill himself, and failed? And tried
again?'

'Oh, he didn't have to *try* again,' said Parvis grimly.

They sat opposite each other in silence, he swinging his eye-glasses thoughtfully about his finger, she motionless, her arms stretched along her knees in an attitude of rigid tension.

'But if you knew all this,' she began at length, hardly able to force her voice above a whisper, 'how is it that when I wrote you at the time of my husband's disappearance you said you didn't understand his letter?'

Parvis received this without perceptible embarrassment. 'Why, I didn't understand it – strictly speaking. And it wasn't the time to talk about it, if I had. The Elwell business was settled when the suit was withdrawn. Nothing I could have told you would have helped you to find your husband.'

Mary continued to scrutinize him. 'Then why are you telling me now?'

Still Parvis did not hesitate. 'Well, to begin with, I supposed you knew more than you appear to – I mean about the circumstances of Elwell's death. And then people are talking of it now; the whole matter's been raked up again. And I thought if you didn't know you ought to.'

She remained silent, and he continued: 'You see, it's only come out lately what a bad state Elwell's affairs were in. His wife's a proud woman, and she fought on as long as she could, going out to work, and taking sewing at home when she got too sick – something with the heart, I believe. But she had his mother to look after, and the children, and she broke down under it, and finally had to ask for help. That called attention to the case, and the papers took it up, and a subscription was started. Everybody out there liked Bob Elwell, and most of the prominent names in the place are down on the list, and people began to wonder why –'

Parvis broke off to fumble in an inner pocket. 'Here,' he continued, 'here's an account of the whole thing from the *Sentinel* – a little sensational, of course. But I guess you'd better look it over.'

He held out a newspaper to Mary, who unfolded it slowly, remembering, as she did so, the evening when, in that same room, the perusal of a clipping from the *Sentinel* had first shaken the depths of her security.

As she opened the paper her eyes, shrinking from the glaring headlines, 'Widow of Boyne's Victim Forced to Appeal for Aid', ran down the column of text to two portraits inserted in it. The first was her husband's, taken from a photograph made the year they had come to England. It was the picture of him that she liked best, the one that stood on the writing-table upstairs in her bedroom. As the eyes in the photograph met hers, she felt it would be impossible to read what was said of him, and closed her lids with the sharpness of the pain.

'I thought if you felt disposed to put your name down —' she heard Parvis continue.

She opened her eyes with an effort, and they fell on the other portrait. It was that of a youngish man, slightly built, with features somewhat blurred by the shadow of a projecting hat-brim. Where had she seen that outline before? She stared at it confusedly, her heart hammering in her ears. Then she gave a cry.

'This is the man – the man who came for my husband!'

She heard Parvis start to his feet, and was dimly aware that she had slipped backwards into the corner of the sofa, and that he was bending above her in alarm. She straightened herself and reached out for the paper, which she had dropped.

'It's the man! I should know him anywhere!' she persisted in a voice that sounded to her own ears like a scream.

Parvis's answer seemed to come to her from far off, down endless fog-muffled windings.

'Mrs Boyne, you're not very well. Shall I call someone? Shall I get a glass of water?'

'No, no, no!' She threw herself towards him, her hand frantically clutching the newspaper. 'I tell you, it's the man! I *know* him! He spoke to me in the garden!'

Parvis took the journal from her, directing his glasses to the portrait. 'It can't be, Mrs Boyne. It's Robert Elwell.'

'Robert Elwell?' Her white stare seemed to travel into space. 'Then it was Robert Elwell who came for him.'

'Came for Boyne? The day he went away from here?' Parvis's voice dropped as hers rose. He bent over, laying a fraternal hand on her, as if to coax her gently back into her seat. 'Why, Elwell was dead! Don't you remember?'

Mary sat with her eyes fixed on the picture, unconscious of what he was saying.

'Don't you remember Boyne's unfinished letter to me – the one you found on his desk that day? It was written just after he'd heard of Elwell's death.' She noticed an odd shake in Parvis's unemotional voice. 'Surely you remember!' he urged her.

Yes, she remembered: that was the profoundest horror of it. Elwell had died the day before her husband's disappearance; and this was Elwell's portrait; and it was the portrait of the man who had spoken to her in the garden. She lifted her head and looked slowly about the library. The library could have borne witness that it was also the portrait of the man who had come in that day to call Boyne from his unfinished letter. Through the misty surgings of her brain she heard the faint boom of half-forgotten words – words spoken by Alida Stair on the lawn at Pangbourne before Boyne and his wife had ever seen the house at Lyng, or had imagined that they might one day live there.

'This was the man who spoke to me,' she repeated.

She looked again at Parvis. He was trying to conceal his disturbance under what he probably imagined to be an expression of indulgent commiseration; but the edges of his lips were blue. 'He thinks me mad, but I'm not mad,' she reflected; and suddenly there flashed upon her a way of justifying her strange affirmation.

She sat quiet, controlling the quiver of her lips, and waiting till she could trust her voice; then she said, looking straight at Parvis: 'Will you answer me one question, please? When was it that Robert Elwell tried to kill himself?'

'When – when?' Parvis stammered.

'Yes; the date. Please try to remember.'

She saw that he was growing still more afraid of her. 'I have a reason,' she insisted.

'Yes, yes. Only I can't remember. About two months before, I should say.'

'I want the date,' she repeated.

Parvis picked up the newspaper. 'We might see here,' he said, still humouring her. He ran his eyes down the page. 'Here it is. Last October – the –'

She caught the words from him. 'The 20th, wasn't it?' With a sharp look at her, he verified. 'Yes, the 20th. Then you *did* know?'

'I know now.' Her gaze continued to travel past him. 'Sunday, the 20th – that was the day he came first.'

Parvis's voice was almost inaudible. 'Came *here* first?'

'Yes.'

'You saw him twice, then?'

'Yes, twice.' She just breathed it at him. 'He came first on the

20th of October. I remember the date because it was the day we went up Meldon Steep for the first time.' She felt a faint gasp of inward laughter at the thought that but for that she might have forgotten.

Parvis continued to scrutinize her, as if trying to intercept her gaze.

'We saw him from the roof,' she went on. 'He came down the lime-avenue towards the house. He was dressed just as he is in that picture. My husband saw him first. He was frightened, and ran down ahead of me; but there was no one there. He had vanished.'

'Elwell had vanished?' Parvis faltered.

'Yes.' Their two whispers seemed to grope for each other. 'I couldn't think what had happened. I see now. He *tried* to come then; but he wasn't dead enough – he couldn't reach us. He had to wait for two months to die; and then he came back again – and Ned went with him.'

She nodded at Parvis with the look of triumph of a child who has worked out a difficult puzzle. But suddenly she lifted her hands with a desperate gesture, pressing them to her temples.

'Oh, my God! I sent him to Ned – I told him him where to go! I sent him to this room!' she screamed.

She felt the walls of books rush towards her, like inward falling ruins; and she heard Parvis, a long way off, through the ruins, crying to her and struggling to get at her. But she was numb to his touch, she did not know what he was saying. Through the tumult she heard but one clear note, the voice of Alida Stair speaking on the lawn at Pangbourne:

'You won't know till afterward,' it said. 'You won't know till long, long afterward.'

The Triumph of Night

It was clear that the sleigh from Weymore had not come; and the shivering young traveller from Boston, who had counted on jumping into it when he left the train at Northridge Junction, found himself standing alone on the open platform, exposed to the full assault of nightfall and winter.

The blast that swept him came off New Hampshire snow-fields and ice-hung forests. It seemed to have traversed interminable leagues of frozen silence, filling them with the same cold roar and sharpening its edge against the same bitter black-and-white landscape. Dark, searching and sword-like, it alternatively muffled and harried its victim, like a bull-fighter now whirling his cloak and now planting his darts. This analogy brought home to the young man the fact that he himself had no cloak, and that the overcoat in which he had faced the relatively temperate air of Boston seemed no thicker than a sheet of paper on the bleak heights of Northridge. George Faxon said to himself that the place was uncommonly well named. It clung to an exposed ledge over the valley from which the train had lifted him, and the wind combed it with teeth of steel that he seemed actually to hear scraping against the wooden sides of the station. Other building there was none; the village lay far down the road and thither – since the Weymore sleigh had not come – Faxon saw himself under the necessity of plodding through several feet of snow.

He understood well enough what had happened: his hostess

103

had forgotten that he was coming. Young as Faxon was, this sad
lucidity of soul had been acquired as the result of long experience, and he knew that the visitors who can least afford to hire a
carriage are almost always those whom their hosts forget to send
for. Yet to say that Mrs Culme had forgotten him was too crude
a way of putting it. Similar incidents led him to think that she
had probably told her maid to tell the butler to telephone the
coachman to tell one of the grooms (if no one else needed him)
to drive over to Northridge to fetch the new secretary; but on a
night like this, what groom who respected his rights would fail to
forget the order?

Faxon's obvious course was to struggle through the drifts to
the village, and there rout out a sleigh to convey him to Weymore;
but what if, on his arrival at Mrs Culme's, no one remembered
to ask him what this devotion to duty had cost? That, again, was
one of the contingencies he had expensively learned to look out
for, and the perspicacity so acquired told him it would be cheaper
to spend the night at the Northridge inn, and advise Mrs Culme
of his presence there by telephone. He had reached this decision,
and was about to entrust his luggage to a vague man with a
lantern, when his hopes were raised by the sound of bells.

Two sleighs were just dashing up to the station, and from the
foremost there sprang a young man muffled in furs.

'Weymore? – No, these are not the Weymore sleighs.'

The voice was that of the youth who had jumped to the platform
– a voice so agreeable that, in spite of the words, it fell consolingly
on Faxon's ears. At the same moment the wandering station-lantern,
casting a transient light on the speaker, showed his features to be
in the pleasantest harmony with his voice. He was very fair and
very young – hardly in the twenties, Faxon thought – but his
face, though full of a morning freshness, was a trifle too thin and
fine-drawn, as though a vivid spirit contended in him with a strain
of physical weakness. Faxon was perhaps the quicker to notice
such delicacies of balance because his own temperament hung on
lightly quivering nerves, which yet, as he believed, would never
quite swing him beyond a normal sensibility.

'You expected a sleigh from Weymore?' the newcomer continued, standing beside Faxon like a slender column of fur.

Mrs Culme's secretary explained his difficulty, and the other
brushed it aside with a contemptuous 'Oh, *Mrs Culme*!' that carried

both speakers a long way towards reciprocal understanding.

'But then you must be—' The youth broke off with a smile of interrogation.

'The new secretary? Yes. But apparently there are no notes to be answered this evening.' Faxon's laugh deepened the sense of solidarity which had so promptly established itself between the two.

His friend laughed also. 'Mrs Culme', he explained, 'was lunching at my uncle's today, and she said you were due this evening. But seven hours is a long time for Mrs Culme to remember anything.'

'Well,' said Faxon philosophically, 'I suppose that's one of the reasons why she needs a secretary. And I've always the inn at Northridge,' he concluded.

'Oh, but you haven't, though! It burned down last week.'

'The deuce it did!' said Faxon; but the humour of the situation struck him before its inconvenience. His life, for years past, had been mainly a succession of resigned adaptations, and he had learned before dealing practically with his embarrassments, to extract from most of them a small tribute of amusement.

'Oh, well, there's sure to be somebody in the place who can put me up.'

'No one *you* could put up with. Besides, Northridge is three miles off, and our place – in the opposite direction – is a little nearer.' Through the darkness, Faxon saw his friend sketch a gesture of self-introduction. 'My name's Frank Rainer, and I'm staying with my uncle at Overdale. I've driven over to meet two friends of his, who are due in a few minutes from New York. If you don't mind waiting till they arrive I'm sure Overdale can do you better than Northridge. We're only down from town for a few days, but the house is always ready for a lot of people.'

'But your uncle—?' Faxon could only object, with the odd sense, through his embarrassment, that it would be magically dispelled by his invisible friend's next words.

'Oh, my uncle – you'll see! I answer for him! I daresay you've heard of him – John Lavington?'

John Lavington! There was a certain irony in asking if one had heard of John Lavington! Even from a post of observation as obscure as that of Mrs Culme's secretary the rumour of John Lavington's money, of his pictures, his politics, his charities and his hospitality, was as difficult to escape as the roar of a cataract in a mountain solitude. It might almost have been said that the one place in which one would not have expected to come upon him was in just such a solitude as now surrounded the speakers – at least in this deepest hour of its desertedness. But it was just like Lavington's brilliant ubiquity to put one in the wrong even there.

'Oh, yes, I've heard of your uncle.'

'Then you *will* come, won't you? We've only five minutes to wait,' young Rainer urged, in the tone that dispels scruples by ignoring them; and Faxon found himself accepting the invitation as simply as it was offered.

A delay in the arrival of the New York train lengthened their five minutes to fifteen; and as they paced the icy platform Faxon began to see why it had seemed the most natural thing in the world to accede to his new acquaintance's suggestion. It was because Frank Rainer was one of the privileged beings who simplify human intercourse by the atmosphere of confidence and good humour they diffuse. He produced this effect, Faxon noted, by the exercise of no gift but his youth, and of no art but his sincerity; and these qualities were revealed in a smile of such sweetness that Faxon felt, as never before, what Nature can achieve when she deigns to match the face with the mind.

He learned that the young man was the ward, and the only nephew, of John Lavington, with whom he had made his home since the death of his mother, the great man's sister. Mr Lavington, Rainer said, had been 'a regular brick' to him – 'But then he is to everyone, you know' – and the young fellow's situation seemed in fact to be perfectly in keeping with his person. Apparently the only shade that had ever rested on him was cast by the physical weakness which Faxon had already detected. Young Rainer had been threatened with tuberculosis, and the disease was so far advanced that, according to the highest authorities, banishment to Arizona or New Mexico was inevitable. 'But luckily my uncle didn't pack me off, as most people would have done, without getting another opinion. Whose? Oh, an awfully clever chap, a young doctor with a lot of new ideas, who simply laughed at my being sent away, and said I'd do perfectly well in New York if I didn't dine out too much, and if I dashed off occasionally to Northridge for a little fresh air. So it's really my uncle's doing that I'm not in exile – and I feel no end better since the new chap told me I needn't bother.' Young Rainer went on to confess that he was extremely fond of dining out, dancing and similar distractions; and Faxon, listening to him, was inclined to think that the physician who had refused to cut him off altogether from these pleasures was probably a better psychologist than his seniors.

'All the same, you ought to be careful, you know.' The sense of elder-brotherly concern that forced the words from Faxon made him, as he spoke, slip his arm through Frank Rainer's.

The latter met the movement with a responsive pressure. 'Oh, I *am*: awfully, awfully. And then my uncle has such an eye on me!'

'But if your uncle has such an eye on you, what does he say to your swallowing knives out here in this Siberian wild?'

Rainer raised his fur collar with a careless gesture. 'It's not that that does it – the cold's good for me.'

'And it's not the dinners and dances? What is it, then?' Faxon good-humouredly insisted; to which his companion answered with a laugh: 'Well, my uncle says it's being bored; and I rather think he's right!'

His laugh ended in a spasm of coughing and a struggle for breath that made Faxon, still holding his arm, guide him hastily into the shelter of the fireless waiting-room.

Young Rainer had dropped down on the bench against the wall and pulled off one of his fur gloves to grope for a handkerchief. He tossed aside his cap and drew the handkerchief across his forehead, which was intensely white, and beaded with moisture, though his face retained a healthy glow. But Faxon's gaze remained fastened to the hand he had uncovered: it was so long, so colourless, so wasted, so much older than the brow he passed it over.

'It's queer – a healthy face but dying hands,' the secretary mused: he somehow wished young Rainer had kept on his glove.

The whistle of the express drew the young men to their feet, and the next moment two heavily furred gentlemen had descended to the platform and were breasting the rigour of the night. Frank Rainer introduced them as Mr Grisben and Mr Balch, and Faxon, while their luggage was being lifted into the second sleigh, discerned them, by the roving lantern-gleam, to be an elderly grey-headed pair, of the average prosperous business cut.

They saluted their host's nephew with friendly familiarity, and Mr Grisben, who seemed the spokesman of the two, ended his greeting with a genial – 'and many many more of them, dear boy!' which suggested to Faxon that their arrival coincided with an anniversary. But he could not press the enquiry, for the seat allotted him was at the coachman's side, while Frank Rainer joined his uncle's guests inside the sleigh.

A swift flight (behind such horses as one could be sure of John Lavington's having) brought them to tall gateposts, an illuminated lodge, and an avenue on which the snow had been levelled to the smoothness of marble. At the end of the avenue the long house loomed up, its principal bulk dark, but one wing sending out a ray of welcome; and the next moment Faxon was receiving a violent impression of warmth and light, of hot-house plants, hurrying servants, a vast, spectacular oak hall like a stage-setting, and, in its unreal middle distance, a small figure, correctly dressed, conventionally featured, and utterly unlike his rather florid conception of the great John Lavington.

The surprise of the contrast remained with him through his hurried dressing in the large, luxurious bedroom to which he had been shown. 'I don't see where he comes in,' was the only way he could put it, so difficult was it to fit the exuberance of Lavington's public personality into his host's contracted frame and manner. Mr Lavington, to whom Faxon's case had been rapidly explained by young Rainer, had welcomed him with a sort of dry and stilted cordiality that exactly matched his narrow face, his stiff hand, and the whiff of scent on his evening handkerchief. 'Make yourself at home – at home!' he had repeated, in a tone that suggested, on his own part, a complete inability to perform the feat he urged on his visitor. 'Any friend of Frank's ... delighted ... make yourself thoroughly at home!'

II

In spite of the balmy temperature and complicated conveniences of Faxon's bedroom, the injunction was not easy to obey. It was wonderful luck to have found a night's shelter under the opulent roof of Overdale, and he tasted the physical satisfaction to the full. But the place, for all its ingenuities of comfort, was oddly cold and unwelcoming. He couldn't have said why, and could only suppose that Mr Lavington's intense personality – intensely negative, but intense all the same – must, in some occult way, have penetrated every corner of his dwelling. Perhaps, though, it was merely that Faxon himself was tired and hungry, more deeply chilled than he had known till he came in from the cold, and unutterably sick of all strange houses, and of the prospect of perpetually treading other people's stairs.

'I hope you're not famished?' Rainer's slim figure was in the doorway. 'My uncle has a little business to attend to with Mr Grisben, and we don't dine for half an hour. Shall I fetch you, or can you find your way down? Come straight to the dining-room – the second door on the left of the long gallery.'

He disappeared, leaving a ray of warmth behind him, and Faxon, relieved, lit a cigarette and sat down by the fire.

Looking about with less haste, he was struck by a detail that had escaped him. The room was full of flowers – a mere 'bachelor's room', in the wing of a house opened only for a few days, in the dead middle of a New Hampshire winter! Flowers were everywhere, not in senseless profusion, but placed with the same conscious art that he had remarked in the grouping of the blossoming shrubs in the hall. A vase of arums stood on the writing-table, a cluster of strange-hued carnations on the stand at his elbow, and from bowls of glass and porcelain clumps of freesia-bulbs diffused their melting fragrance. The fact implied acres of glass – but that was the least interesting part of it. The flowers themselves, their quality, selection and arrangement, attested on someone's part – and on whose but John Lavington's? – a solicitous and sensitive passion for that particular form of beauty. Well, it simply made the man, as he had appeared to Faxon, all the harder to understand!

·The half-hour elapsed, and Faxon, rejoicing at the prospect of food, set out to make his way to the dining-room. He had not noticed the direction he had followed in going to his room, and was puzzled, when he left it, to find that two staircases, of apparently equal importance, invited him. He chose the one to his right, and reached, at its foot, a long gallery such as Rainer had described. The gallery was empty, the doors down its length were closed; but Rainer had said: 'The second to the left', and Faxon, after pausing for some chance enlightenment which did not come, laid his hand on the second knob to the left.

The room he entered was square, with dusky picture-hung walls. In its centre, about a table lit by veiled lamps, he fancied Mr Lavington and his guests to be already seated at dinner; then he perceived that the table was covered not with viands but with papers, and that he had blundered into what seemed to be his host's study. As he paused Frank Rainer looked up.

'Oh, here's Mr Faxon. Why not ask him—?'

Mr Lavington, from the end of the table, reflected his nephew's smile in a glance of impartial benevolence.

'Certainly. Come in, Mr Faxon. If you won't think it a liberty—'

Mr Grisben, who sat opposite his host, turned his head towards the door. 'Of course Mr Faxon's an American citizen?'

Frank Rainer laughed. 'That's all right! . . . Oh, no, not one of your pin-pointed pens, Uncle Jack. Haven't you got a quill somewhere?'

Mr Balch, who spoke slowly, and as if reluctantly, in a muffled voice, of which there seemed to be very little left, raised his hand to say: 'One moment: you acknowledge this to be —?'

'My last will and testament? Rainer's laugh redoubled. 'Well, I won't answer for the "last". It's the first, anyway.'

'It's a mere formula,' Mr Balch explained.

'Well, here goes.' Rainer dipped his quill in the inkstand his uncle had pushed in his direction, and dashed a gallant signature across the document.

Faxon, understanding what was expected of him, and conjecturing that the young man was signing his will on the attainment of his majority, had placed himself behind Mr Grisben, and stood awaiting his turn to affix his name to the instrument, Rainer, having signed, was about to push the paper across the table to Mr Balch; but the latter, again raising his hand, said in his sad, imprisoned voice: 'The seal —?'

'Oh, does there have to be a seal?'

Faxon, looking over Mr Grisben at John Lavington, saw a faint frown between his impassive eyes. 'Really, Frank!' He seemed, Faxon thought, slightly irritated by his nephew's frivolity.

'Who's got a seal?' Frank Rainer continued, glancing about the table. 'There doesn't seem to be one here.'

Mr Grisben interposed. 'A wafer will do. Lavington, have you a wafer?'

Mr Lavington had recovered his serenity. 'There must be some in one of the drawers. But I'm ashamed to say I don't know where my secretary keeps these things. He ought to have seen to it that a wafer was sent with the document.'

'Oh, hang it —' Frank Rainer pushed the paper aside: 'It's the hand of God – and I'm as hungry as a wolf. Let's dine first, Uncle Jack.'

'I think I've a seal upstairs,' said Faxon.

Mr Lavington sent him a barely perceptible smile. 'So sorry to give you the trouble —'

'Oh, I say, don't send him after it now. Let's wait till after dinner!'

Mr Lavington continued to smile on his guest, and the latter, as if under the faint coercion of the smile, turned from the room and ran upstairs. Having taken the seal from his writing-case he came down again, and once more opened the door of the study. No one was speaking when he entered – they were evidently awaiting his return with the mute impatience of hunger, and he put the seal in Rainer's reach, and stood watching while Mr Grisben struck a match and held it to one of the candles flanking the inkstand. As the wax descended on the paper Faxon remarked again the strange emaciation, the premature physical weariness, of the hand that held it; he wondered if Mr Lavington had ever noticed his nephew's hand, and if it were not poignantly visible to him now.

With this thought in his mind, Faxon raised his eyes to look at Mr Lavington. The great man's gaze rested on Frank Rainer with an expression of untroubled benevolence; and at the same instant Faxon's attention was attracted by the presence in the room of another person, who must have joined the group while he was upstairs searching for the seal. The newcomer was a man of about Mr Lavington's age and figure, who stood just behind his chair, and who, at the moment when Faxon first saw him, was gazing at young Rainer with an equal intensity of attention. The likeness between the two men – perhaps increased by the fact that the hooded lamps on the table left the figure behind the chair in shadow – struck Faxon the more because of the contrast in their expression. John Lavington, during his nephew's clumsy attempt to drop the wax and apply the seal, continued to fasten on him a look of half-amused affection; while the man behind the chair, so oddly reduplicating the lines of his features and figure, turned on the boy a face of pale hostility.

The impression was so startling that Faxon forgot what was going on about him. He was just dimly aware of young Rainer's exclaiming: 'Your turn, Mr Grisben!', of Mr Grisben's protesting:

'No – no; Mr Faxon first', and of the pen's being thereupon transferred to his own hand. He received it with a deadly sense of being unable to move, or even to understand what was expected of him, till he became conscious of Mr Grisben's paternally pointing out the precise spot on which he was to leave his autograph. The effort to fix his attention and steady his hand prolonged the process of signing, and when he stood up – a strange weight of fatigue on all his limbs – the figure behind Mr Lavington's chair was gone.

Faxon felt an immediate sense of relief. It was puzzling that the man's exit should have been so rapid and noiseless, but the door behind Mr Lavington was screened by a tapestry hanging, and Faxon concluded that the unknown looker-on had merely had to raise it to pass out. At any rate he was gone, and with his withdrawal the strange weight was lifted. Young Rainer was lighting a cigarette, Mr Balch inscribing his name at the foot of the document, Mr Lavington – his eyes no longer on his nephew – examining a strange white-winged orchid in the vase at his elbow. Everything suddenly seemed to have grown natural and simple again, and Faxon found himself responding with a smile to the affable gesture with which his host declared: 'And now, Mr Faxon, we'll dine.'

III

'I wonder how I blundered into the wrong room just now; I thought you told me to take the second door to the left,' Faxon said to Frank Rainer as they followed the older men down the gallery.

'So I did; but I probably forgot to tell you which staircase to take. Coming from your bedroom, I ought to have said the fourth door to the right. It's a puzzling house, because my uncle keeps adding to it from year to year. He built this room last summer for his modern pictures.'

Young Rainer, pausing to open another door, touched an electric button which sent a circle of light about the walls of a long room hung with canvases of the French impressionist school.

Faxon advanced, attracted by a shimmering Monet, but Rainer laid a hand on his arm.

'He bought that last week. But come along – I'll show you all this after dinner. Or *he* will, rather – he loves it.'

'Does he really love things?'

Rainer stared, clearly perplexed at the question. 'Rather! Flowers and pictures especially! Haven't you noticed the flowers? I suppose you think his manner's cold: it seems so at first; but he's really awfully keen about things.'

Faxon looked quickly at the speaker. 'Has your uncle a brother?'

'Brother? No – never had. He and my mother were the only ones.'

'Or any relation who – who looks like him? Who might be mistaken for him?'

'Not that I ever heard of. Does he remind you of someone?'

'Yes.'

'That's queer. We'll ask him if he's got a double. Come on!'

But another picture had arrested Faxon, and some minutes elapsed before he and his young host reached the dining-room. It was a large room, with the same conventionally handsome furniture and delicately grouped flowers; and Faxon's first glance showed him that only three men were seated about the dining-table. The man who had stood behind Mr Lavington's chair was not present, and no seat awaited him.

When the young men entered, Mr Grisben was speaking, and his host, who faced the door, sat looking down at his untouched soup-plate and turning the spoon about in his small, dry hand.

'It's pretty late to call them rumours – they were devilish close to facts when we left town this morning,' Mr Grisben was saying, with an unexpected incisiveness of tone.

Mr Lavington laid down his spoon and smiled interrogatively. 'Oh, facts – what *are* facts? Just the way a thing happens to look at a given minute. . . .'

'You haven't heard anything from town?' Mr Grisben persisted.

'Not a syllable. So you see . . . Balch, a little more of that *petite marmite*. Mr Faxon . . . between Frank and Mr Grisben, please.'

The dinner progressed through a series of complicated courses, ceremoniously dispensed by a prelatical butler attended by three tall footmen, and it was evident that Mr Lavington took a certain satisfaction in the pageant. That, Faxon, reflected, was probably the joint in his armour – that and the flowers. He had changed the subject – not abruptly but firmly – when the young men entered, but Faxon perceived that it still possessed the thoughts of the two elderly visitors, and Mr Balch presently observed, in a voice that seemed to come from the last survivor down a mine-shaft: 'If it *does* come, it will be the biggest crash since '93.'

Mr Lavington looked bored but polite. 'Wall Street can stand crashes better than it could then. It's got a robuster constitution.'

'Yes; but —'

'Speaking of constitutions,' Mr Grisben intervened: 'Frank, are you taking care of yourself?'

A flush rose to young Rainer's cheeks.

'Why, of course! Isn't that what I'm here for?'

'You're here about three days in a month, aren't you? And the rest of the time it's crowded restaurants and hot ballrooms in town. I thought, you were to be shipped off to New Mexico?'

'Oh, I've got a new man who say that's rot.'

'Well, you don't look as if your new man were right,' said Mr Grisben bluntly.

Faxon saw the lad's colour fade, and the rings of shadow deepen under his gay eyes. At the same moment his uncle turned to him with a renewed intensity of attention. There was such solicitude in Mr Lavington's gaze that it seemed almost to fling a shield between his nephew and Mr Grisben's tactless scrutiny.

'We think Frank's a good deal better,' he began; 'this new doctor —'

The butler, coming up, bent to whisper a word in his ear, and the communication caused a sudden change in Mr Lavington's expression. His face was naturally so colourless that it seemed not so much to pale as to fade, to dwindle and recede into something blurred and blotted out. He half rose, sat down again and sent a rigid smile about the table.

'Will you excuse me? The telephone. Peters, go on with the dinner.' With small, precise steps he walked out of the door which one of the footmen had thrown open.

A momentary silence fell on the group; then Mr Grisben once more addressed himself to Rainer. 'You ought to have gone, my boy; you ought to have gone.'

The anxious look returned to the youth's eyes. 'My uncle doesn't think so, really.'

'You're not a baby, to be always governed by your uncle's opinion. You came of age today, didn't you? Your uncle spoils you . . . that's what's the matter. . . . '

The thrust evidently went home, for Rainer laughed, and looked down with a slight accession of colour.

'But the doctor —'

'Use your common sense, Frank! You had to try twenty doctors to find one to tell you what you wanted to be told.'

A look of apprehension overshadowed Rainer's gaiety. 'Oh, come – I say! . . . What would *you* do?' he stammered.

'Pack up and jump on the first train.' Mr Grisben leaned forward and laid his hand kindly on the young man's arm. 'Look here: my nephew, Jim Grisben, is out there ranching on a big scale. He'll take you in, and be glad to have you. You say your new doctor thinks it won't do you any good; but he doesn't pretend to say it will do you harm, does he? Well, then – give it a trial. It'll take you out of hot theatres and night restaurants, anyhow . . . And all the rest of it . . . Eh, Balch?'

'Go!' said Mr Balch hollowly. 'Go *at once*,' he added, as if a closer look at the youth's face had impressed on him the need of backing up his friend.

Young Rainer had turned ashy-pale. He tried to stiffen his mouth into a smile. 'Do I look as bad as all that?'

Mr Grisben was helping himself to terrapin. 'You look like the day after an earthquake,' he said.

The terrapin had encircled the table, and been deliberately enjoyed by Mr Lavington's three visitors (Rainer, Faxon noticed, left his plate untouched) before the door was thrown open to readmit their host.

Mr Lavington advanced with an air of recovered composure. He seated himself, picked up his napkin and consulted the gold-monogrammed menu. 'No, don't bring back the fillet. . . . Some, terrapin, yes. . . .' He looked affably about the table. 'Sorry to have deserted you, but the storm has played the deuce with the wires, and I had to wait a long time before I could get a good connection. It must be blowing up for a blizzard.'

'Uncle Jack,' young Rainer broke out, 'Mr Grisben's been lecturing me.'

Mr Lavington was helping himself to terrapin. 'Ah – what about?'

He thinks I ought to have given New Mexico a show.'

'I want him to go straight out to my nephew at Santa Paz and stay there till his next birthday.' Mr Lavington signed to the butler to hand the terrapin to Mr Grisben who, as he took a second helping, addressed himself again to Rainer. 'Jim's in New York now, and going back the day after tomorrow in Olyphant's private car. I'll ask Olyphant to squeeze you in if you'll go. And when you've been out there a week or two, in the saddle all day and sleeping nine hours a night, I suspect you won't think much of the doctor who prescribed New York.'

Faxon spoke up, he knew not why. 'I was out there once: it's a splendid life. I saw a fellow – oh, a really *bad* case – who'd been simply made over by it.'

'It *does* sound jolly,' Rainer laughed, a sudden eagerness in his tone.

His uncle looked at him gently. 'Perhaps Grisben's right. It's an opportunity –'

Faxon glanced up with a start: the figure dimly perceived in the study was now more visibly and tangibly planted behind Mr Lavington's chair.

'That's right, Frank: you see your uncle approves. And the trip out there with Olyphant isn't a thing to be missed. So drop a few dozen dinners and be at the Grand Central the day after tomorrow at five.'

Mr Grisben's pleasant grey eye sought corroboration of his host, and Faxon, in a cold anguish of suspense, continued to watch him as he turned his glance on Mr Lavington. One could not look at Lavington without seeing the presence at his back, and it was clear that, the next minute, some change in Mr Grisben's expression must give his watcher a clue.

But Mr Grisben's expression did not change: the gaze he fixed on his host remained unperturbed, and the clue he gave was the startling one of not seeming to see the other figure.

Faxon's first impulse was to look away, to look anywhere else, to resort again to the champagne glass the watchful butler had already brimmed; but some fatal attraction, at war in him with an overwhelming physical resistance, held his eyes upon the spot they feared.

The figure was still standing, more distinctly, and therefore more resembling, at Mr Lavington's back; and while the latter continued to gaze affectionately at his nephew, his counterpart, as before, fixed young Rainer with eyes of deadly menace.

Faxon, with what felt like an actual wrench of the muscles, dragged his own eyes from the sight to scan the other countenances about the able; but not one revealed the least consciousness of what he saw, and a sense of mortal isolation sank upon him.

'It's worth considering, certainly —' he heard Mr Lavington continue; and as Rainer's face lit up, the face behind his uncle's chair seemed to gather into its look all the fierce weariness of old unsatisfied hates. That was the thing that, as the minutes laboured by, Faxon was becoming most conscious of. The watcher behind the chair was no longer merely malevolent: he had grown suddenly, unutterably tired. His hatred seemed to well up out of the very depths of balked effort and thwarted hopes, and the fact made him more pitiable, and yet more dire.

Faxon's look reverted to Mr Lavington, as if to surprise in him a corresponding change. At first none was visible: his pinched smile was screwed to his blank face like a gas-light to a white-washed wall. Then the fixity of the smile became ominous: Faxon saw that its wearer was afraid to let it go. It was evident that Mr Lavington was unutterably tired, too, and the discovery sent a colder current through Faxon's veins. Looking down at his untouched plate, he caught the soliciting twinkle of the champagne glass; but the sight of the wine turned him sick.

'Well, we'll go into the details presently,' he heard Mr Lavington say, still on the question of his nephew's future. 'Let's have a cigar first. No – not here, Peters.' He turned his smile on Faxon. 'When we've had coffee I want to show you my pictures.'

'Oh, by the way, Uncle Jack – Mr Faxon wants to know if you've got a double?'

'A double?' Mr Lavington, still smiling, continued to address himself to his guest. 'Not that I know of. Have you seen one, Mr Faxon?'

Faxon thought: 'My God, if I look up now they'll *both* be looking at me!' To avoid raising his eyes he made as though to lift the glass to his lips; but his hand sank inert, and he looked up. Mr Lavington's glance was politely bent on him, but with a loosening of the strain about his heart he saw that the figure behind the chair still kept its gaze on Rainer.

'Do you think you've seen my double, Mr Faxon?'

Would the other face turn if he said yes? Faxon felt a dryness in his throat. 'No,' he answered.

'Ah! It's possible I've a dozen. I believe I'm extremely usual-looking.' Mr Lavington went on conversationally; and still the other face watched Rainer.

'It was . . . a minute . . . a confusion of memory . . .' Faxon heard himself stammer. Mr Lavington pushed back his chair, and as he did so Mr Grisben suddenly leaned forward.

'Lavington! What have we been thinking of? We haven't drunk Frank's health!'

Mr Lavington reseated himself. 'My dear boy! . . . Peters, another bottle. . . . ' He turned to his nephew. 'After such a sin of omission I don't presume to propose the toast myself . . . but Frank knows. . . . Go ahead, Grisben!'

The boy shone on his uncle. 'No, no, Uncle Jack! Mr Grisben won't mind. Nobody but *you* – today!'

The butler was replenishing the glasses. He filled Mr Lavington's last, and Mr Lavington put out his small hand to raise it. . . . As he did so Faxon looked away.

'Well, then – all the good I've wished you in all the past years . . . I put it into the prayer that the coming ones may be healthy and happy and many . . . and *many*, dear boy!'

Faxon saw the hands about him reach out for their glasses. Automatically, he reached for his. His eyes were still on the table, and he repeated to himself with a trembling vehemence: 'I won't look up! I won't . . . I won't. . . . '

His fingers clasped the glass and raised it to the level of his lips. He saw the other hands making the same motion. He heard Mr Grisben's genial 'Hear! Hear!' and Mr Balch's hollow echo. He said to himself, as the rim of the glass touched his lips: 'I won't look up! I swear I won't' – and he looked.

The glass was so full that it required an extraordinary effort to hold it there, brimming and suspended, during the awful interval before he could trust his hand to lower it again, untouched, to the table. It was this merciful preoccupation which saved him, kept him from crying out, from losing his hold, from slipping down into the bottomless blackness that gaped for him. As long as the problem of the glass engaged him he felt able to keep his seat, manage his muscles, fit unnoticeably into the group; but as the glass touched the table his last link with safety snapped. He stood up and dashed out of the room.

IV

In the gallery, the instinct of self-preservation helped him to turn back and sign to young Rainer not to follow. He stammered out something about a touch of dizziness, and joining them presently; and the boy nodded sympathetically and drew back.

At the foot of the stairs Faxon ran against a servant. 'I should like to telephone to Weymore,' he said with dry lips.

'Sorry, sir, wires all down. We've been trying the last hour to get New York again for Mr Lavington.'

Faxon shot on to his room, burst into it, and bolted the door. The lamplight lay on furniture, flowers, books; in the ashes a log still glimmered. He dropped down on the sofa and hid his face. The room was profoundly silent, the whole house was still: nothing about him gave a hint of what was going on, darkly and dumbly, in the room he had flown from, and with the covering of his eyes oblivion and reassurance seemed to fall on him. But they fell for a moment only; then his lids opened again to the monstrous vision. There it was, stamped on his pupils, a part of him forever, an indelible horror burnt into his body and brain. But why into his – just his? Why had he alone been chosen to see what he had seen? What business was it of *his*, in God's name? Any one of the others, thus enlightened, might have exposed the horror and defeated it; but *he*, the one weaponless and defenceless spectator, the one whom none of the others would believe or understand if he attempted to reveal what he knew – *he* alone had been singled out, as the victim of this dreadful initiation!

Suddenly he sat up, listening: he had heard a step on the stairs. Someone, no doubt, was coming to see how he was – to urge him, if he felt better, to go down and join the smokers. Cautiously he opened his door; yes, it was young Rainer's step. Faxon looked down the passage, remembered the other stairway and darted to it. All he wanted was to get out of the house. Not another instant would he breathe its abominal air! What business was it of *his*, in God's name?

He reached the opposite end of the lower gallery, and beyond it saw the hall by which he had entered. It was empty, and on a long table he recognized his coat and cap. He got into his coat, unbolted the door, and plunged into the purifying night.

The darkness was deep, and the cold so intense that for an instant it stopped his breathing. Then he perceived that only a thin snow was falling, and resolutely he set his face for flight. The trees along the avenue marked his way as he hastened with long strides over the beaten snow. Gradually, while he walked,

the tumult in his brain subsided. The impulse to fly still drove
him forward, but he began to feel that he was flying from a
terror of his own creating, and that the most urgent reason for
escape was the need of hiding his state, of shunning other eyes
till he should regain his balance.

He had spent the long hours in the train in fruitless broodings
on a discouraging situation, and he remembered how his bitter-
ness had turned to exasperation when he found that the Weymore
sleigh was not awaiting him. It was absurd, of course; but, though
he had joked with Rainer over Mrs Culme's forgetfulness, to confess
it had cost a pang. That was what his rootless life had brought
him to: for lack of a personal stake in things his sensibility was
at the mercy of such trifles. . . . Yes, that, and the cold and fatigue, the absence of hope and the haunting sense of starved ap-
titudes, all these had brought him to the perilous verge over which,
once or twice before, his terrified brain had hung.

Why else, in the name of any imaginable logic, human or devilish,
should he, a stranger, be singled out for this experience? What
could it mean to him, how was he related to it, what bearing had
it on his case? . . . Unless, indeed, it was just because he was a
stranger – a stranger everywhere – because he had no personal
life, no warm screen of private egotisms to shield him from exposure,
that he had developed this abnormal sensitiveness to the vicissitudes
of others. The thought pulled him up with a shudder. No! Such a
fate was too abominable; all that was strong and sound in him
rejected it. A thousand times better regard himself as ill, disor-
ganized, deluded, than as the predestined victim of such warnings!

He reached the gates and paused before the darkened lodge.
The wind had risen and was sweeping the snow into his face.
The cold had him in its grasp again, and he stood uncertain.
Should he put his sanity to the test and go back? He turned and
looked down the dark drive to the house. A single ray shone
through the trees, evoking a picture of the lights, the flowers, the
faces grouped about that fatal room. He turned and plunged out
into the road. . . .

He remembered that, about a mile from Overdale, the coachman had pointed out the road to Northridge, and he began to
walk in that direction. Once in the road he had the gale in his
face, and the wet snow in his moustache and eyelashes instantly
hardened to ice. The same ice seemed to be driving a million

blades into his throat and lungs, but he pushed on, the vision of the warm room pursuing him.

The snow in the road was deep and uneven. He stumbled across ruts and sank into drifts, and the wind drove against him like a granite cliff. Now and then he stopped, gasping, as if an invisible hand had tightened an iron band about his body; then he started again, stiffening himself against the stealthy penetration of the cold. The snow continued to descend out of a pall of inscrutable darkness, and once or twice he paused, fearing he had missed the road to Northridge; but seeing no sign of a turn, he ploughed on.

At last, feeling sure that he had walked for more than a mile, he halted and looked back. The act of turning brought immediate relief, first because it put his back to the wind, and then because, far down the road, it showed him the gleam of a lantern. A sleigh was coming – a sleigh that might, perhaps, give him a lift to the village! Fortified by the hope, he began to walk back towards the light. It came forward very slowly, with unaccountable zigzags and waverings; and even when he was within a few yards of it he could catch no sound of sleigh bells. Then it paused and became stationary by the roadside, as though carried by a pedestrian who had stopped, exhausted by the cold. The thought made Faxon hasten on, and a moment later he was stooping over a motionless figure huddled against the snow-bank. The lantern had dropped from its bearer's hand, and Faxon, fearfully raising it, threw its light into the face of Frank Rainer.

'Rainer! What on earth are you doing her?'

The boy smiled back through his pallor. 'What are *you*, I'd like to know?' he retorted; and, scrambling to his feet with a clutch on Faxon's arm, he added gaily: 'Well, I've run you down!'

Faxon stood confounded, his heart sinking. The lad's face was grey.

'What madness —' he began.

'Yes, it *is*. What on earth did you do it for?'

'I? Do what? . . . Why I . . . I was just taking a walk . . . I often walk at night . . . '

Frank Rainer burst into a laugh. 'On such nights? Then you hadn't bolted?'

'Bolted?'

'Because I'd done something to offend you? My uncle thought you had.'

Faxon grasped his arm. 'Did your uncle send you after me?'

'Well, he gave me an awful rowing for not going up to your room with you when you said you were ill. And when we found you'd gone we were frightened – and he was awfully upset – so I said I'd catch you. . . . You're *not* ill, are you?'

'Ill? No. Never better.' Faxon picked up the lantern. 'Come; let's go back. It was awfully hot in that dining-room.'

'Yes; I hoped it was only that.'

They trudged on in silence for a few minutes; then Faxon questioned: 'You're not too done up?'

'Oh, no. It's a lot easier with the wind behind us.'

'All right. Don't talk any more.'

They pushed ahead, walking, in spite of the light that guided them, more slowly than Faxon had walked alone into the gale. The fact of his companion's stumbling against a drift gave Faxon a pretext for saying: 'Take hold of my arm,' and Rainer obeying, gasped out: 'I'm blown!'

'So am I. Who wouldn't be?'

'What a dance you led me! If it hadn't been for one of the servants happening to see you —'

'Yes; all right. And now, won't you kindly shut up?'

Rainer laughed and hung on him. 'Oh, the cold doesn't hurt me. . . . '

For the first few minutes after Rainer had overtaken him, anxiety for the lad had been Faxon's only thought. But as each labouring step carried them nearer to the spot he had been fleeing, the reasons for his flight grew more ominous and more insistent. No, he was not ill, he was not distraught and deluded – he was the instrument singled out to warn and save; and here he was, irresistibly driven, dragging the victim back to his doom!

The intensity of the conviction had almost checked his steps. But what could he do or say? At all costs he must get Rainer out of the cold, into the house and into his bed. After that he would act.

The snowfall was thickening, and as they reached a stretch of the road between open fields the wind took them at an angle, lashing their faces with barbed thongs. Rainer stopped to take breath, and Faxon felt the heavier pressure of his arm.

'When we get to the lodge, can't we telephone to the stable for a sleigh?'

'If they're not all asleep at the lodge.'

'Oh, I'll manage. Don't talk!' Faxon ordered; and they plodded on. . . .

At length the lantern ray showed ruts that curved away from the road under tree-darkness.

Faxon's spirits rose. 'There's the gate! We'll be there in five minutes.

As he spoke he caught, above the boundary hedge, the gleam of a light at the farther end of the dark avenue. It was the same light that had shone on the scene of which every detail was burnt into his brain; and he felt again its overpowering reality. No – he couldn't let the boy go back!

They were at the lodge at last, and Faxon was hammering on the door. He said to himself: 'I'll get him inside first, and make them give him a hot drink. Then I'll see – I'll find an argument.'

There was no answer to his knocking, and after an interval Rainer said: 'Look here – we'd better go on.'

'No!'

'I can, perfectly —'

'You shan't go to the house, I say!' Faxon redoubled his blows, and at length steps sounded on the stairs. Rainer was leaning against the jamb, and as the door opened the light from the hall flashed on his pale face and fixed eyes. Faxon caught him by the arm and drew him in.

'It *was* cold out there,' he sighed; and then, abruptly, as if invisible shears at a single stroke had cut every muscle in his body, he swerved, drooped on Faxon's arm, and seemed to sink into nothing at his feet.

The lodge-keeper and Faxon bent over him, and somehow, between them, lifted him into the kitchen and laid him on a sofa by the stove.

The lodge-keeper, stammering: 'I'll ring up the house,' dashed out of the room. But Faxon heard the words without heeding them: omens mattered nothing now, beside this woe fulfilled. He knelt down to undo the fur collar about Rainer's throat, and as he did so he felt a warm moisture on his hands. He held them up, and they were red. . . .

V

The palms threaded their endless line along the yellow river. The little steamer lay at the wharf; and George Faxon, sitting in the verandah of the wooden hotel, idly watched the coolies carrying the freight across the gangplank.

He had been looking at such scenes for two months. Nearly five had elapsed since he had descended from the train at Northridge and strained his eyes for the sleigh that was to take him to Weymore: Weymore, which he was never to behold! . . . Part of the interval – the first part – was still a great grey blur. Even now he could not be quite sure how he had got back to Boston, reached the house of a cousin, and been thence transferred to a quiet room looking out on snow under bare trees. He looked out a long time at the same scene, and finally one day a man he had known at Harvard came to see him, and invited him to go out on a business trip to the Malay Peninsula.

'You've had a bad shake-up, and it'll do you no end of good to get away from things.'

When the doctor came the next day it turned out that he knew of the plan and approved it. 'You ought to be quiet for a year. Just loaf and look at the landscape,' he advised.

Faxon felt the first faint stirrings of curiosity.

'What's been the matter with me, anyway?'

'Well, overwork, I suppose. You must have been bottling up for a bad breakdown before you started for New Hampshire last December. And the shock of that poor boy's death did the rest.'

Ah, yes – Rainer had died. He remembered. . . .

He started for the East, and gradually, by imperceptible degrees, life crept back into his weary bones and leaden brain. His friend was patient and considerate, and they travelled slowly and talked little. At first Faxon had felt a great shrinking from whatever touched on familiar things. He seldom looked at a newspaper, and he never opened a letter without a contraction of the heart. It was not that he had any special cause for apprehension, but merely that a great trail of darkness lay on everything. He had looked too deep down into the abyss. . . . But little by little health and energy returned to him, and with them the common promptings of curiosity. He was beginning to wonder how the world was going, and when, presently, the hotel-keeper told him there were no letters for him in the steamer's mailbag, he felt a distinct sense of disappointment. His friend had gone into the jungle on a long excursion, and he was lonely, unoccupied and wholesomely bored. He got up and strolled into the stuffy reading-room.

There he found a game of dominoes, a mutilated picture-puzzle, some copies of *Zion's Herald* and a pile of New York and London newspapers.

He began to glance through the papers, and was disappointed to find that they were less recent than he had hoped. Evidently the last numbers had been carried off by luckier travellers. He continued to turn them over, picking out the American ones first. These, as it happened, were the oldest: they dated back to December and January. To Faxon, however, they had all the flavour of novelty, since they covered the precise period during which he had virtually ceased to exist. It had never before occurred to him to wonder what had happened in the world during that interval of obliteration; but now he felt a sudden desire to know.

To prolong the pleasure, he began by sorting the papers chronologically, and as he found and spread out the earliest number, the date at the top of the page entered into his consciousness like a key slipping into a lock. It was the 17th of December: the date of the day after his arrival at Northridge. He glanced at the first page and read in blazing characters: 'Reported Failure of Opal Cement Company. Lavington's Name Involved. Gigantic Exposure of Corruption Shakes Wall Street to its Foundations.'

He read on, and when he had finished the first paper he turned to the next. There was a gap of three days, but the Opal Cement 'Investigation' still held the centre of the stage. From its complex revelations of greed and ruin his eye wandered to the death notices, and he read: 'Rainer, suddenly, at Northridge, New Hampshire, Francis John, only son of the late ... '

His eyes clouded, and he dropped the newspaper and sat for a long time with his face in his hands. When he looked up again he noticed that his gesture had pushed the other papers from the table and scattered them at his feet. The uppermost lay spread out before him, and heavily his eyes began their search again. 'John Lavington comes forward with plan for reconstructing company. Offers to put in ten millions of his own. The proposal under consideration by the District Attorney.'

Ten millions ... ten millions of his own. But if John Lavington

was ruined? . . . Faxon stood up with a cry. That was it, then –
that was what the warning meant! And if he had not fled from it,
dashed wildly away from it into the night, he might have broken
the spell of iniquity, the powers of darkness might not have prevailed!
He caught up the pile of newspapers and began to glance through
each in turn for the headline: 'Wills Admitted to Probate'. In the
last of all he found the paragraph he sought, and it stared up at
him as if with Rainer's dying eyes.

That – *that* was what he had done! The powers of pity had
singled him out to warn and save, and he had closed his ears to
their call, and washed his hands of it, and fled. Washed his hands
of it! That was the word. It caught him back to the dreadful
moment in the lodge when, raising himself up from Rainer's side,
he had looked at his hands and seen that they were red. . . .

Bewitched

I

The snow was still falling thickly when Orrin Bosworth, who farmed the land south of Lonetop, drove up in his cutter to Saul Rutledge's gate. He was surprised to see two other cutters ahead of him. From them descended two muffled figures. Bosworth, with increasing surprise, recognized Deacon Hibben, from North Ashmore, and Sylvester Brand, the widower, from the old Bearcliff farm on the way to Lonetop.

It was not often that anybody in Hemlock County entered Saul Rutledge's gate; least of all in the dead of winter, and summoned (as Bosworth, at any rate, had been) by Mrs Rutledge, who passed, even in that unsocial region, for a woman of cold manners and solitary character. The situation was enough to excite the curiosity of a less imaginative man than Orrin Bosworth.

As he drove in between the broken-down white gateposts topped by fluted urns the two men ahead of him were leading their horses to the adjoining shed. Bosworth followed, and hitched his horse to a post. Then the three tossed off the snow from their shoulders, clapped their numb hands together, and greeted each other.

'Hallo, Deacon.'

'Well, well, Orrin –' They shook hands.

''Day, Bosworth,' said Sylvester Brand, with a brief nod. He seldom put any cordiality into his manner, and on this occasion he was still busy about his horse's bridle and blanket.

Orrin Bosworth, the youngest and most communicative of the three, turned back to Deacon Hibben, whose long face, queerly blotched and mouldy-looking, with blinking peering eyes, was yet less forbidding than Brand's heavily hewn countenance.

'Queer, our all meeting here this way. Mrs Rutledge sent me a message to come,' Bosworth volunteered.

The Deacon nodded. 'I got a word from her too – Andy Pond come with it yesterday noon. I hope there's no trouble here –'

He glanced through the thickening fall of snow at the desolate front of the Rutledge house, the more melancholy in its present neglected state because, like the gateposts, it kept traces of former elegance. Bosworth had often wondered how such a house had come to be built in that lonely stretch between North Ashmore and Cold Corners. People said there had once been other houses like it, forming a little township called Ashmore, a sort of mountain colony created by the caprice of an English Royalist officer, one Colonel Ashmore, who had been murdered by the Indians, with all his family, long before the Revolution. This tale was confirmed by the fact that the ruined cellars of several smaller houses were still to be discovered under the wild growth of the adjoining slopes, and that the Communion plate of the moribund Episcopal church of Cold Corners was engraved with the name of Colonel Ashmore, who had given it to the church of Ashmore in the year 1723. Of the church itself no traces remained. Doubtless it had been a modest edifice, built on piles, and the conflagration which had burnt the other houses to the ground's edge had reduced it utterly to ashes. The whole place, even in summer, wore a mournful solitary air, and people wondered why Saul Rutledge's father had gone there to settle.

'I never knew a place,' Deacon Hibben said, 'as seemed as far away from humanity. And yet it ain't so in miles.'

'Miles ain't the only distance,' Orrin Bosworth answered; and the two men, followed by Sylvester Brand, walked across the drive to the front door. People in Hemlock County did not usually come and go by their front doors, but all three men seemed to feel that, on an occasion which appeared to be so exceptional, the usual and more familiar approach by the kitchen would not be suitable.

They had judged rightly; the Deacon had hardly lifted the knocker when the door opened and Mrs Rutledge stood before them.

'Walk right in,' she said in her usual dead-level tone; and Bosworth, as she followed the others, thought to himself: 'Whatever's happened, she'd not going to let it show in her face.'

It was doubtful, indeed, if anything unwonted could be made to show in Prudence Rutledge's face, so limited was its scope, so fixed were its features. She was dressed for the occasion in a black calico with white spots, a collar of crochet-lace fastened by a gold brooch, and a grey woollen shawl crossed under her arms and tied at the back. In her small narrow head the only marked prominence was that of the brow projecting roundly over pale spectacled eyes. Her dark hair, parted above this prominence, passed tight and flat over the tips of her ears into a small braided coil at the nape; and her contracted head looked still narrower from being perched on a long hollow neck with cord-like throat-muscles. Her eyes were of a pale cold grey, her complexion was an even white. Her age might have been anywhere from thirty-five to sixty.

The room into which she led the three men had probably been the dining-room of the Ashmore house. It was now used as a front parlour, and black stove planted on a sheet of zinc stuck out from the delicately fluted panels of an old wooden mantel. A newly lit fire smouldered reluctantly, and the room was at once close and bitterly cold.

'Andy Pond,' Mrs Rutledge cried to some one at the back of the house, 'step out and call Mr Rutledge. You'll likely find him in the wood-shed, or round the barn somewheres.' She joined her visitors. 'Please suit yourselves to seats,' she said.

The three men, with an increasing air of constraint, took the chairs she pointed out, and Mrs Rutledge sat stiffly down upon a fourth, behind a rickety head-work table. She glanced from one to the other of her visitors.

'I presume you folks are wondering what it is I asked you to come here for,' she said in her dead-level voice. Orrin Bosworth and Deacon Hibben murmured an assent; Sylvester Brand sat silent, his eyes, under their great thicket of eyebrows, fixed on the huge boot-tip swinging before him.

'Well, I allow you didn't expect it was for a party,' continued Mrs Rutledge.

No one ventured to respond to this ·chill pleasantry, and she continued: 'We're in trouble here, and that's the fact. And we need advice – Mr Rutledge and myself do.' She cleared her throat, and added in a lower tone, her pitilessly clear eyes looking straight before her: 'There's a spell been cast over Mr Rutledge.'

The Deacon looked up sharply, an incredulous smile pinching his thin lips. 'A spell?'

'That's what I said: he's bewitched.'

Again the three visitors were silent; then Bosworth, more at ease or less tongue-tied than the others, asked with an attempt at humour: 'Do you see the word in the strict Scripture sense, Mrs Rutledge?'

She glanced at him before replying: 'That's how *he* uses it.'

The Deacon coughed and cleared his long rattling throat. 'Do you care to give us more particulars before your husband joins us?'

Mrs Rutledge looked down at her clasped hands, as if considering the question. Bosworth noticed that the inner fold of her lids was of the same uniform white as the rest of her skin, so that when she dropped them her rather prominent eyes looked like the sightless orbs of a marble statue. The impression was unpleasing, and he glanced away at the text over the mantelpiece, which read:

The Soul That Sinneth It Shall Die.

'No,' she said at length, 'I'll wait.'

At this moment Sylvester Brand suddenly stood up and pushed back his chair. 'I don't know', he said, in his rough bass voice, 'as I've got any particular lights on Bible mysteries; and this happens to be the day I was to go down to Starkfield to close a deal with a man.'

Mrs Rutledge lifted one of her long thin hands. Withered and wrinkled by hard work and cold, it was nevertheless of the same leaden white as her face. 'You won't be kept long,' she said. 'Won't you be seated?'

Farmer Brand stood irresolute, his purplish underlip twitching. 'The Deacon here – such things is more in his line. . . . '

'I want you should stay,' said Mrs Rutledge quietly; and Brand sat down again.

A silence fell, during which the four persons present seemed all to be listening for the sound of a step; but none was heard, and after a minute or two Mrs Rutledge began to speak again.

'It's down by the old shack on Lamer's pond; that's where they meet,' she said suddenly.

Bosworth, whose eyes were on Sylvester Brand's face, fancied he saw a sort of inner flush darken the farmer's heavy leather skin. Deacon Hibben leaned forward, a glitter of curiosity in his eyes.

'They – *who*, Mrs Rutledge?'

'My husband, Saul Rutledge ... and her. ...'

Sylvester Brand again stirred in his seat. 'Who do you mean by *her?*' he asked abruptly, as if roused out of some far-off musing.

Mrs Rutledge's body did not move; she simply revolved her head on her long neck and looked at him.

'Your daughter, Sylvester Brand.'

The man staggered to his feet with an explosion of inarticulate sounds. 'My – my daughter? What the hell are you talking about? My daughter? It's a damned lie ... it's ... it's ... '

'Your daughter *Ora*, Mr Brand,' said Mrs Rutledge slowly.

Bosworth felt an icy chill down his spine. Instinctively he turned his eyes away from Brand, and they rested on the mildewed countenance of Deacon Hibben. Between the blotches it had become as white as Mrs Rutledge's, and the Deacon's eyes burned in the whiteness like live embers among ashes.

Brand gave a laugh: the rusty creaking laugh of one whose springs of mirth are never moved by gaiety. 'My daughter *Ora?*' he repeated.

'Yes.'

'My *dead* daughter?'

'That's what he says.'

'Your husband?'

'That's what Mr Rutledge says.'

Orrin Bosworth listened with a sense of suffocation; he felt as if he were wrestling with long-armed horrors in a dream. He could no longer resist letting his eyes return to Sylvester Brand's face. To his surprise it had resumed a natural imperturbable expression. Brand rose to his feet. 'Is that all?' he queried contemptuously.

'All? Ain't it enough? How long is it since you folks seen Saul Rutledge, any of you?' Mrs Rutledge flew out at them.

Bosworth, it appeared, had not seen him for nearly a year; the Deacon had only run across him once, for minute, at the North Ashmore post-office, the previous autumn, and acknowledged that he wasn't looking any too good then. Brand said nothing, but stood irresolute.

'Well, if you wait a minute you'll see with your own eyes; and he'll tell you with his own words. That's what I've got you here for – to see for yourselves what's come over him. Then you'll talk different,' she added, twisting her head abruptly towards Sylvester Brand.

The Deacon raised a lean hand of interrogation.

'Does your husband know we've been sent for on this business, Mrs Rutledge?'

Mrs Rutledge signed assent.

'It was with his consent, then –?'

She looked coldly at her questioner. 'I guess it had to be,' she said. Again Bosworth felt the chill down his spine. He tried to dissipate the sensation by speaking with an affectation of energy.

'Can you tell us, Mrs Rutledge, how this trouble you speak of shows itself ... what makes you think ... ?'

She looked at him for a moment; then she leaned forward across the rickety bead-work table. A thin smile of disdain narrowed her colourless lips. 'I don't think – I know.'

'Well – but how?'

She leaned closer, both elbows on the table, her voice dropping. 'I seen 'em.'

In the ashen light from the veiling of snow beyond the windows the Deacon's little screwed-up eyes seemed to give out red sparks. 'Him and the dead?'

'Him and the dead.'

'Saul Rutledge and – and Ora Brand?'

'That's so.'

Sylvester Brand's chair fell backward with a crash. He was on his feet again, crimson and cursing. 'It's a God-damned fiend-begotten lie. . . . '

'Friend Brand ... Friend Brand ... ' The Deacon protested.

'Here, let me get out of this. I want to see Saul Rutledge himself, and tell him –'

'Well, here he is,' said Mrs Rutledge.

The outer door had opened; they heard the familiar stamping and shaking of a man who rids his garments of their last snowflakes before penetrating to the sacred precincts of the best parlour. Then Saul Rutledge entered.

II

As he came in he faced the light from the north window, and Bosworth's first thought was that he looked like a drowned man fished out from under the ice – 'self-drowned', he added. But the snow-light plays cruel tricks with a man's colour, and even with the shape of his features; it must have been partly that, Bosworth reflected, which transformed Saul Rutledge from the straight muscular fellow he had been a year before into the haggard wretch now before them.

The Deacon sought for a word to ease the horror. 'Well, now, Saul – you look's if you'd ought to set right up to the stove. Had a touch of ague, maybe?'

The feeble attempt was unvailing. Rutledge neither moved nor answered. He stood among them silent, incommunicable, like one risen from the dead.

Brand grasped him roughly by the shoulder. 'See her, Saul Rutledge, what's this dirty lie your wife tells us you've been putting about?'

Still Rutledge did not move. 'It's no lie,' he said.

Brand's hand dropped from his shoulder. In spite of the man's rough bullying power he seemed to be undefinably awed by Rutledge's look and tone.

'No lie? You've gone plumb crazy, then, have you?'

Mrs Rutledge spoke. 'My husband's not lying, nor he ain't gone crazy. Don't I tell you I seen 'em?'

Brand laugh again. 'Him and the dead?'

'Yes.'

'Down by the Lamer pond, you say?'

'Yes.'

'And when was that, if I might ask?'

'Day before yesterday.'

A silence fell on the strangely assembled group. The Deacon at length broke it to say to Mr Brand: 'Brand, in my opinion we've got to see this thing through.'

Brand stood for a moment in speechless contemplation: there was something animal and primitive about him, Bosworth thought, as he hung thus, lowering and dumb, a little foam beading the corners of that heavy purplish underlip. He let himself slowly down into his chair. 'I'll see it through.'

The two other men and Mrs Rutledge had remained seated. Saul Rutledge stood before them, like a prisoner at the bar, or rather like a sick man before the physicians who were to heal him. As Bosworth scrutinized that hollow face, so wan under the dark sunburn, so sucked inward and consumed by some hidden fever, there stole over the sound healthy man the thought that perhaps, after all, husband and wife spoke the truth, and that they were all at that moment really standing on the edge of some forbidden mystery. Things that the rational mind would reject without a thought seemed no longer so easy to dispose of as one looked at the actual Saul Rutledge and remembered the man he had been a year before. Yes; as the Deacon said, they would have to see it through. . . .

'Sit down then, Saul; draw up to us, won't you?' the Deacon suggested, trying again for a natural tone.

Mrs Rutledge pushed a chair forward, and her husband sat down on it. He stretched out his arms and grasped his knees in his brown bony fingers; in that attitude he remained, turning neither his head nor his eyes.

'Well, Saul,' the Deacon continued, 'your wife says you thought mebbe we could do something to help you through this trouble, whatever it is.'

Rutledge's grey eyes widened a little. 'No; I didn't think that. It was her idea to try what could be done.'

'I presume, though, since you've agreed to our coming, that you don't object to our putting a few questions?'

Rutledge was silent for a moment; then he said with a visible effort: 'No, I don't object.'

'Well – you've heard what your wife says?'

Rutledge made a slight motion of assent.

'And – what have you got to answer? How do you explain . . . ?'

Mrs Rutledge intervened. 'How can he explain? I seen 'em.'

There was a silence; then Bosworth, trying to speak in an easy reassuring tone, queried: 'That so, Saul?'

'That's so.'

Brand lifted up his brooding head. 'You mean to say you . . . you sit here before us all and say . . . '

The Deacon's hand again checked him. 'Hold on, friend Brand. We're all of us trying for the facts, ain't we?' He turned to Rutledge. 'We've heard what Mrs Rutledge says. What's your answer?'

'I don't know as there's any answer. She found us.'

'And you mean to tell me the person with you was ... was what you took to be. ...' The Deacon's thin voice grew thinner: 'Ora Brand?'

Saul Rutledge nodded.

'You knew ... or thought you knew ... you were meeting with the dead?'

Rutledge bent his head again. The snow continued to fall in a steady unwavering sheet against the window, and Bosworth felt as if a winding-sheet were descending from the sky to envelop them all in a common grave.

'Think what you're saying! It's against our religion! Ora ... poor child ... died over a year ago. I saw you at her funeral, Saul. How can you make such a statement?'

'What else can he do?' thrust in Mrs Rutledge.

There was another pause. Bosworth's resources had failed him, and Brand once more sat plunged in dark meditation. The Deacon laid his quivering fingertips together and moistened his lips.

'Was the day before yesterday the first time?' he asked.

The movement of Rutledge's head was negative.

'Not the first? Then when ... '

'Nigh on a year ago, I reckon.'

'God! And you mean to tell us that ever since –?'

'Well ... look at him,' said his wife. The three men lowered their eyes.

After a moment Bosworth, trying to collect himself, glanced at the Deacon. 'Why not ask Saul to make his own statement, if that's what we're here for?'

'That's so,' the Deacon assented. He turned to Rutledge. 'Will you try and give us your idea ... of ... of how it began?'

There was another silence. Then Rutledge tightened his grasp on his gaunt knees, and still looking straight ahead, with his curiously clear unseeing gaze: 'Well,' he said, 'I guess it begun away back, afore even I was married to Mrs Rutledge. ... ' He spoke in a low automatic tone, as if some invisible agent were dictating his words, or even uttering them for him. 'You know,' he added, 'Ora and me was to have been married.'

Sylvester Band lifted his head. 'Straighten that statement out first, please,' he interjected.

'What I mean is, we kept company. But Ora she was very young.

Mr Brand here he sent her away. She was gone nigh to three years, I guess. When she come back I was married.'

'That's right,' Brand said, relapsing once more into his sunken attitude.

'And after she came back did you meet her again?' the Deacon continued.

'Alive?' Rutledge questioned.

A perceptible shudder ran through the room.

'Well – of course,' said the Deacon nervously.

Rutledge seemed to consider. 'Once I did – only once. There was a lot of other people round. At Cold Corners fair it was.'

'Did you talk with her then?'

'Only a minute.'

'What did she say?'

His voice dropped. 'She said she was sick and knew she was going to die, and when she was dead she'd come back to me.'

'And what did you answer?'

'Nothing.'

'Did you think anything of it at the time?'

'Well, no. Not till I heard she was dead I didn't. After that I thought of it – and I guess she drew me.' He moistened his lips.

'Drew you down to that abandoned house by the pond?'

Rutledge made a faint motion of assent, and the Deacon added: 'How did you know it was there she wanted you to come?'

'She . . . just drew me. . . .'

There was a long pause. Bosworth felt, on himself and the other two men, the oppressive weight of the next question to be asked. Mrs Rutledge opened and closed her narrow lips once or twice, like some beached shellfish gasping for the tide. Rutledge waited.

'Well, now, Saul, won't you go on with what you was telling us?' the Deacon at length suggested.

'That's all. There's nothing else.'

The Deacon lowered his voice. 'She just draws you?'

'Yes.'

'Often?'

'That's as it happens. . . .'

'But if it's always there she draws you, man, haven't you the strength to keep away from the place?'

For the first time, Rutledge wearily turned his head towards his questioner. A spectral smile narrowed his colourless lips. 'Ain't any use. She follers after me. . . .'

There was another silence. What more could they ask, then and there? Mrs Rutledge's presence checked the next question. The Deacon seemed hopelessly to revolve the matter. At length he spoke in a more authoritative tone. 'These are forbidden things. You know that, Saul. Have you tried prayer?'

Rutledge shook his head.

'Will you pray with us now?'

Rutledge cast a glance of freezing indifference on his spiritual adviser. 'If you folks want to pray, I'm agreeable,' he said. But Mrs Rutledge intervened.

'Prayer ain't any good. In this kind of thing it ain't no manner of use; you know it ain't. I called you here, Deacon, because you remember the last case in this parish. Thirty years ago it was, I guess; but you remember. Lefferts Nash – did praying help *him*? I was a little girl then, but I used to hear my folks talk of it winter nights. Lefferts Nash and Hannah Cory. They drove a stake through her breast. That's what cured him.'

'Oh –' Orrin Bosworth exclaimed.

Sylvester Brand raised his head. 'You're speaking of that old story as if this was the same sort of thing?'

'Ain't it? Ain't my husband pining away the same as Lefferts Nash did? The Deacon here knows –'

The Deacon stirred anxiously in his chair. 'These are forbidden things,' he repeated. 'Supposing your husband is quite sincere in thinking himself haunted, as you might say. Well, even then, what proof have we that the . . . the dead woman . . . is the spectre of that poor girl?'

'Proof! don't he say so? Didn't she tell him? Ain't I seen 'em?' Mrs Rutledge almost screamed.

The three men sat silent, and suddenly the wife burst out: 'A stake through the breast! That's the old way; and it's the only way. The Deacon knows it!'

'It's against our religion to disturb the dead.'

'Ain't it against your religion to let the living perish as my husband is perishing?' She sprang up with one of her abrupt movements and took the family Bible from the what-not in a corner of the parlour. Putting the book on the table, and moistening a livid fingertip, she turned the pages rapidly, till she came to one on which she laid her hand like a stony paperweight. 'See here,' she said, and read out in her level chanting voice:

'*Thou shalt not suffer a witch to live.*'

'That's in Exodus, that's where it is,' she added, leaving the book open as if to confirm the statement.

Bosworth continued to glance anxiously from one to the other of the four people about the table. He was younger than any of them, and had had more contact with the modern world; down in Starkfield, in the bar of the Fielding House, he could hear himself laughing with the rest of the men at such old wives' tales. But it was not for nothing that he had been born under the icy shadow of Lonetop, and had shivered and hungered as a lad through the bitter Hemlock County winters. After his parents died, and he had taken hold of the farm himself, he had got more out of it by using improved methods, and by supplying the increasing throng of summer-boarders over Stotesbury way with milk and vegetables. He had been made a selectman of North Ashmore; for so young a man he had a standing in the county. But the roots of the old life were still in him. He could remember, as a little boy, going twice a year with his mother to that bleak hill-farm out beyond Sylvester Brand's, where Mrs Bosworth's aunt, Cressidora Cheney, had been shut up for years in a cold clean room with iron bars in the windows. When little Orrin first saw Aunt Cressidora she was a small white old woman, whom her sisters used to 'make decent' for visitors the day that Orrin and his mother were expected. The child wondered why there were bars to the window. 'Like a canary-bird,' he said to his mother. The phrase made Mrs Bosworth reflect. 'I do believe they keep Aunt Cressidora too lonesome,' she said; and the next time she went up the mountain with the little boy he carried to his great-aunt a canary in a little wooden cage. It was a great excitement; he knew it would make her happy.

The old woman's motionless face lit up when she saw the bird, and her eyes began to glitter. 'It belongs to me,' she said instantly, stretching her soft bony hand over the cage.

'Of course it does, Aunt Cressy,' said Mrs Bosworth, her eyes filling.

But the bird, startled by the shadow of the old woman's hand, began to flutter and beat its wings distractedly. At the sight, Aunt Cressidora's calm face suddenly became a coil of twitching features. 'You she-devil, you!' she cried in a high squealing voice; and thrusting her hand into the cage she dragged out the terrified bird and wrung its neck. She was plucking the hot body, and squealing 'she-devil, she-devil!' as they drew little Orrin from the room. On the way down the mountain his mother wept a great deal, and said: 'You must never tell anybody that poor Auntie's crazy, or the men would come and take her down to the asylum at Starkfield, and the shame of it would kill us all. Now promise.' The child promised.

He remembered the scene now, with its deep fringe of mystery, secrecy and rumour. It seemed related to a great many other things below the surface of his thoughts, things which stole up anew, making him feel that all the old people he had known, and who 'believed in these things', might after all be right. Hadn't a witch been burned at North Ashmore? Didn't the summer folk still drive over in jolly buckboard loads to see the meeting-house where the trial had been held, the pond where they had ducked her and she had floated? . . . Deacon Hibben believed; Bosworth was sure of it. If he didn't, why did people from all over the place come to him when their animals had queer sicknesses, or when there was a child in the family that had to be kept shut up because it fell down flat and foamed? Yes, in spite of his religion, Deacon Hibben *knew*. . . .

And Brand? Well, it came to Bosworth in a flash: that North Ashmore woman who was burned had the name of Brand. The same stock, no doubt; there had been Brands in Hemlock County ever since the white men had come there. And Orrin, when he was a child, remembered hearing his parents say that Sylvester Brand hadn't ever oughter married his own cousin, because of the blood. Yet the couple had had two healthy girls, and when Mrs Brand pined away and died nobody suggested that anything had been wrong with her mind. And Vanessa and Ora were the handsomest girls anywhere round. Brand knew it, and scrimped and saved all he could do to send Ora, the eldest, down to Starkfield to learn bookkeeping. 'When she's married I'll send you,' he used to say to little Venny, who was his favourite. But Ora never married. She was away three years, during which Venny ran wild on the slopes of Lonetop; and when Ora came back she sickened and died – poor girl! Since then Brand had grown more savage and morose. He was a hard-working farmer, but there wasn't much to be got out of those barren Bearcliff acres. He was said to have taken to drink since his wife's death; now and then men ran across him in the 'dives' of Stotesbury. But not often. And between times he laboured hard on his stony acres and did his best for his daughters. In the neglected graveyard of Cold Corners there was a slanting headstone marked with his wife's name; near it, a year since, he had laid his eldest daughter. And sometimes, at dusk, in the autumn, the village people saw him walk slowly by, turn in between the graves, and stand looking down on the two stones. But he never brought a flower there, or planted a bush; nor Venny either. She was too wild and ignorant. . . .

Mrs Rutledge repeated: 'That's in Exodus.'

The three visitors remained silent, turning about their hats in reluctant hands. Rutledge faced them, still with that empty pellucid gaze which frightened Bosworth. What was he seeing?

'Ain't any of you folks got the grit –?' his wife burst out again, half hysterically.

Deacon Hibben held up his hand. 'That's no way, Mrs Rutledge. This ain't a question of having grit. What we want first of all is . . . proof. . . . '

'That's so,' said Bosworth, with an explosion of relief, as if the words had lifted something black and crouching from his breast. Involuntarily the eyes of both men had turned to Brand. He stood there smiling grimly, but did not speak.

'Ain't it so, Brand?' the Deacon prompted him.

'Proof that spooks walk?' the other sneered.

'Well – I presume you want this business settled too?'

The old farmer squared his shoulders. 'Yes – I do. But I ain't a sperritualist. How the hell are you going to settle it?'

Deacon Hibben hesitated; then he said, in a low incisive tone: 'I don't see but one way – Mrs Rutledge's.'

There was a silence.

'What?' Brand sneered again. 'Spying?'

The Deacon's voice sank lower. 'If the poor girl *does* walk . . . her that's your child . . . wouldn't you be the first to want her laid quiet? We all know there've been such cases . . . mysterious visitations . . . Can any one of us here deny it?'

'I seen 'em,' Mrs Rutledge interjected.

There was another heavy pause. Suddenly Brand fixed his gaze on Rutledge. 'See here, Saul Rutledge, you've got to clear up this damned calumny, or I'll know why. You say my dead girl comes to you.' He laboured with his breath, and then jerked out: 'When? You tell me that, and I'll be there.'

Rutledge's head drooped a little, and his eyes wandered to the window. 'Round about sunset, mostly.'

'You know beforehand?'

Rutledge made a sign of assent.

'Well, then – tomorrow, will it be?'

Rutledge made the same sign.

Brand turned to the door. 'I'll be there.' That was all he said. He strode out between them without another glance or word. Deacon Hibben looked at Mrs Rutledge. 'We'll be there too,' he said as if she had asked him; but she had not spoken, and Bosworth saw that her thin body was trembling all over. He was glad when he and Hibben were out again in the snow.

III

They thought that Brand wanted to be left to himself, and to give him time to unhitch his horse they made a pretence of hanging about in the doorway while Bosworth searched his pockets for a pipe he had no mind to light.

But Brand turned back to them as they lingered. 'You'll meet me down by Lamer's pond tomorrow?' he suggested. 'I want witnesses. Round about sunset.'

They nodded their acquiescence, and he got into his sleigh, gave the horse a cut across the flanks, and drove off under the snow-smothered hemlocks. The other two men went to the shed.

'What do you make of this business, Deacon?' Bosworth asked, to break the silence.

The Deacon shook his head. 'The man's a sick man – that's sure. Something's sucking the life clean out of him.'

But already, in the biting outer air, Bosworth was getting himself under better control. 'Looks to me like a bad case of the ague, as you said.'

'Well – ague of the mind, then. It's his brain that's sick.'

Bosworth shrugged. 'He ain't the first in Hemlock County.'

'That's so,' the Deacon agreed. ' It's a worm in the brain, solitude is.'

'Well, we'll know this time tomorrow, maybe,' said Bosworth. He scrambled into his sleigh, and was driving off in his turn when he heard his companion calling after him. The Deacon explained that his horse had cast a shoe; would Bosworth drive him down to the forge near North Ashmore, if it wasn't too much out of his way? He didn't want the mare slipping about on the freezing snow, and he could probably get the blacksmith to drive him back and shoe her in Rutledge's shed. Bosworth made room for him under the bearskin, and the two men drove off, pursued by a puzzled whinny from the Deacon's old mare.

The road they took was not the one that Bosworth would have followed to reach his own home. But he did not mind that. The shortest way to the forge passed close by Lamer's pond, and Bosworth, since he was in for the business, was not sorry to look the ground over. They drove on in silence.

The snow had ceased, and a green sunset was spreading upward into the crystal sky. A stinging wind barbed with ice-flakes caught them in the face on the open ridges, but when they dropped down into the hollow by Lamer's pond the air was as soundless and empty as an unswung bell. They jogged along slowly, each thinking his own thoughts.

'That's the house . . . that tumbledown shack over there, I suppose?' the Deacon said, as the road drew near the edge of the frozen pond.

'Yes: that's the house. A queer hermit-fellow built it years ago, my father used to tell me. Since then I don't believe it's ever been used but by the gypsies.'

Bosworth had reined in his horse, and sat looking through pine-trunks purpled by the sunset at the crumbling structure. Twilight already lay under the trees, though day lingered in the open. Between two sharply patterned pine-boughs he saw the evening star, like a white boat in a sea of green.

His gaze dropped from that fathomless sky and followed the blue-white undulations of the snow. It gave him a curious agitated feeling to think that here, in this icy solitude, in the tumbledown house he had so often passed without heeding it, a dark mystery, too deep for thought, was being enacted. Down that very slope, coming from the graveyard at Cold Corners, the being they called 'Ora' must pass towards the pond. His heart began to beat stiflingly. Suddenly he gave an exclamation: 'Look!'

He had jumped out of the cutter and was stumbling up the bank towards the slope of snow. On it, turned in the direction of the house by the pond, he had detected a woman's footprints; two; then three; then more. The Deacon scrambled out after him, and they stood and stared.

'God – barefoot!' Hibben gasped. 'Then it *is* . . . the dead. . . .'

Bosworth said nothing. But he knew that no live woman would travel with naked feet across that freezing wilderness. Here, then, was the proof the Deacon had asked for – they held it. What should they do with it?

'Supposing we was to drive up nearer – round the turn of the pond, till we get close to the house,' the Deacon proposed in a colourless voice. 'Mebbe then . . .'

Postponement was a relief. They got into the sleigh and drove on. Two or three hundred yards farther the road, a mere lane under steep bushy banks, turned sharply to the right, following the bend of the pond. As they rounded the turn they saw Brand's cutter ahead of them. It was empty, the horse tied to a tree-trunk. The two men looked at each other again. This was not Brand's nearest way home.

Evidently he had been actuated by the same impulse which had made them rein in their horse by the pond-side, and then hasten on to the deserted hovel. Had he, too, discovered those spectral footprints? Perhaps it was for that very reason that he had left his cutter and vanished in the direction of the house. Bosworth found himself shivering all over under his bearskin. 'I wish to God the dark wasn't coming on,' he muttered. He tethered his own horse near Brand's, and without a word he and the Deacon ploughed through the snow, in the track of Brand's huge feet. They had only a few yards to walk to overtake him. He did not hear them following him, and when Bosworth spoke his name, and he stopped short and turned, his heavy face was dim and confused, like a darker blot on the dusk. He looked at them dully, but without surprise.

'I wanted to see the place,' he merely said.

The Deacon cleared his throat. 'Just take a look . . . yes. . . . We thought so. . . . But I guess there won't be anything to *see*. . . .' He attempted a chuckle.

The other did not seem to hear him, but laboured on ahead through the pines. The three men came out together in the cleared space before the house. As they emerged from beneath the trees they seemed to have left night behind. The evening star shed a lustre on the speckless snow, and Brand, in that lucid circle, stopped with a jerk, and pointed to the same light footprints turned towards the house – the track of a woman in the snow. He stood still, his face working. 'Bare feet . . .' he said.

The Deacon piped up in a quavering voice: 'The feet of the dead.'

Brand remained motionless. 'The feet of the dead,' he echoed.

Deacon Hibben laid a frightened hand on his arm. 'Come away now, Brand; for the love of God come away.'

The father hung there, gazing down at those light tracks on the snow – light as fox or squirrel trails they seemed, on the white immensity. Bosworth thought to himself: 'The living couldn't walk so light – not even Ora Brand couldn't have, when she lived. . . .' The cold seemed to have entered into his very marrow. His teeth were chattering.

Brand swung about on them abruptly. '*Now!*' he said, moving on as if to an assault, his head bowed forward on his bull neck.

'Now – now? Not in there?' gasped the Deacon. 'What's the use? It was tomorrow he said –' He shook like a leaf.

'It's now,' said Brand. He went up to the door of the crazy house, pushed it inward, and meeting with an unexpected resistance, thrust his heavy shoulder against the pane. The door collapsed like a playing-card, and Brand stumbled after it into the darkness of the hut. The others, after a moment's hesitation, followed.

Bosworth was never quite sure in what order the events that succeeded took place. Coming in out of the snow-dazzle, he seemed to be plunging into total blackness. He groped his way across the threshold, caught a sharp splinter of the fallen door in his palm, seemed to see something white and wraith-like surge up out of the darkest corner of the hut, and then heard a revolver shot at his elbow, and a cry –

Brand had turned back, and was staggering past him out into the lingering daylight. The sunset, suddenly flushing through the trees, crimsoned his face like blood. He held a revolver in his hand and looked about him in his stupid way.

'They *do* walk, then,' he said and began to laugh. He bent his head to examine his weapon. 'Better here than in the churchyard. They shan't dig her up *now*,' he shouted out. The two men caught him by the arms, and Bosworth got the revolver away from him.

IV

The next day Bosworth's sister Loretta, who kept house for him, asked him, when he came in for his midday dinner, if he had heard the news.

Bosworth had been sawing wood all the morning, and in spite of the cold and the driving snow, which had begun again in the night, he was covered with an icy sweat, like a man getting over a fever.

'What news?'

'Venny Brand's down sick with pneumonia. The Deacon's been there. I guess she's dying.'

Bosworth looked at her with listless eyes. She seemed far off from him, miles away. 'Venny Brand?' he echoed.

'You never liked her, Orrin.'

'She's a child. I never knew much about her.'

'Well,' repeated his sister, with the guileless relish of the unimaginative for bad news, 'I guess she's dying.' After a pause she added: 'It'll kill Sylvester Brand, all alone up there.'

Bosworth got up and said: 'I've got to see to poulticing the grey's fetlock.' He walked out into the steadily falling snow.

Venny Brand was buried three days later. The Deacon read the service; Bosworth was one of the pall-bearers. The whole countryside turned out, for the snow had stopped falling, and at any season a funeral offered an opportunity for an outing that was not to be missed. Besides, Venny Brand was young and handsome – at least some people thought her handsome, though she was so swarthy – and her dying like that, so suddenly, had the fascination of tragedy.

'They say her lungs filled right up... Seems she'd had bronchial troubles before... I always said both them girls was frail... Look at Ora, how she took and wasted away! And it's colder'n all outdoors up there to Brand's... Their mother, too, *she* pined away just the same. They don't ever make old bones on the mother's side of the family... There's that young Bedlow over there; they say Venny was engaged to him... Oh, Mrs Rutledge, excuse *me*... Step right into the pew; there's a seat for you alongside of grandma....'

Mrs Rutledge was advancing with deliberate step down the narrow aisle of the bleak wooden church. She had on her best bonnet, a monumental structure which no one had seen out of her trunk since old Mrs Silsee's funeral, three years before. All the women remembered it. Under its perpendicular pile her narrow face, swaying on the long thin neck, seemed whiter than ever; but her air of fretfulness had been composed into a suitable expression of mournful immobility.

'Looks as if the stonemason had carved her to put atop of Venny's grave,' Bosworth thought as she glided past him; and then shivered at his own sepulchral fancy. When she bent over her hymn book her lowered lids reminded him again of marble eyeballs; the bony hands clasping the book were bloodless. Bosworth had never seen such hands since he had seen old Aunt Cressidora Cheney strangle the canary-bird because it fluttered.

The service was over, the coffin of Venny Brand had been lowered into her sister's grave, and the neighbours were slowly dispersing. Bosworth, as pall-bearer, felt obliged to linger and say a word to the stricken father. He waited till Brand had turned from the grave with the Deacon at his side. The three men stood together for a moment; but not one of them spoke. Brand's face was the closed door of a vault, barred with wrinkles like bands of iron.

Finally the Deacon took his hand and said: 'The Lord gave—'

Brand nodded and turned away towards the shed where the horses were hitched. Bosworth followed him. 'Let me drive along home with you,' he suggested.

Brand did not so much as turn his head. 'Home? What home?' he said; and the other fell back.

Loretta Bosworth was talking with the other women while the men unblanketed their horses and backed the cutters out into the heavy snow. As Bosworth waited for her, a few feet off, he saw Mrs Rutledge's tall bonnet lording it above the group. Andy Pond, the Rutledge farm-hand, was backing out the sleigh.

'Saul ain't here today, Mrs Rutledge, is he?' one of the village elders piped, turning a benevolent old tortoise-head about on a loose neck, and blinking up into Mrs Rutledge's marble face.

Bosworth heard her measure out her answer in slow incisive words. 'No. Mr Rutledge he ain't here. He would 'a' come for certain, but his aunt Minorca Cummins is being buried down to Stotesbury this very day and he had to go down there. Don't it sometimes seem zif we was all walking right in the Shadow of Death?'

As she walked towards the cutter, in which Andy Pond was already seated, the Deacon went up to her with visible hesitation. Involuntarily Bosworth also moved nearer. He heard the Deacon say: 'I'm glad to hear that Saul is able to be up and around.'

She turned her small head on her rigid neck, and lifted the lids of marble.

'Yes, I guess he'll sleep quieter now – And *her* too, maybe, now she don't lay there alone any longer,' she added in a low voice, with a sudden twist of her chin towards the fresh black stain in the graveyard snow. She got into the cutter, and said in a clear tone to Andy Pond: ' 'S long as we're down here I don't know but what I'll just call round and get a box of soap at Hiram Pringle's.'

A Bottle of Perrier

A two days' struggle over the treacherous trails in a well-intentioned but short-winded 'flivver', and a ride of two more on a hired mount of unamiable temper, had disposed young Medford, of the American School of Archaeology at Athens, to wonder why his queer English friend, Henry Almodham, had chosen to live in the desert.

Now he understood.

He was leaning against the roof parapet of the old building, half Christian fortress, half Arab palace, which had been Almodham's pretext; or one of them. Below, in an inner court, a little wind, rising as the sun sank, sent through a knot of palms the rain-like rattle so cooling to the pilgrims of the desert. An ancient fig tree, enormous, exuberant, writhed over a whitewashed well-head, sucking life from what appeared to be the only source of moisture within the walls. Beyond these, on every side, stretched away the mystery of the sands, all golden with promise, all livid with menace, as the sun alternately touched or abandoned them.

Young Medford, somewhat weary after his journey from the coast, and awed by his first intimate sense of the omnipresence of the desert, shivered and drew back. Undoubtedly, for a scholar and a misogynist, it was a wonderful refuge; but one would have to be, incurably, both.

'Let's take a look at the house,' Medford said to himself, as if speedy contact with man's handiwork were necessary to his reassurance.

The house, he already knew, was empty save for the quick cosmopolitan manservant, who spoke a sort of palimpsest Cockney lined with Mediterranean tongues and desert dialects – English, Italian or Greek, which was he? – and two or three burnoused underlings who, having carried Medford's bags to his room, had relieved the place of their gliding presences. Mr Almodham, the servant told him, was away; suddenly summoned by a friendly chief to visit some unexplored ruins to the south, he had ridden off at dawn, too hurriedly to write, but leaving messages of excuse and regret. That evening late he might be back, or next morning.

Almodham, as young Medford knew, was always making these archaeological explorations; they had been his ostensible reason for settling in that remote place, and his desultory search had already resulted in the discovery of several early Christian ruins of great interest.

Medford was glad that his host had not stood on ceremony, and rather relieved, on the whole, to have the next few hours to himself. He had had a malarial fever the previous summer, and in spite of his cork helmet he had probably caught a touch of the sun; he felt curiously, helplessly tired, yet deeply content.

And what a place it was to rest in! The silence, the remoteness, the illimitable air! And in the heart of the wilderness green leafage, water, comfort – he had already caught a glimpse of wide wicker chairs under the palms – a humane and welcoming habitation. Yes, he began to understand Almodham. To anyone sick of the Western fret and fever the very walls of this desert fortress exuded peace.

As his foot was on the ladder-like stair leading down from the roof, Medford saw the manservant's head rising towards him. It rose slowly and Medford had time to remark that it was sallow, bald on the top, diagonally dented with a long white scar, and ringed with thick ash-blond hair. Hitherto Medford had noticed only the man's face – youngish, but sallow also – and been chiefly struck by its wearing an odd expression which could best be defined as surprise.

The servant, moving aside, looked up, and Medford perceived that his air of surprise was produced by the fact that his intensely blue eyes were rather wider open than most eyes, and fringed with thick ash-blond lashes; otherwise there was nothing noticeable about him.

'Just to ask – what wine for dinner, sir? Champagne, or –'

'No wine, thanks.'

The man's disciplined lips were played over by a faint flicker of depracation or irony, or both.

'Not any at all, sir?'

Medford smiled back. 'Well, no; I've been rather seedy, and wine's forbidden.'

The servant remained incredulous. 'Just a little light Moselle, though, to colour the water, sir?'

'No wine at all,' said Medford, growing bored. He was still in the stage of convalescence when it is irritating to be argued with about one's dietary.

'Oh – what's your name, by the way?' he added, to soften the curtness of his refusal.

'Gosling,' said the other unexpectedly, though Medford didn't in the least know what he had expected him to be called.

'You're English, then?'

'Oh, yes, sir.'

'You've been in these parts a good many years, though?'

Yes, he had, Gosling said; rather too long for his own liking; and added that he had been born at Malta. 'But I know England well too.' His deprecating look returned. 'I will confess, sir, I'd like to have 'ad a look at Wembley.* Mr Almodham 'ad promised me – but there –' As if to minimize the *abandon* of this confidence, he followed it up by a ceremonious request for Medford's keys, and an enquiry as to when he would like to dine. Having received a reply, he still lingered, looking more surprised than ever.

'Just a mineral water, then, sir?'

'Oh, yes – anything.'

'Shall we say a bottle of Perrier?'

Perrier in the desert! Medford smiled assentingly, surrendered his keys and strolled away.

The house turned out to be smaller than he had imagined, or at least the habitable part of it; for above this towered mighty dilapidated walls of yellow stone, and in their crevices clung plaster chambers, one above the other, cedar-beamed, crimson-shuttered but crumbling. Out of this jumble of masonry and stucco, Christian

---

* ·The famous exhibition at Wembley, near London, took place in 1924.

and Muslim, the latest tenant of the fortress had chosen a cluster of rooms tucked into an angle of the ancient keep. These apartments opened on the uppermost court, where the palms chattered and the fig tree coiled above the well. On the broken marble pave-ment, chairs and a low table were grouped, and a few geraniums and blue morning-glories had been coaxed to grow between the slabs.

A white-skirted boy with watchful eyes was watering the plants; but at Medford's approach he vanished like a wisp of vapour.

There was something vaporous and insubstantial about the whole scene; even the long arcaded room opening on the court, furnished with saddlebag cushions, divans with gazelle skins, and rough indigenous rugs; even the table piled with old *Times* and ultra-modern French and English reviews – all seemed, in that clear mocking air, born of the delusion of some desert wayfarer.

A seat under the fig tree invited Medford to doze, and when he woke the hard blue dome above him was gemmed with stars and the night breeze gossiped with the palms.

Rest – beauty – peace. Wise Almodham!

Wise Almodham! Having carried out – with somewhat disappointing results – the excavation with which an archaeological society had charged him twenty-five years ago, he had lingered on, taken possession of the Crusaders' stronghold, and turned his attention from ancient to medieval remains. But even these investigations, Medford suspected, he prosecuted only at intervals, when the enchantment of his leisure did not lie on him too heavily.

The young American had met Henry Almodham at Luxor the previous winter; had dined with him at old Colonel Swordsley's, on that perfumed starlit terrace above the Nile; and having somehow awakened the archaeologist's interest, had been invited to look him up in the desert the following year.

They had spent only that one evening together, with old Swordsley blinking at them under memory-laden lids, and two or three charming women from the Winter Palace chattering and exclaiming; but the two men had ridden back to Luxor together in the moonlight, and during that ride Medford fancied he had puzzled out the essential lines of Henry Almodham's character. A nature saturnine yet sentimental; chronic indolence alternating with spurts of highly intelligent activity; gnawing self-distrust soothed by intimate self-appreciation; a craving for complete solitude coupled with the inability to tolerate it for long.

There was more, too, Medford suspected; a dash of Victorian romance, gratified by the setting, the remoteness, the inaccessibility of his retreat, and by being known as *the* Henry Almodham – 'the one who lives in a Crusaders' castle, you know' – the gradual imprisonment in a pose assumed in youth, and into which middle age had slowly stiffened; and something deeper, darker, too, perhaps, though the young man doubted that; probably just the fact that living in that particular way had brought healing to an old wound, an old mortification, something which years ago had touched a vital part and left him writhing. Above all, in Almodham's hesitating movements and the dreaming look of his long well-featured brown face with its shock of grey hair, Medford detected an inertia, mental and moral, which life in this castle of romance must have fostered and excused.

'Once here, how easy not to leave!' he mused.

'Dinner, sir,' Gosling announced.

The table stood in an open arch of the living-room; shaded candles made a rosy pool in the dusk. Each time he emerged into their light the servant, white-jacketed, velvet-footed, looked more competent and more surprised then ever. Such dishes, too – the cook also a Maltese? Gosling bridled, smiled his acknowledgement, and started to fill the guest's glass with Chablis.

'No wine,' said Medford patiently.

'Sorry, sir. But the fact is –'

'You said there was Perrier?'

'Yes, sir; but I find there's none left. It's been awfully hot, and Mr Almodham has been and drank it all up. The new supply isn't due till next week. We 'ave to depend on the caravans going south.'

'No matter. Water, then. I really prefer it.'

Gosling's surprise widened to amazement. 'Not water, sir? Water – in these parts?'

Medford's irritability stirred again. 'Something wrong with your water? Boil it then, can't you? I won't –' He pushed away the half-filled wineglass.

'Oh – boiled? Certainly, sir.' The man's voice dropped almost to a whisper. He placed on the table a succulent mess of rice and mutton, and vanished.

Medford leaned back, surrendering himself to the night, the coolness, the ripple of wind in the palms.

One agreeable dish succeeded another. As the last appeared, the dinner began to feel the pangs of thirst, and at the same moment a beaker of water was placed at his elbow. 'Boiled, sir, and I squeezed a lemon into it.'

'Right. I suppose at the end of the summer your water gets a bit muddy?'

'That's it, sir. But you'll find this all right, sir.'

Medford tasted. 'Better than Perrier.' He emptied the glass, leaned back and groped in his pocket. A tray was instantly at his hand with cigars and cigarettes.

'You don't – smoke, sir?'

Medford, for answer, held up his cigar to the man's light. 'What do you call this?'

'Oh, just so. I meant the other style.' Gosling glanced discreetly at the opium pipes of jade and amber which were laid out on the low table.

Medford shrugged away the invitation – and wondered. Was that perhaps Almodham's other secret – or one of them? For he began to think there might be many; and all, he was sure, safely stored away behind Gosling's vigilant brow.

'No news yet of Mr Almodham?'

Gosling was gathering up the dishes with dexterous gestures. For a moment he seemed not to hear. Then – from beyond the candle gleam – 'News, sir? There couldn't 'ardly be, could there? There's no wireless in the desert, sir; not like London.' His respectful tone tempered the slight irony. 'But tomorrow evening ought to see him riding in.' Gosling paused, drew nearer, swept one of his swift hands across the table in pursuit of the last crumbs, and added tentatively: 'You'll surely be able, sir, to stay till then?'

Medford laughed. The night was too rich in healing; it sank on his spirit like wings. Time vanished, fret and trouble were no more. 'Stay? I'll stay a year if I have to!'

'Oh – a year?' Gosling echoed it playfully, gathered up the dessert dishes and was gone.

Medford had said that he would wait for Almodham a year; but the next morning he found that such arbitrary terms had lost their meaning. There were no time measures in a place like this.

The silly face of his watch told its daily tale to emptiness. The wheeling of the constellations over those ruined walls marked only the revolutions of the earth; the spasmodic motions of man meant nothing.

The very fact of being hungry, that stroke of the inward clock, was minimized by the slightness of the sensation – just the ghost of a pang, that might have been quieted by dried fruit and honey. Life and the light monotonous smoothness of eternity.

Towards sunset Medford shook off this queer sense of otherwhereness and climbed to the roof. Across the desert he spied for Almodham. Southward the Mountains of Alabaster hung like a blue veil lined with light. In the west a great column of fire shot up, spraying into plumy cloudlets which turned the sky to a fountain of rose-leaves, the sands beneath to gold.

No riders specked them. Medford watched in vain for his absent host till night fell, and the punctual Gosling invited him once more to table.

In the evening Medford absently fingered the ultramodern reviews – three months old, and already so stale to the touch – then tossed them aside, flung himself on a divan and dreamed. Almodham must spend a lot of time in dreaming; that was it. Then, just as he felt himself sinking down into torpor, he would be off on one of these dashes across the desert in quest of unknown ruins. Not such a bad life.

Gosling appeared with Turkish coffee in a cup cased in filigree.

'Are there any horses in the stable?' Medford suddenly asked.

'Horses? Only what you might call pack-horses, sir. Mr Almodham has the two best saddle-horses with him.'

'I was thinking I might ride out to meet him.'

Gosling considered. 'So you might, sir.'

'Do you know which way he went?'

'Not rightly, sir. The caid's man was to guide them.'

'Them? Who went with him?'

'Just one of our men, sir. They've got the two thoroughbreds. There's a third but he's lame.' Gosling paused. 'Do you know the trails, sir? Excuse me, but I don't think I ever saw you here before.'

'No,' Medford acquiesced, 'I've never been here before.'

'Oh, then' – Gosling's gesture added: 'In that case, even the best thoroughbred wouldn't help you.'

'I suppose he may still turn up tonight?'

'Oh, easily, sir. I expect to see you both breakfasting here tomorrow morning,' said Gosling cheerfully.

Medford sipped his coffee. 'You said you'd never seen me here before. How long have you been here yourself?'

Gosling answered instantly, as though the figures were never long out of his memory: 'Eleven years and seven months altogether, sir.'

'Nearly twelve years! That's a longish time.'

'Yes, it is.'

'And I don't suppose you often get away?'

Gosling was moving off with the tray. He halted, turned back, and said with sudden emphasis: 'I've never once been away. Not since Mr Almodham first brought me here.'

'Good Lord! Not a single holiday?'

'Not one, sir.'

'But Mr Almodham goes off occasionally. I met him at Luxor last year.'

'Just so, sir. But when he's here he needs me for himself; and when he's away he needs me to watch over the others. So you see –'

'Yes, I see. But it must seem to you devilish long.'

'It seems long, sir.'

'But the others? You mean they're not – wholly trustworthy?'

'Well, sir, they're just Arabs,' said Gosling with careless contempt.

'I see. And not a single old reliable among them?'

'The term isn't in their language, sir.'

Medford was busy lighting his cigar. When he looked up he found that Gosling still stood a few feet off.

'It wasn't as if it 'adn't been a promise, you know, sir,' he said, almost passionately.

'A promise?'

'To let me 'ave my holiday, sir. A promise – agine and agine.'

'And the time never came?'

'No, sir. The days just drifted by –'

'Ah. They would, here. Don't sit up for me,' Medford added. 'I think I shall wait for Mr Almodham.'

Gosling's stare widened. 'Here, sir? Here in the court?'

The young man nodded, and the servant stood still regarding him, turned by the moonlight to a white spectral figure, the unquiet ghost of a patient butler who might have died without his holiday.

'Down here in this court all night, sir? It's a lonely spot. I couldn't 'ear you if you was to call. You're best in bed, sir. The air's bad. You might bring your fever on again.'

Medford laughed and stretched himself in his long chair. 'Decidedly,' he thought, 'the fellow needs a change.' Aloud he remarked: 'Oh, I'm all right. It's you who are nervous, Gosling. When Mr Almodham comes back I mean to put in a word for you. You shall have your holiday.'

Gosling still stood motionless. For a minute he did not speak. 'You would, sir, you would?' He gasped it out on a high cracked note, and the last word ran into a laugh – a brief shrill cackle, the laugh of one long unused to such indulgences.

'Thank you, sir. Good night, sir.' He was gone.

'You do boil my drinking water, always?' Medford questioned, his hand clasping the glass without lifting it.

The tone was amicable, almost confidential; Medford felt that since his rash promise to secure a holiday for Gosling he and Gosling were on terms of real friendship.

'Boil it? Always, sir. Naturally.' Gosling spoke with a slight note of reproach, as though Medford's question implied a slur – unconscious, he hoped – on their newly established relation. He scrutinized Medford with his astonished eyes, in which a genuine concern showed itself through the glaze of professional indifference.

'Because, you know, my bath this morning –'

Gosling was in the act of receiving from the hands of a gliding Arab a fragrant dish of *kuskus*. Under his breath he whispered to the native: 'You damned aboriginy, you, can't you even 'old a dish steady? Ugh!' The Arab vanished before the imprecation, and Gosling, with a calm deliberate hand, set the dish before Medford. 'All alike, they are.' Fastidiously he wiped a trail of grease from his linen sleeve.

'Because, you know, my bath this morning simply stank,' said Medford, plunging fork and spoon into the dish.

'Your bath, sir?' Gosling stressed the word. Astonishment, to the exclusion of all other emotion, again filled his eyes as he rested them on Medford. 'Now, I wouldn't 'ave 'ad that 'appen for the world,' he said self-reproachfully.

'There's only the one well here, eh? The one in the court?'

Gosling aroused himself from absorbed consideration of the visitor's complaint. 'Yes, sir; only the one.'

'What sort of well is it? Where does the water come from?'

'Oh, it's just a cistern, sir. Rain water. There's never been any other here. Not that I ever knew it to fail; but at this season sometimes it does turn queer. Ask any o' them Arabs, sir; they'll tell you. Liars as they are, they won't trouble to lie about that.'

Medford was cautiously tasting the water in his glass. 'This seems all right,' he pronounced.

Sincere satisfaction was depicted on Gosling's countenance. 'I seen to its being boiled myself, sir. I always do. I 'ope that Perrier'll turn up tomorrow, sir.'

'Oh, tomorrow' – Medford shrugged, taking a second helping. 'Tomorrow I may not be here to drink it.'

'What – going away, sir?'

Medford, wheeling around abruptly, caught a new and incomprehensible look in Gosling's eyes. The man had seemed to feel a sort of dog-like affection for him; had wanted, Medford could have sworn, to keep him on, persuade him to patience and delay; yet now, Medford could equally have sworn, there was relief in his look, satisfaction, almost, in his voice.

'So soon, sir?'

'Well, this is the fifth day since my arrival. And as there's no news yet of Mr Almodham, and you say he may very well have forgotten all about my coming –'

'Oh, I don't say that, sir; not forgotten! Only, when one of those old piles of stones takes 'old of him, he does forget about the time, sir. That's what I meant. The days drift by – 'e's in a dream. Very likely he thinks you're just due now, sir.' A small thin smile sharpened the lustreless gravity of Gosling's features. It was the first time that Medford had seen him smile.

'Oh, I understand. But still –' Medford paused. Through the spell of inertia laid on him by the drowsy place and its easeful comforts his instinct of alertness was struggling back. 'It's odd–'

'What's odd?' Gosling echoed unexpectedly, setting the dried dates and figs on the table.

'Everything,' said Medford.

He leaned back in his chair and glanced up through the arch at the lofty sky from which noon was pouring down in cataracts of blue and gold. Almodham was out there somewhere under that canopy of fire, perhaps, as the servant said, absorbed in his dream. The land was full of spells.

'Coffee, sir?' Gosling reminded him. Medford took it.

'It's odd that you say you don't trust any of these fellows – these Arabs – and yet that you don't seem to feel worried at Mr Almodham's being off God knows where, all alone with them.'

Gosling received this attentively, impartially; he saw the point. 'Well, sir, no – you wouldn't understand. It's the very thing that can't be taught, when to trust 'em and when not. It's 'ow their interests lie, of course, sir; and their religion, as they call it.' His contempt was unlimited. 'But even to begin to understand why I'm not worried about Mr Almodham, you'd 'ave to 'ave lived among them, sir, and you'd 'ave to speak their language.'

'But I –' Medford began. He pulled himself up short and bent above his coffee.

'Yes, sir?'

'But I've travelled among them more or less.'

'Oh, travelled!' Even Gosling's intonation could hardly conciliate respect with derision in his reception of this boast.

'This makes the fifth day, though,' Medford continued argumentatively. The midday heat lay heavy even on the shaded side of the court, and the sinews of his will were weakening.

'I can understand, sir, a gentleman like you 'aving other engagements – being pressed for time, as it were,' Gosling reasonably conceded.

He cleared the table, committed its freight to a pair of Arab arms that just showed and vanished, and finally took himself off while Medford sank into the divan. A land of dreams . . .

The afternoon hung over the place like a great velarium of cloth-of-gold stretched across the battlements and drooping down in ever slacker folds upon the heavy-headed palms. When at length the gold turned to violet, and the west to a bow of crystal clasping the dark sands, Medford shook off his sleep and wandered out. But this time, instead of mounting to the roof, he took another direction.

He was surprised to find how little he knew of the place after five days of loitering and waiting. Perhaps this was to be his last evening alone in it. He passed out of the court by a vaulted stone passage which led to another walled enclosure. At his approach two of three Arabs who had been squatting there rose and melted out of sight. It was as if the solid masonry had received them.

Beyond, Medford heard a stamping of hoofs, the stir of a stable at nightfall. He went under another archway and found himself among horses and mules. In the fading light an Arab was rubbing down one of the horses, a powerful young chestnut. He too seemed to vanish; but Medford caught him by the sleeve.

'Go on with your work,' he said in Arabic.

The man, who was young and muscular, with a lean Bedouin face, stopped and looked at him.

'I didn't know your Excellency spoke our language.'

'Oh, yes,' said Medford.

The man was silent, one hand on the horse's restless neck, the other thrust into his woollen girdle. He and Medford examined each other in the faint light.

'Is that the horse that's lame?' Medford asked.

'Lame?' The Arab's eyes ran down the animal's legs. 'Oh, yes; lame,' he answered vaguely.

Medford stooped and felt the horse's knees and fetlocks. 'He seems pretty fit. Couldn't he carry me for a canter this evening if I felt like it?'

The Arab considered; he was evidently perplexed by the weight of responsibility which the question placed on him.

'Your Excellency would like to go for a ride this evening?'

'Oh, just a fancy. I might or I might not.' Medford lit a cigarette and offered one to the groom, whose white teeth flashed his gratification. Over the shared match they drew nearer and the Arab's diffidence seemed to lessen.

'Is this one of Mr Almodham's own mounts?' Medford asked.

'Yes, sir, it's his favourite,' said the groom, his hand passing proudly down the horse's bright shoulder.

'His favourite? Yet he didn't take him on this long expedition?'

The Arab fell silent and stared at the ground.

'Weren't you surprised at that?' Medford queried.

The man's gesture declared that it was not his business to be surprised.

The two remained without speaking while the quick blue night descended.

At length Medford said carelessly: 'Where do you suppose your master is at this moment?'

The moon, unperceived in the radiant fall of day, had now suddenly possessed the world, and a broad white beam lay full on the Arab's white smock, his brown face and the turban of camel's hair knotted above it. His agitated eyeballs glistened like jewels.

'If Allah would vouchsafe to let us know!'

'But you suppose he's safe enough, don't you? You don't think it's necessary yet for a party to go out in search of him?'

The Arab appeared to ponder this deeply. The question must have taken him by surprise. He flung a brown arm about the horse's neck and continued to scrutinize the stones of the court.

'When the master is away Mr Gosling is our master.'

'And he doesn't think it necessary?'

The Arab sighed: 'Not yet.'

'But if Mr Almodham were away much longer –'

The man was again silent, and Medford continued: 'You're the head groom, I suppose?'

'Yes, Excellency.'

There was another pause. Medford half turned away; then, over his shoulder: 'I suppose you know the direction Mr Almodham took? The place he's gone to?'

'Oh, assuredly, Excellency.'

'Then you and I are going to ride after him. Be ready an hour before daylight. Say nothing to anyone – Mr Gosling or anybody else. We two ought to be able to find him without other help.'

The Arab's face was all a responsive flash of eyes and teeth. 'Oh, sir, I undertake that you and my master shall meet before tomorrow night. And none shall know of it.'

'He's as anxious about Almodham as I am,' Medford thought; a faint shiver ran down his back.

'All right. Be ready,' he repeated.

He strolled back and found the court empty of life, but fantastically peopled by palms of beaten silver and a white marble fig tree.

'After all,' he thought irrelevantly, 'I'm glad I didn't tell Gosling that I speak Arabic.'

He sat down and waited till Gosling, approaching from the living-room, ceremoniously announced for the fifth time that dinner was served.

Medford sat up in bed with the jerk which resembles no other. Someone was in his room. The fact reached him not by sight or sound – for the moon had set, and the silence of the night was complete – but by a peculiar faint disturbance of the invisible currents that enclose us.

He was awake in an instant, caught up his electric hand-lamp and flashed it into two astonished eyes. Gosling stood above the bed.

'Mr Almodham – he's back?' Medford exclaimed.

'No, sir; he's not back.' Gosling spoke in low controlled tones. His extreme self-possession gave Medford a sense of danger – he couldn't say why, or of what nature. He sat upright, looking hard at the man.

'Then what's the matter?'

'Well, sir, you might have told me you talk Arabic' – Gosling's tone was now wistfully reproachful – 'before you got 'obnobbing with that Selim. Making randyvoos with 'im by night in the desert.'

Medford reached for his matches and lit the candle by the bed. He did not know whether to kick Gosling out of the room or to listen to what the man had to say; but a quick movement of curiosity made him determine on the latter course.

'Such folly! First I thought I'd lock you in. I might 'ave.' Gosling drew a key from his pocket and held it up. 'Or again I might 'ave let you go. Easier than not. But there was Wembley.'

'Wembley?' Medford echoed. He began to think the man was going mad. One might, so conceivably, in that place of postponements and enchantments! He wondered whether Almodham himself were not a little mad.

'Wembley. You promised to get Mr Almodham to give me an 'oliday – to let me go back to England in time for a look at Wembley. Every man 'as 'is fancies, 'asn't 'e, sir? And that's mine. I've told Mr Almodham so, agine and agine. He'd never listen, or only make believe to; say: "We'll see, now, Gosling, we'll see"; and no more 'eard of it. But you was different, sir. You said it, and I knew you meant it – about my 'oliday. So I'm going to lock you in.'

Gosling spoke composedly, but with an underthrill of emotion in his queer Mediterranean-Cockney voice.

'Lock me in?'

'Prevent you somehow from going off with that murderer. You don't suppose you'd ever 'ave come back alive from that ride, do you?'

A shiver ran over Medford, as it had the evening before when he had said to himself that the Arab was as anxious as he was about Almodham. He gave a slight laugh.

'I don't know what you're talking about. But you're not going to lock me in.'

The effect of this was unexpected. Gosling's face was drawn up into a convulsive grimace and two tears rose to his pale eyelashes and ran down his cheeks.

'You don't trust me, after all,' he said plaintively.

Medford leaned on his pillow and considered. Nothing as queer had ever before happened to him. The fellow looked almost ridiculous enough to laugh at; yet his tears were certainly not simulated. Was he weeping for Almodham, already dead, or for Medford, about to be committed to the same grave?

'I should trust you at once,' said Medford, 'if you'd tell me where your master is.'

Gosling's face resumed its usual guarded expression, though the trace of the tears still glittered on it.

'I can't do that, sir.'

'Ah, I thought so!'

'Because – 'ow do I know?'

Medford thrust a leg out of bed. One hand, under the blanket, lay on his revolver.

'Well, you may go now. Put that key down on the table first. And don't try to do anything to interfere with my plans. If you do I'll shoot you,' he added concisely.

'Oh, no, you wouldn't shoot a British subject; it makes such a fuss. Not that I'd care – I've often thought of doing it myself. Sometimes in the sirocco season. That don't scare me. And you shan't go.'

Medford was on his feet now, the revolver visible. Gosling eyed it with indifference.

'Then you do know where Mr Almodham is? And you're determined that I shan't find out?' Medford challenged him.

'Selim's determined,' said Gosling, 'and all the others are. They all want you out of the way. That's why I've kept 'em to their quarters – done all the waiting on you myself. Now will you stay here? For God's sake, sir! The return caravan is going through to the coast the day after tomorrow. Join it, sir – it's the only safe way! I darsn't let you go with one of our men, not even if you was to swear you'd ride straight for the coast and let this business be.'

'This business? What business?'

'This worrying about where Mr Almodham is, sir. Not that there's anything to worry about. The men all know that. But the plain fact is they've stolen some money from his box, since he's been gone, and if I hadn't winked at it they'd 'ave killed me; and all they want is to get you to ride out after 'im, and put you safe away under a 'eap of sand somewhere off the caravan trails. Easy job. There; that's all, sir. My word it is.'

There was a long silence. In the weak candle-light the two men stood considering each other.

Medford's wits began to clear as the sense of peril closed in on him. His mind reached out on all sides into the enfolding mystery, but it was everywhere impenetrable. The odd thing was that, though he did not believe half of what Gosling had told him, the man yet inspired him with a queer sense of confidence as far as their mutual relation was concerned.

Medford laid his revolver on the table. 'Very well,' he said. 'I won't ride out to look for Mr Almodham, since you advise me not to. But I won't leave by the caravan; I'll wait here till he comes back.'

He saw Gosling whiten under his sallowness. 'Oh, don't do that, sir; I couldn't answer for them if you was to wait. The caravan'll take you to the coast the day after tomorrow as easy as if you was riding in Rotten Row.'

'Ah, then you know that Mr Almodham won't be back by the day after tomorrow?' Medford caught him up.

'I don't know anything, sir.'

'Not even where he is now?'

Gosling reflected. 'He's been gone too long, sir, for me to know that.'

The door closed on him.

Medford found sleep unrecoverable. He leaned in his window and watched the stars fade and the dawn break in all its holiness. As the stir of life rose among the ancient walls he marvelled at the contrast between that fountain of purity welling up into the heavens and the evil secrets clinging bat-like to the nest of masonry below.

He no longer knew what to believe or whom. Had some enemy of Almodham's lured him into the desert and bought the conniv-ance of his people? Or had the servants had some reason of their own for spiriting him away, and was Gosling possibly telling the truth when he said that the same fate would befall Medford?

Medford, as the light brightened, felt his energy return. The very impenetrableness of the mystery stimulated him. He would stay, and he would find out the truth.

It was always Gosling himself who brought up the water for Medford's bath; but this morning he failed to appear with it, and when he came it was to bring the breakfast tray. Medford noticed that his face was of a pasty pallor, and that his lids were reddened as if with weeping. The contrast was unpleasant, and a dislike for Gosling began to shape itself in the young man's breast.

'My bath?' he queried.

'Well, sir, you complained yesterday of the water –'

'Can't you boil it?'

'I 'ave, sir.'

'Well, then –'

Gosling went out sullenly and presently returned with a brass jug. 'It's the time of year – we're dying for rain,' he grumbled, pouring a scant measure of water into the tub.

Yes, the well must be pretty low, Medford thought. Even boiled, the water had the disagreeable smell that he had noticed the day before, though of course in a slighter degree. But a bath was a necessity in that climate.

He spent the day in rather fruitlessly considering his situation. He had hoped the morning would bring counsel, but it brought only courage and resolution, and these were of small use without enlightenment. Suddenly he remembered that the caravan going south from the coast would pass near the castle that afternoon. Gosling had dwelt on the date often enough, for it was the caravan which was to bring the box of Perrier water.

'Well, I'm not sorry for that,' Medford reflected, with a slight shrinking of the flesh. Something sick and viscous, half smell, half substance, seemed to have clung to his skin since his morning bath, and the idea of having to drink that water again was nauseating.

But his chief reason for welcoming the caravan was the hope of finding in it some European, or at any rate some native official from the coast, to whom he might confide his anxiety. He hung about, listening and waiting, and then mounted to the roof to gaze northward along the trail. But in the afternoon glow he saw only three Bedouins guiding laden packmules towards the castle.

As they mounted the steep path he recognized some of Almodham's men, and guessed at once that the southward caravan trail did not actually pass under the walls and that the men had been out to meet it, probably at a small oasis behind some fold of the sandhills. Vexed at his own thoughtlessness in not foreseeing such a possibility, Medford dashed down to the court, hoping the men might have brought back some news of Almodham.

As Medford reached the court, angry vociferations, and retorts as vehement, rose from the stableyard. He leaned over the wall and listened.

Gosling, master of all the desert dialects, was cursing his subordinates in a half-dozen.

'And you didn't bring it – and you tell me it wasn't there, and I tell you it was, and that you know it, and that you either left it on a sand-heap while you were jawing with some of those slimy fellows from the coast, or else fastened it on to the horse so carelessly that it fell off on the way – and all of you too sleepy to notice. Oh, you sons of females I wouldn't soil my lips by naming! Well, back you go to hunt it up, that's all!'

'By Allah and the tomb of his Prophet, you wrong us unpardonably. There was nothing left at the oasis, nor yet dropped off on the way back. It was not there, and that is the truth in its purity.'

'Truth! Purity! You miserable lot of shirks and liars, you – and the gentleman here not touching a drop of anything but water – as you profess to do, you liquor-swilling humbugs!'

Medford drew back from the parapet with a smile of relief. It was nothing but a case of Perrier – the missing case – which had raised the passions of these grown men to the pitch of frenzy! The anticlimax lifted a load from his breast. If Gosling, the calm and self-controlled, could waste his wrath on so slight a hitch in the working of the commissariat, he at least must have a free mind. How absurd this homely incident made Medford's speculations seem!

He was at once touched by Gosling's solicitude, and annoyed that he should have been so duped by the hallucinating fancies of the East.

Almodham was off on his own business; very likely the men

knew where and what the business was; and even if they had robbed him in his absence, and quarreled over the spoils, Medford did not see what he could do. It might even be that his eccentric host – with whom, after all, he had had but one evening's acquaintance – repenting of an invitation too rashly given, had ridden away to escape the boredom of entertaining him. As this alternative occurred to Medford it seemed so plausible that he began to wonder if Almodham had not simply withdrawn to some secret suite of that intricate dwelling, and were waiting there for his guest's departure.

So well would this explain Gosling's solicitude to see the visitor off – so completely account for the man's nervous and contradictory behaviour – that Medford, smiling at his own obtuseness, hastily resolved to leave on the morrow. Tranquillized by this decision, he lingered about the court till dusk fell, and then, as usual, went up to the roof. But today his eyes, instead of raking the horizon, fastened on the clustering edifice of which, after six days' residence, he knew so little. Aerial chambers, jutting out at capricious angles, baffled him with closely shuttered windows, or here and there with the enigma of painted panes. Behind which window was his host concealed, spying, it might be, at this very moment on his guest?

The idea that that strange moody man, with his long brown face and shock of white hair, his half-guessed selfishness and tyranny, and his morbid self-absorption, might be actually within a stone's throw, gave Medford, for the first time, a sharp sense of isolation. He felt himself shut out, unwanted – the place, now that he imagined someone might be living in it unknown to him, became lonely, inhospitable, dangerous.

'Fool that I am – he probably expected me to pack up and go as soon as I found he was away!' the young man reflected. Yes; decidedly, he would leave the next morning.

Gosling had not shown himself all the afternoon. When at length, belatedly, he came to set the table, he wore a look of sullen, almost surly, reserve which Medford had not yet seen on his face. He hardly returned the young man's friendly 'Hallo – dinner?' and when Medford was seated handed him the first dish in silence. Medford's glass remained unfilled till he touched its brim.

'Oh, there's nothing to drink, sir. The men lost the case of Perrier – or dropped it and smashed the bottles. They say it never came. 'Ow do I know when they never open their 'eathen lips but to lie!' Gosling burst out with sudden violence.

He set down the dish he was handing, and Medford saw that he had been obliged to do so because his whole body was shaking as if with fever.

'My dear man, what does it matter? You're going to be ill,' Medford exclaimed, laying his hand on the servant's arm. But the latter, muttering: 'Oh, God, if I'd only 'a' gone for it myself,' jerked away and vanished from the room.

Medford sat pondering; it certainly looked as if poor Gosling were on the edge of a breakdown.

No wonder, when Medford himself was so oppressed by the uncanniness of the place. Gosling reappeared after an interval, correct, close-lipped, with the dessert and a bottle of white wine. 'Sorry, sir.'

To pacify him, Medford sipped the wine and then pushed his chair away and returned to the court. He was making for the fig tree by the well when Gosling, slipping ahead, transferred his chair and wicker table to the other end of the court.

'You'll be better here – there'll be a breeze presently,' he said. 'I'll fetch your coffee.'

He disappeared again, and Medford sat gazing up at the pile of masonry and plaster, and wondering whether he had not been moved away from his favourite corner to get him out of – or into? – the angle of vision of the invisible watcher. Gosling, having brought the coffee, went away and Medford sat on.

At length he rose and began to pace up and down as he smoked.

Medford went back to his seat; but as soon as he had resumed it he fancied that the gaze of his hidden watcher was jealously fixed on the red spark of his cigar. The sensation became increasingly distasteful; he could almost feel Almodham reaching out long ghostly arms from somewhere above him in the darkness. He moved back into the living-room, where a shaded light hung from the ceiling; but the room was airless, and finally he went out again and dragged his seat to its old place under the fig tree. From there the windows which he suspected could not command him, and he felt easier, though the corner was out of the breeze and the heavy air seemed tainted with the exhalation of the adjoining well.

'The water must be very low,' Medford mused. The smell, though faint, was unpleasant. He drowsed.

When he woke the moon was pushing up its ponderous orange disk above the walls, and the darkness in the court was less dense. He must have slept for an hour or more. The night was delicious, or would have been anywhere but there. Medford felt a shiver of his old fever and remembered that Gosling had warned him that the court was unhealthy at night.

'On account of the well, I suppose. I've been sitting too close to it,' he reflected. His head ached, and he fancied that the sweetish foulish smell clung to his face as it had after his bath. He stood up and approached the well to see how much water was left in it. But the moon was not yet high enough to light those depths, and he peered down into blackness.

Suddenly he felt both shoulders gripped from behind and forcibly pressed forward, as if by someone seeking to push him over the edge. An instant later, almost coinciding with his own swift resistance, the push became a strong tug backwards, and he swung round to confront Gosling, whose hands immediately dropped from his shoulders.

'I thought you had the fever, sir – I seemed to see you pitching over,' the man stammered.

Medford's wits returned. 'We must both have it, for I fancied you were pitching me,' he said with a laugh.

'Me, sir?' Gosling gasped. 'I pulled you back as 'ard as ever –'

'Of course. I know.'

Gosling was silent. At length he asked: 'Aren't you going up to bed, sir?'

'No,' said Medford, 'I prefer to stay here.'

Gosling's face took on an expression of dogged anger. 'Well, then, I prefer that you shouldn't.'

Medford laughed again. 'Why? Because it's the hour when Mr Almodham comes out to take the air?'

The effect of this question was unexpected. Gosling dropped back a step or two and flung up his hands, pressing them to his lips as if to stifle a low outcry.

'Come! Own up that he's here and have done with it!' cried Medford.

'Here? What do you mean by "here"? You 'aven't seen 'im, 'ave you?' Before the words were out of the man's lips he flung up his arms again, stumbled forward and fell in a heap at Medford's feet.

Medford, still leaning against the well-head, smiled down contemptuously at the stricken wretch. His conjecture had been the right one, then.

'Get up, man. Don't be a fool! It's not your fault if I guessed that Mr Almodham walks here at night –'

'Walks here!' wailed the other, still cowering.

'Well, doesn't he? He won't kill you for owning up, will he?'

'Kill me? Kill me? I wish I'd killed *you*!' Gosling half got to his feet, his head thrown back in ashen terror. 'And I might 'ave, too, so easy! You felt me pushing of you over, didn't you? Coming 'ere spying and sniffing –'

Medford had not changed his position. The very abjectness of the creature at his feet gave him an easy sense of power. But Gosling's last cry had suddenly deflected the course of his speculations. Almodham was here, then; that was certain; but just where was he, and in what shape? A new fear scuttled down Medford's spine.

'So you did want to push me over?' he said. 'Why? As the quickest way of joining your master?'

The effect was more immediate than he had foreseen.

Gosling, getting to his feet, stood there bowed and shrunken in the accusing moonlight.

'Oh, God – and I 'ad you 'arf over! You know I did! And then – it was what you said about Wembley. So help me, sir, I felt you meant it, and it 'eld me back.' The man's face was again wet with tears, but this time Medford recoiled from them as if they had been drops splashed up by a falling body from the foul waters below.

Medford was silent.

Gosling continued to ramble on.

'And if only that Perrier 'ad of come. I don't believe it'd ever 'ave crossed your mind, if only you'd 'ave had your Perrier regular, now would it? But you say 'e walks – and I knew he would! Only – what was I to do with him, with you turning up like that the very day?'

Still Medford did not move.

'And 'im driving me to madness, sir, sheer madness, that same morning. Will you believe it? The very week before you come, I was to sail for England and 'ave my 'oliday, a 'ole month, sir – and I was entitled to six, if there was any justice – a 'ole month in 'Ammersmith, sir, in a cousin's 'ouse, and the chance to see Wembley thoroughly; and then 'e 'eard you was coming, sir, and 'e was bored and lonely 'ere, you understand – 'e 'ad to have new excitements provided for 'im or 'e'd go off 'is bat – and when 'e 'eard you were coming, 'e come out of his black mood in a flash and was 'arf crazy with pleasure, and said: "I'll keep 'im 'ere all winter – a remarkable young man, Gosling – just my kind." And when I says to him: "And 'ow about my 'oliday?" he stares at me with those stony eyes of 'is and says: "'Oliday? Oh, to be sure; why, next year – we'll see what can be done about it next year." Next year, sir, as if 'e was doing me a favour! And that's the way it 'ad been for nigh on twelve years.

'But this time, if you 'adn't 'ave come I do believe I'd 'ave got away, for he was getting used to 'aving Selim about 'im and his 'ealth was never better – and, well, I told 'im as much, and 'ow a man 'ad his rights after all, and my youth was going, and me that 'ad served him so well chained up 'ere like 'is watchdog, and always next year and next year – and, well, sir, 'e just laughed, sneering-like, and lit 'is cigarette. "Oh, Gosling, cut it out," 'e says.

'He was standing on the very spot where you are now, sir; and he turned to walk into the 'ouse. And it was then I 'it 'im. He was a heavy man, and he fell against the well curb. And just when you were expected any minute – oh, my God!'

Gosling's voice died out in a strangled murmur.

Medford, at his last words, had involuntarily shrunk back a few feet. The two men stood in the middle of the court and stared at each other without speaking. The moon, swinging high above the battlements, sent a searching spear of light down into the guilty darkness of the well.

The Looking-Glass

I

Mrs Attlee had never been able to understand why there was any harm in giving people a little encouragement when they needed it.

Sitting back in her comfortable armchair by the fire, her working days over, and her muscular masseuse's hands lying swollen and powerless on her knee, she was at leisure to turn the problem over, and ponder it as there had never been time to do before.

Mrs Attlee was so infirm now, that when her widowed daughter-in-law was away for the day, her granddaughter Moyra Attlee had to stay with her until the kitchen girl had prepared the cold supper, and could come in and sit in the parlour.

'You'd be surprised, you know, my dear, to find how discouraged the grand people get, in those big houses with all the help, and the silver dinner plates, and a bell always handy if the fire wants poking, or the pet dog asks for a drink.... And what'd a masseuse be good for, if she didn't jolly up their minds a little along with their muscles? – as Dr Welbridge used to say to me many a time, when he'd given me a difficult patient. And he always gave me the most difficult,' she added proudly.

She paused, aware (for even now little escaped her) that Moyra had ceased to listen, but accepting the fact resignedly, as she did most things in the slow decline of her days.

'It's a fine afternoon,' she reflected, 'and likely she's fidgety because there's a new movie on; or that young fellow's fixed it up to get back earlier from New York. . . .'

She relapsed into silence, following her thoughts; but presently, as happens with old people, they came to the surface again.

'And I hope I'm a good Catholic, as I said to Father Divott the other day, and at peace with heaven, if ever I was took suddenly – but no matter what happens I've got to risk my punishment for the wrong I did to Mrs Clingsland, because as long as I've never repented it there's no use telling Father Divott about it. Is there?'

Mrs Attlee heaved an introspective sigh. Like many humble persons of her kind and creed, she had a vague idea that a sin unrevealed was, as far as the consequences went, a sin uncommitted; and this conviction had often helped her in the difficult task of reconciling doctrine and practice.

II

Moyra Attlee interrupted her listless stare down the empty Sunday street of the New Jersey suburb, and turned an astonished glance on her grandmother.

'Mrs Clingsland? A wrong you did to Mrs Clingsland?'

Hitherto she had lent an inattentive ear to her grandmother's ramblings; the talk of old people seemed to be a language hardly worth learning. But it was not always so with Mrs Attlee's. Her activities among the rich had ceased before the first symptoms of the financial depression; but her tenacious memory was stored with pictures of the luxurious days of which her granddaughter's generation, even in a wider world, knew only by hearsay. Mrs Attlee had a gift for evoking in a few words scenes of half-understood opulence and leisure, like a guide leading a stranger through the gallery of a palace in the twilight, and now and then lifting a lamp to a shimmering Rembrandt or a jewelled Rubens; and it was particularly when she mentioned Mrs Clingsland that Moyra caught these dazzling glimpses. Mrs Clingsland had always been something more than a name to the Attlee family. They knew (though they did not know why) that it was through her help that Grandmother Attlee had been able, years ago, to buy the little house at Montclair, with a patch of garden behind it, where, all through the Depression, she had held out, thanks to fortunate investments made on the advice of Mrs Clingsland's great friend, the banker.

'She had so many friends, and they were all high-up people, you understand. Many's the time she'd say to me: "Cora" (think of the loveliness of her calling me Cora), "Cora, I'm going to buy some Golden Flyer shares on Mr Stoner's advice; Mr Stoner of the National Union Bank, you know. He's getting me in on the ground floor, as they say, and if you want to step in with me, why come along. There's nothing too good for you, in my opinion," she used to say. And, as it turned out, those shares have kept their head above water all through the bad years, and now I think they'll see me through, and be there when I'm gone, to help out you children.'

Today Moyra Attlee heard the revered name with a new interest. The phrase: 'The wrong I did to Mrs Clingsland,' had struck through her listlessness, rousing her to sudden curiosity. What could her grandmother mean by saying she had done a wrong to the benefactress whose bounties she was never tired of recording? Moyra believed her grandmother to be a very good woman – certainly she had been wonderfully generous in all her dealings with her children and grandchildren; and it seemed incredible that, if there had been one grave lapse in her life, it should have taken the form of an injury to Mrs Clingsland. True, whatever the lapse was, she seemed to have made peace with herself about it; yet it was clear that its being unconfessed lurked disquietingly in the back of her mind.

'How can you say you ever did harm to a friend like Mrs Clingsland, Gran?'

Mrs Attlee's eyes grew sharp behind her spectacles, and she fixed them half distrustfully on the girl's face. But in a moment she seemed to recover herself. 'Not harm, I don't say; I'll never think I harmed her. Bless you, it wasn't to harm her I'd ever have lifted a finger. All I wanted was to help. But when you try to help too many people at once, the devil sometimes takes note of it. You see, there's quotas nowadays for everything, doing good included, my darling.'

Moyra made an impatient movement. She did not care to hear her grandmother philosophize. 'Well – but you said you did a wrong to Mrs Clingsland.'

Mrs Attlee's sharp eyes seemed to draw back behind a mist of age. She sat silent, her hands lying heavily over one another in their tragic uselessness.

'What would *you* have done, I wonder,' she began suddenly, 'if
you'd ha' come in on her that morning, and seen her laying in
her lovely great bed, with the lace a yard deep on the sheets, and
her face buried in the pillows, so I knew she was crying? Would
you have opened your bag same as usual, and got out your coco-
nut cream and talcum powder, and the nail polishers, and all the
rest of it, and waited there like a statue till she turned over to
you; or'd you have gone up to her, and turned her softly round,
like you would a baby, and said to her: "Now, my dear, I guess
you can tell Cora Attlee what's the trouble"? Well, that's what I
did, anyhow; and there she was, with her face streaming with
tears, and looking like a martyred saint on an altar, and when I
said to her: "Come, now, you tell me, and it'll help you", she
just sobbed out: "Nothing can ever help me, now I've lost it"'.

'"Lost what?" I said, thinking first of her boy, the Lord help me,
though I'd heard him whistling on the stairs as I went up; but she
said: "My beauty, Cora – I saw it suddenly slipping out of the
door from me this morning...." Well, at that I had to laugh,
and half angrily too. "Your beauty," I said to her, "and is that
all? And me that thought it was your husband, or your son – or
your fortune even. If it's only your beauty, can't I give it back to
you with these hands of mine? But what are you saying to me
about beauty, with that seraph's face looking up at me this minute?"
I said to her, for she angered me as if she'd been blaspheming.'

'Well, was it true?' Moyra broke in, impatient and yet curious.

'True that she'd lost her beauty?' Mrs Attlee paused to consider. 'Do you know how it is, sometimes when you're doing a
bit of fine darning sitting by the window in the afternoon; and
one minute it's full daylight, and your needle seems to find the
way of itself; and the next minute you say: "Is it my eyes?" because the work seems blurred; and presently you see it's the daylight going, stealing away, softlike, from your corner, though there's
plenty left overhead. Well – it was the way with her....'

But Moyra had never done fine darning, or strained her eyes in
fading light, and she intervened again, more impatiently: 'Well,
what did she do?'

Mrs Attlee once more reflected. 'Why, she made me tell her
every morning that it wasn't true; and every morning she believed
me a little less. And she asked everybody in the house, beginning
with her husband, poor man – him so bewildered when you asked

him anything outside of his business, or his club or his horses, and never noticing any difference in her looks since the day he'd led her home as his bride, twenty years before, maybe. . . .

'But there – nothing he could have said, if he'd had the wit to say it, would have made any difference. From the day she saw the first little line around her eyes she thought of herself as an old woman, and the thought never left her for more than a few minutes at a time. Oh, when she was dressed up, and laughing, and receiving company, then I don't say the faith in her beauty wouldn't come back to her, and go to her head like champagne; but it wore off quicker than champagne, and I've seen her run upstairs with the foot of a girl, and then, before she'd tossed off her finery, sit down in a heap in front of one of her big looking-glasses – it was looking-glasses everywhere in her room – and stare and stare till the tears ran down over her powder.'

'Oh, well, I suppose it's always hateful growing old,' said Moyra, her indifference returning.

Mrs Attlee smiled retrospectively. 'How can I say that, when my own old age has been made so peaceful by all her goodness to me?'

Moyra stood up with a shrug. 'And yet you tell me you acted wrong to her. How am I to know what you mean?'

Her grandmother made no answer. She closed her eyes, and leaned her head against the little cushion behind her neck. Her lips seemed to murmur, but no words came. Moyra reflected that she was probably falling asleep, and that when she woke she would not remember what she had been about to reveal.

'It's not much fun sitting here all this time, if you can't even keep awake long enough to tell me what you mean about Mrs Clingsland,' she grumbled.

Mrs Attlee roused herself with a start.

III

Well (she began) you know what happened in the war – I mean, the way all the fine ladies, and the poor shabby ones too, took to running to the mediums and the clairvoyants, or whatever the stylish folk call 'em. The women had to have news of their men; and they were made to pay high enough for it. . . . Oh, the stories I used to hear – and the price paid wasn't only money, either! There was a fair lot of swindlers and blackmailers in the business there was. I'd sooner have trusted a gypsy at a fair ... but the women just *had* to go to them.

Well, my dear, I'd always had a way of seeing things; from the cradle, even. I don't mean reading the tea leaves, or dealing the cards; that's for the kitchen. No, no; I mean, feeling there's things about you, behind you, whispering over your shoulder.... Once my mother, on the Connemara hills, saw the leprechauns at dusk; and she said they smelt fine and high, too.... Well, when I used to go from one grand house to another, to give my massage and face treatment, I got more and more sorry for those poor wretches that the soothsaying swindlers were dragging the money out of for a pack of lies; and one day I couldn't stand it any longer, and though I knew the Church was against it, when I saw one lady nearly crazy, because for months she'd had no news of her boy at the front, I said to her: 'If you'll come over to my place tomorrow, I might have a word for you.' And the wonder of it was that I *had*! For that night I dreamt a message came saying there was good news for her, and the next day, sure enough, she had a cable, telling her her son had escaped from a German camp....

After that the ladies came in flocks – in flocks fairly ... you're too young to remember, child; but your mother could tell you. Only she wouldn't, because after a bit the priest got wind of it, and then it had to stop ... so she won't even talk of it any more. But I always said: how could I help it? For I *did* see things, and hear things, at that time.... And of course the ladies were supposed to come just for the face treatment ... and was I to blame if I kept hearing those messages for them, poor souls, or seeing things they wanted me to see?

It's no matter now, for I made it all straight with Father Divott years ago; and now nobody comes after me anymore, as you can see for yourself. And all I ask is to be left alone in my chair....

But with Mrs Clingsland – well, that was different. To begin with, she was the patient I liked best. There was nothing she wouldn't do for you, if ever for a minute you could get her to stop thinking of herself ... and that's saying a good deal, for a rich lady. Money's an armour, you see; and there's few cracks in it. But Mrs Clingsland was a loving nature, if only anybody'd shown her how to love.... Oh, dear, and wouldn't she have been surprised if you'd told her that! Her that thought she was living up to her chin in love and love-making. But as soon as the lines began to come about her eyes, she didn't believe in it anymore. And she had to be always hunting for new people to tell her she was as beautiful as ever; because she wore the others out, forever asking them: 'Don't you think I'm beginning to go off a little?' – till finally fewer and fewer came to the house, and as far as a poor masseuse like me can judge, I didn't much fancy the looks of those that did; and I saw Mr Clingsland didn't either.

But there was the children, you'll say. I know, I know! And she did love her children in a way; only it wasn't their way. The girl, who was a good bit the eldest, took after her father: a plain face and plain words. Dogs and horses and athletics. With her mother she was cold and scared; so her mother was cold and scared with her. The boy was delicate when he was little, so she could curl him up, and put him into black velvet pants, like that boy in the book – little Lord Something. But when his long legs grew out of the pants, and they sent him to school, she said he wasn't her own little cuddly baby anymore; and it riles a growing boy to hear himself talked about like that.

She had good friends left, of course; mostly elderly ladies they were, of her own age (for she *was* elderly now; the change had come), who used to drop in often for a gossip; but, bless your heart, they weren't much help, for what she wanted, and couldn't do without, was the gaze of men struck dumb by her beauty. And that was what she couldn't get any longer, except she paid for it. And even so –!

For, you see, she was too quick and clever to be humbugged long by the kind that tried to get things out of her. How she used to laugh at the old double-chinners trotting round to the night-clubs with their boy-friends! She laughed at old ladies in love; and yet she couldn't bear to be out of love, though she knew she was getting to be an old lady herself.

Well, I remember one day another patient of mine, who'd never had much looks beyond what you can buy in Fifth Avenue, laughing at me about Mrs Clingsland, about her dread of old age, and her craze for admiration – and as I listened, I suddenly thought: 'Why, we don't either of us know anything about what a beautiful woman suffers when she loses her beauty. For you and me, and thousands like us, beginning to grow old is like going from a bright warm room to one a little less warm and bright; but to a beauty like Mrs Clingsland it's like being pushed out of an illuminated

ballroom, all flowers and chandeliers, into the winter night and
the snow.' And I had to bite the words back, not to say them to
my patient. . . .

IV

Mrs Clingsland brightened up a little when her own son grew up
and went to college. She used to go over and see him now and
again; or he'd come home for the holidays. And he used to take
her out for lunch, or to dance at those cabaret places; and when
the headwaiters took her for his sweetheart she'd talk about it
for a week. But one day a hall porter said: 'Better hurry up,
mister. There's your mother waiting for you over there, looking
clean fagged out'; and after that she didn't go round with him so
much.

For a time she used to get some comfort out of telling me
about her early triumphs; and I used to listen patiently, because I
knew it was safer for her to talk to me than to the flatterers who
were beginning to get round her.

You mustn't think of her, though, as an unkind woman. She
was friendly to her husband, and friendly to her children; but
they meant less and less to her. What she wanted was a looking-
glass to stare into; and when her own people took enough notice
of her to serve as looking-glasses, which wasn't often, she didn't
much fancy what she saw there. I think this was about the worst
time of her life. She lost a tooth; she began to dye her hair; she
went into retirement to have her face lifted, and then got frightened, and came out again looking like a ghost, with a pouch
under one eye, where they'd begun the treatment. . . .

I began to be really worried about her then. She got sour and
bitter towards everybody, and I seemed to be the only person she
could talk out to. She used to keep me by for hours, always
paying for the appointments she made me miss, and going over
the same thing again and again; how when she was young and
came into a ballroom, or a restaurant or a theatre, everybody
stopped what they were doing to turn and look at her – even the
actors on the stage did, she said; and it was the truth, I dare say.
But that was over. . . .

Well, what could I say to her? She'd heard it all often enough.
But there were people prowling about in the background that I

didn't like the look of; people, you understand, who live on weak women that can't grow old. One day she showed me a love letter. She said she didn't know the man who'd sent it; but she knew about him. He was a Count Somebody; a foreigner. He'd had adventures. Trouble in his own country, I guess. . . . She laughed and tore the letter up. Another came from him, and I saw that too – but I didn't see her tear it up.

'Oh, I know what he's after,' she said. 'Those kind of men are always looking out for silly old women with money. . . . Ah,' says she, 'it was different in old times. I remember one day I'd gone into a florist's to buy some violets, and I saw a young fellow there; well, maybe he was a little younger than me – but I looked like a girl still. And when he saw me he just stopped short with what he was saying to the florist, and his face turned so white I thought he was going to faint. I bought my violets; and as I went out a violet dropped from the bunch, and I saw him stoop and pick it up, and hide it away as if it had been money he'd stolen. . . .Well,' she says, 'a few days after that I met him at a dinner, and it turned out he was the son of a friend of mine, a woman older than myself, who'd married abroad. He'd been brought up in England, and had just come to New York to take up a job there. . . .'

She lay back with her eyes closed, and a quiet smile on her poor tormented face. 'I didn't know it then, but I suppose that was the only time I've ever been in love. . . .' For a while she didn't say anything more, and I noticed the tears beginning to roll down her cheeks. 'Tell me about it, now do, you poor soul,' I says; for I thought, this is better for her than fandangoing with that oily count whose letter she hasn't torn up.

'There's so little to tell,' she said. 'We met only four or five times – and then Harry went down on the *Titanic*.'

'Mercy,' says I, 'and was it all those years ago?'

'The years don't make any difference, Cora,' she says. 'The way he looked at me I know no one ever worshipped me as he did.'

'And did he tell you so?' I went on, humouring her; though I felt kind of guilty towards her husband.

'Some things don't have to be told,' says she, with the smile of a bride. 'If only he hadn't died, Cora. . . . It's the sorrowing for him that's made me old before my time.' (Before her time! And her well over fifty.)

Well, a day or two after that I got a shock. Coming out of Mrs Clingsland's front door as I was going into it I met a woman I'd know among a million if I was to meet her again in hell – where I will, I know, if I don't mind my steps.... You see, Moyra, though I broke years ago with all that crystal-reading, and table-rapping, and what the Church forbids, I was mixed up in it for a time (till Father Divott ordered me to stop), and I knew, by sight at any rate, most of the big mediums and their touts. And this woman on the doorstep was a tout, one of the worst and most notorious in New York; I knew cases where she'd sucked people dry selling them the news they wanted, like she was selling them a forbidden drug. And all of a sudden it came to me that I'd heard it said that she kept a foreign count, who was sucking *her* dry – and I gave one jump home to my own place, and sat down there to think it over.

I saw well enough what was going to happen. Either she'd persuade my poor lady that the count was mad over her beauty, and get a hold over her that way; or else – and this was worse – she'd make Mrs Clingsland talk, and get at the story of the poor young man called Harry, who was drowned, and bring her messages from him; and that might go on for ever, and bring in more money than the count....

Well, Moyra, could I help it? I was so sorry for her, you see. I could see she was sick and fading away, and her will weaker than it used to be; and if I was to save her from those gangsters I had to do it right away, and make it straight with my conscience afterwards – if I could....

V

I don't believe I ever did such hard thinking as I did that night. For what was I after doing? Something that was against my Church and against my own principles; and if ever I got found out, it was all up with me – me, with my thirty years' name of being the best masseuse in New York, and none honester, nor more respectable!

Well, then, I says to myself, what'll happen if that woman gets hold of Mrs Clingsland? Why, one way or another, she'll bleed her white, and then leave her without help or comfort. I'd seen households where that had happened, and I wasn't going to let it happen to my poor lady. What I was after was to make her believe in herself again, so that she'd be in a kindlier mind towards others ... and by the next day I'd thought my plan out, and set it going.

It wasn't so easy, neither; and I sometimes wonder at my nerve. I'd figured it out that the other woman would have to work the stunt of the young man who was drowned, because I was pretty sure Mrs Clingsland, at the last minute, would shy away from the count. Well, then, thinks I, I'll work the same stunt myself – but how?

You see, dearie, those big people, when they talk and write to each other, they use lovely words we ain't used to; and I was afraid if I began to bring messages to her, I'd word them wrong, and she'd suspect something. I knew I could work it the first day or the second; but after that I wasn't so sure. But there was no time to lose, and when I went back to her next morning I said: 'A queer thing happened to me last night. I guess it was the way you spoke to me about that gentleman – the one on the *Titanic*. Making me see him as clear as if he was in the room with us–' and at that I had her sitting up in bed with her great eyes burning into me like gimlets. 'Oh, Cora, perhaps he *is*! Oh, tell me quickly what happened!'

'Well, when I was laying in my bed last night something came to me from him. I knew at once it was from him; it was a word he was telling me to bring you....'

I had to wait then, she was crying so hard, before she could listen to me again; and when I went on she hung on to me, saving the word, as if I'd been her Saviour. The poor woman!

The message I'd hit on for that first day was easy enough. I said he'd told me to tell her he'd always loved her. It went down her throat like honey, and she just lay there and tasted it. But after a while she lifted up her head. 'Then why didn't he tell me so?' says she.

'Ah,' says I, 'I'll have to try to reach him again, and ask him that.' And that day she fairly drove me off on my other jobs, for fear I'd be late getting home, and too tired to hear him if he came again. 'And he *will* come, Cora; I know he will! And you must be ready for him, and write down everything. I want every word written down the minute he says it, for fear you'll forget a single one.'

Well, that was a new difficulty. Writing wasn't ever my strong point; and when it came to finding the words for a young gentleman in love who'd gone down on the *Titanic,* you might as well have asked me to write a Chinese dictionary. Not that I couldn't imagine how he'd have felt; but I didn't for Mary's grace know how to say it for him.

But it's wonderful, as Father Divott says, how Providence sometimes seems to be listening behind the door. That night when I got home I found a message from a patient, asking me to go to see a poor young fellow she'd befriended when she was better off – he'd been her children's tutor, I believe – who was down and out, and dying in a miserable rooming house down here at Montclair. Well, I went; and I saw at once why he hadn't kept this job, or any other job. Poor fellow, it was the drink; and now he was dying of it. It was a pretty bad story, but there's only a bit of it belongs to what I'm telling you.

He was a highly educated gentleman, and as quick as a flash; and before I'd half explained, he told me what to say, and wrote out the message for me. I remember it now. 'He was so blinded by your beauty that he couldn't speak – and when he saw you the next time, at the dinner, in your bare shoulders and your pearls, he felt farther away from you than ever. And he walked the streets till morning, and then went home, and wrote you a letter; but he didn't dare to send it after all.'

This time Mrs Clingsland swallowed it down like champagne. Blinded by her beauty; struck dumb by love of her! Oh, but that's what she'd been thirsting and hungering for all these years. Only, once it had begun, she had to have more of it, and always more ... and my job didn't get any easier.

Luckily, though, I had that young fellow to help me; and after a while, when I'd given him a hint of what it was all about, he got as much interested as I was, and began to fret for me the days I didn't come.

But, my, what questions she asked. 'Tell him, if it's true that I took his breath away that first evening at dinner, to describe to you how I was dressed. They must remember things like that even in the other world, don't you think so? And you say he noticed my pearls?'

Luckily she'd described that dress to me so often that I had no difficulty about telling the young man what to say – and so it went on, and it went on, and one way or another I managed each time to have an answer that satisfied her. But one day, after Harry'd sent her a particularly lovely message from the Over There (as those people call it) she burst into tears and cried out: 'Oh, why did he never say things like that to me when we were together?'

That was a poser, as they say; I couldn't imagine why he hadn't. Of course I knew it was all wrong and immoral, anyway; but, poor thing, I don't see who it can hurt to help the love-making between a sick woman and a ghost. And I'd taken care to say a Novena against Father Divott finding me out.

Well, I told the poor young man what she wanted to know, and he said: 'Oh, you can tell her an evil influence came between them. Someone who was jealous, and worked against him – here, give me a pencil, and I'll write it out. . . .' and he pushed out his hot twitching hand for the paper.

That message fairly made her face burn with joy. 'I knew it – I always knew it!' She flung her thin arms about me, and kissed me. 'Tell me again, Cora, how he said I looked the first day he saw me. . . .'

'Why, you must have looked as you look now,' says I to her, 'for there's twenty years fallen from your face.' And so there was.

What helped me to keep on was that she'd grown so much gentler and quieter. Less impatient with the people who waited on her, more understanding with the daughter and Mr Clingsland. There was a different atmosphere in the house. And sometimes she'd say: 'Cora, there must be poor souls in trouble, with nobody to hold out a hand to them; and I want you to come to me when you run across anybody like that.' So I used to keep that poor young fellow well looked after, and cheered up with little dainties. And you'll never make me believe there was anything wrong in that – or in letting Mrs Clingsland help me out with the new roof on this house, either.

But there was a day when I found her sitting up in bed when I came in, with two red spots on her thin cheeks. And all the peace had gone out of her poor face. 'Why, Mrs Clingsland, my dear, what's the matter?' But I could see well enough what it was. Somebody'd been undermining her belief in spirit communications, or whatever they call them, and she'd been crying herself into a fever, thinking I'd made up all I'd told her. 'How do I know you're a medium, anyhow,' she flung out at me with pitiful furious eyes, 'and not taking advantage of me with all this stuff every morning?'

Well, the queer thing was that I took offense at that, not because I was afraid of being found out, but because – heaven help us! – I'd somehow come to believe in that young man Harry and his love-making, and it made me angry to be treated as a fraud. But I kept my temper and my tongue, and went on with the message as if I hadn't heard her; and she was ashamed to say any more to me. The quarrel between us lasted a week; and then one day, poor soul, she said, whimpering like a drug taker: 'Cora, I can't get on without the messages you bring me. The ones I get through other people don't sound like Harry – and yours do.'

I was so sorry for her then that I had hard work not to cry with her; but I kept my head, and answered quietly: 'Mrs Clingsland, I've been going against my Church, and risking my immortal soul, to get those messages through to you; and if you've found others that can help you, so much the better for me, and I'll go and make my peace with Heaven this very evening,' I said.

'But the other messages don't help me, and I don't want to disbelieve in you,' she sobbed out. 'Only lying awake all night and turning things over, I get so miserable. I shall die if you can't prove to me that it's really Harry speaking to you.'

I began to pack up my things. 'I can't prove that, I'm afraid,' I says in a cold voice, turning away my head so she wouldn't see the tears running down my cheeks.

'Oh, but you must, Cora, or I shall die!' she entreated me; and she looked as if she would, the poor soul. 'How I can prove it to you?' I answered. For all my pity for her, I still resented the way she'd spoken; and I thought how glad I'd be to get the whole business off my soul that very night in the confessional.

She opened her great eyes and looked up at me; and I seemed to see the wraith of her young beauty looking out of them. 'There's only one way,' she whispered.

'Well,' I said, still offended, 'what's the way?'

'You must ask him to repeat to you that letter he wrote, and didn't dare send to me. I'll know instantly then if you're in communication with him, and if you are I'll never doubt you any more.'

Well, I sat down and gave a laugh. 'You think it's as easy as that to talk with the dead, do you?'

'I think he'll know I'm dying too, and have pity on me, and do as I ask.' I said nothing more, but packed up my things and went away.

IV

That letter seemed to me a mountain in my path; and the poor young man, when I told him, thought so too. 'Ah, that's too difficult,' he said. But he told me he'd think it over, and do his best – and I was to come back the next day if I could. 'If only I knew more about her – or about *him*. It's damn difficult, making love for a dead man to a woman you've never seen,' says he with his little cracked laugh. I couldn't deny that it was; but I knew he'd do what he could, and I could see that the difficulty of it somehow spurred him on, while me it only cast down.

So I went back to his room the next evening; and as I climbed the stairs I felt one of those sudden warnings that sometimes used to take me by the throat.

'It's as cold as ice on these stairs,' I thought, 'and I'll wager there's no one made up the fire in his room since morning.' But it wasn't really the cold I was afraid of; I could tell there was worse than that waiting for me.

I pushed open the door and went in. 'Well,' says I, as cheerful as I could, 'I've got a pint of champagne and a thermos of hot soup for you; but before you get them you've got to tell me–'

He laid there in his bed as if he didn't see me, though his eyes were open; and when I spoke to him he didn't answer. I tried to laugh. 'Mercy!' I says, 'are you so sleepy you can't even look round to see the champagne? Hasn't that slut of a woman been in to 'tend to the stove for you? The room's as cold as death –' I says, and at the word I stopped short. He neither moved nor spoke; and I felt that the cold came from him, and not from the empty stove. I took hold of his hand, and held the cracked looking-glass to his lips; and I knew he was gone to his Maker. I drew his lids down, and fell on my knees beside the bed. 'You shan't go without a prayer, you poor fellow,' I whispered to him, pulling out my beads.

But though my heart was full of mourning I dursn't pray for long, for I knew I ought to call the people of the house. So I just muttered a prayer for the dead, and then got to my feet again. But before calling in anybody I took a quick look around; for I said to myself it would be better not to leave about any of those bits he'd written down for me. In the shock of finding the poor young man gone I'd clean forgotten all about the letter; but I looked among his few books and papers for anything about the spirit messages, and found nothing. After that I turned back for a last look at him, and a last blessing; and then it was, fallen on the floor and half under the bed, I saw a sheet of paper scribbled over in pencil in his weak writing. I picked it up, and, holy Mother, it was the letter! I hid it away quick in my bag, and I stooped down and kissed him. And then I called the people in.

Well, I mourned the poor young man like a son, and I had a busy day arranging things, and settling about the funeral with the lady that used to befriend him. And with all there was to do I never went near Mrs Clingsland nor so much as thought of her, that day or the next; and the day after that there was a frantic message, asking what had happened, and saying she was very ill, and I was to come quick, no matter how much else I had to do.

I didn't more than half believe in the illness; I've been about too long among the rich not to be pretty well used to their scares and fusses. But I knew Mrs Clingsland was just pining to find out if I'd got the letter, and that my only chance of keeping my hold over her was to have it ready in my bag when I went back. And if I didn't keep my hold over her, I knew what slimy hands were waiting in the dark to pull her down.

Well, the labour I had copying out that letter was so great that I didn't hardly notice what was in it; and if I thought about it at all, it was only to wonder if it wasn't worded too plainlike, and if there oughtn't to have been more long words in it, coming from a gentleman to his lady. So with one thing and another I wasn't any too easy in my mind when I appeared again at Mrs Clingsland's; and if ever I wished myself out of a dangerous job, my dear, I can tell you that was the day. . . .

I went up to her room, the poor lady, and found her in bed, and tossing about, her eyes blazing, and her face full of all the wrinkles I'd worked so hard to rub out of it; and the sight of her softened my heart. After all, I thought, these people don't know what real trouble is; but they've manufactured something so like it that it's about as bad as the genuine thing.

'Well,' she said in a fever, 'well, Cora – the letter? Have you brought me the letter?'

I pulled it out of my bag, and handed it to her; and then I sat down and waited, my heart in my boots. I waited a long time, looking away from her; you couldn't stare at a lady who was reading a message from her sweetheart, could you?

I waited a long time; she must have read the letter very slowly, and then reread it. Once she sighed, ever so softly; and once she said: 'Oh, Harry, no, no – how foolish' . . . and laughed a little under her breath. Then she was still again for so long that at last I turned my head and took a stealthy look at her. And there she lay on her pillows, the hair waving over them, the letter clasped tight in her hands, and her face smoothed out the way it was years before, when I first knew her. Yes – those few words had done more for her than all my labour.

'Well – ?' said I, smiling a little at her.

'Oh, Cora – now at last he's spoken to me, really spoken.' And the tears were running down her young cheeks.

I couldn't hardly keep back my own, the heart was so light in me. 'And now you'll believe in me, I hope, ma'am, won't you?'

'I was mad ever to doubt you, Cora. . . .' She lifted the letter to her breast, and slipped it in among her laces. 'How did you manage to get it , you darling, you?'

Dear me, thinks I, and what if she asks me to get her another one like it, and then another? I waited a moment, and then I spoke very gravely. 'It's not an easy thing, ma'am, coaxing a letter like that from the dead.' And suddenly, with a start, I saw that I'd spoken the truth. It *was* from the dead that I'd got it.

'No, Cora; I can well believe it. But this is a treasure I can live on for years. Only you must tell me how I can repay you. . . . In a hundred years I could never do enough for you,' she says.

Well, that word went to my heart; but for a minute I didn't know how to answer. For it was true I'd risked my soul, and that was something she couldn't pay me for; but then maybe I'd saved hers, in getting her away from those foul people, so the whole business was more of a puzzle to me than ever. But then I had a thought that made me easier.

'Well, ma'am, the day before yesterday I was with a young man about the age of – of your Harry; a poor young man, without health or hope, lying sick in a mean rooming house. I used to got there and see him sometimes –'

Mrs Clingsland sat up in bed in a flutter of pity. 'Oh, Cora, how dreadful! Why did you never tell me? You must hire a better room for him at once. Has he a doctor? Has he a nurse? Quick – give me my checkbook!'

'Thank you, ma'am. But he don't need no nurse nor no doctor; and he's in a room underground by now. All I wanted to ask you for,' said I at length, though I knew I might have got a king's ransom from her, 'is money enough to have a few masses said for his soul – because maybe there's no one else to do it.'

I had hard work making her believe there was no end to the masses you could say for a hundred dollars; but somehow it's comforted me ever since that I took no more from her that day. I saw to it that Father Divott said the masses and got a good bit of the money; so he was a sort of accomplice too, though he never knew it.